A NOTE FROM THE AUTHOR

The reader should be aware that the following is a work of fiction and a pastiche of New Mexico's history. Many of the places, festivals, historical figures and events are real but altered for the sake of the story. For instance, the burning of the Zozobra is an actual festival that takes place in early September rather than late October as portrayed in this book. Stranger yet, Billy the Kid's tombstone was for a fact stolen from Fort Sumner in the year 1950, shortly after a visit from a man who claimed to be a surviving Billy the Kid. The tombstone was recovered in Granbury, Texas, in 1976, after which it was returned to Fort Sumner. That town— its renowned Tombstone Race and all—is basically the same in real life as it appears in this story with alterations made to the schooling system and town layout to suit the needs of the novel. Ultimately, this book is simply an attempt to intertwine some of the stranger legends of the Land of Enchantment into one story. Beyond using real places and events as a jumping-off point, there is no great aim towards historical accuracy. All characters in this book, including the ones "descended" from real people like Pat Garrett and Billy the Kid, are purely fictitious. None is based in any way on a real person, living or dead.

21 GUNS

VOL. I BOOK 1

JOHN LEMAY

WITH ILLUSTRATIONS BY
LOGAN PACK

BICEP BOOKS ·
ROSWELL, NEW MEXICO

For information regarding wholesale/bulk purchases look up this title's ISBN on Ingramspark.

An *Original* Publication of BICEP BOOKS.

Printed in the United States of America

ISBN: 978-1-953221-42-1

For my parents

October 29, 1976
Dingus Dumez
New Mexico History,
Professor Mendez
Second Period.

"My Report on Billy the Kid"

Back in olden times, about one hunerd years ago, lived a desperato by the name of Billy the Kid. He was born as William H. Bonney in the slums of New York in 1859 and moved West here to New Mexico with his mother. But then pour Billy's mother died in Silver City in 1874, leaving Billy an orphan and on his own at 15. In the late 1870s, Billy came to the town of Lincoln. At that time a wild fight was going on between different factions of rich and powerful men in the county. They fought over land and cattle, mostly. One side had Billy and some other cowboys on it, and the other side had the Santa Fe Ring and their hired hands on it. It was known as the Lincoln County War, and eventually said war ended. Even though Billy was a good guy during the war, after it ended, Billy became an outlaw and a sheriff named Pat Garrett was elected to hunt him down. In July of 1881, Pat shot Billy dead right here in Fort Sumner.

This is where the story gets confusing, because some people say that Pat Garrett and Billy the Kid used to be good friends, but there ain't no one around who can prove if that is true or not anymore since most everyone who lived back then is now dead. Some folks even say Pat helped Billy fake his death and in his coffin they buried two bags of sand to give it some weight and planted it in the ground quick as they could the next day. That's why they say nobody here got to see the body.

Many years later, about 1950, this old man called Tumbleweed Williams showed up claiming that he was Billy the Kid and that he didn't really die. Tumbleweed Williams even visited the grave at Fort Sumner to point out that he was still alive and kicking. Right after that, the tombstone from Billy's grave disappeared and Tumbleweed Williams dropped dead of a heart attack before it could ever be proved he was the Kid. It was a crying shame too about the tombstone, because my old man told me that tombstone and Billy's grave was darn near the only reason people even past through Fort Sumner.

A few months ago, Billy the Kid's tombstone was finally found again in a field somewhere in Texas and returned to here in Fort Sumner after 26 hole years. How did it end up in Texas? We do not know. But surely it is one of the biggest mysteries of the Twentiuth Century.

Of course, you know all of this already and I'll never understand why you teachers are always wanting us to write reports on things you already know good and well. Please don't flunk me and I'm sorry again about the time I tied that dead skunk under your car. I've told you several times that I thought it was Mr. Harrison's car, not yours.

Sincerely,

Dingus Dumez

I
THE
NOTED
DESPERADO
PANCHO
DUMEZ

PROLOGUE
CEMETERY WITHOUT CROSSES

Digging my own grave wasn't exactly how I pictured myself spending the weekend, but it's what I was doing just the same. Stretched out on the sofa watching TV at home would have been more likely, or maybe swimming out in the slough if I was feeling ambitious. But being left for dead in the middle of the desert? Not a chance I would've imagined that last Thursday when school let out.

It was perfect weather for grave digging, too—at least a little over 100 degrees. Not to mention the perfect place to do it. After all, you never see someone being forced to dig their own grave at gunpoint somewhere nice. We were surrounded by miles and miles of nothing but dry, hard earth and an old half-dead tree that didn't look like it was long for the world. The only thing missing was a vulture flying overhead, but I was sure one would show up eventually.

Sweat stung my eyes, and for once I wished I didn't have a mop of wavy long black hair. My shovel slammed into the hard ground again. The deeper I went, the harder it got. I thought about asking the guard for a pic ax, then realized I didn't really want to speed this up.

At least I wasn't alone. My older brother Dorado was next to me digging his own hole as though he didn't have a care in the world. I know, you'd think we'd both be more upset, but truthfully this wasn't the worst situation we'd been in over the past few days.

"Care to wager on how they plan to kill us?" I decided I might as well make a little small talk with my brother. It might be the last conversation we'd ever have, but somehow I doubted it.

"That tree looks promising for a hanging," he said casually as though we were talking about the weather. "But I personally think they're going to bury us up to our necks in the sand, cover our faces in honey, and turn an ant den loose on our heads like the Indians used to do." He stopped digging to wipe the sweat off his brow and added, "And if they really want to go the extra mile, they might even slice off our eyelids just so we can't blink during the whole thing."

Even our stoic guard looked disturbed after that one. "Son, what kind of sick Spaghetti Western have you been watching?" he asked in disgust.

"Actually, I'm more of a *Little House on the Prairie* fan myself. The early stuff mind you, before they caved to the censors."

The guard kicked a pile of dirt in Dorado's face. "Son, shut your mouth and get back to digging already," he said, shaking his head in disbelief at Dorado's imagination. "I swear if the sheriff weren't so keen on killing you personally I might just do it myself."

The guard plunked down on the ground and took a swig of water while me and Dorado went back to digging. I partially had my smartass brother to thank for this whole situation, but not entirely. It really all started with our dad and his tombstone-stealing twin brother, but now isn't really a good time to try and tell that story. Not yet, anyway.

"Try not to tick him off again," I whispered. "Cade knows we're here, and if Xander hasn't caught him yet, there's a chance he can help us."

Dorado grunted. "Are you kidding? If our lives are in Cade's hands, we're dead for sure."

I couldn't argue with that. Our cousin Cade wasn't too bright. I looked down at my potential grave, and, for the first time, a feeling of dread washed over me. I had gotten out of a lot of tight spots in the past few days, but maybe this time, my luck had finally run out. The irony also struck me that tomorrow, if I lived, I'd turn fifteen.

"Excuse me," Dorado turned to the guard raising his hand. "Are we expected to fashion our own crosses as well? Because if you splurged to get us nice marble grave markers, I do have some thoughts on the inscription."

Now he'd done it.

"Okay, that's it, smart ass!" The guard jumped to his feet, swung his shotgun around and raised it in the air about to hit Dorado with the butt. Before he could, a gunshot rang out.

Flanked by two men was Xander Garrett walking our way. He was dressed in his usual black duster and cowboy hat and holding a smoking pistol. I had to look away after a second; the glint from his sheriff's badge caught my eye.

"Just what the hell's going on here, Ralf?" Xander yelled.

Ralf reluctantly lowered his weapon. "I was just gonna teach him a lesson, Sheriff. Boy's been mouthing off since you left 'im with me."

Xander stood over Dorado's grave as he holstered his pistol. "These two fine upstanding young men been giving you trouble? I can't imagine." He looked down at us. "You boys get out of those holes you dug yourselves into. Come on. You been digging long enough."

I felt a nervous flutter in my stomach. Just because he sounded happy didn't mean Xander was a nice guy. He's usually happiest when he's about to do something terrible.

"I don't suppose you just wanted to teach us a lesson and then let us go?" I asked as I climbed out of my hole. It was worth a shot. "Just scare us straight and all that instead of kill us?"

Xander stared at me for a second. "Pancho, you're right. I ain't really gonna kill you." He turned to look at his men. "Truthfully, we don't got the heart to kill a couple of teenaged kids. Do we boys?"

The two new guards shook their heads; but not the one called Ralf. He really did want to kill us.

Dorado and I looked at each other and grinned in relief. Maybe we weren't going to die after all.

"You two are going to kill each other." Xander cut into our jubilation.

"Wait. What?" we said in unison.

Xander held up the noose of a rope, smiled, and pointed at the tree.

"Think of a good plan yet?" I whispered to Dorado sarcastically.

"No."

"Well, maybe when that noose tightens around your neck, you'll finally think of something."

"I do work well under pressure."

Believe it or not, my life wasn't always this interesting. Only a few days ago, things were a lot simpler. And just how exactly did my brother and I get into this mess? Well, believe it or not, it all started with a goat...

I.

NO COUNTRY FOR OLD GOATS

3 DAYS AGO…THURSDAY, OCTOBER 28, 1976

*A*nd so there I was, disguised as a cheerleader, skirt and all, peddling a bicycle as fast as I could down the hallways of Pat Garrett High. My cousin, Dingus, was doing his best to sit on the handlebars and hold onto the poor baby goat we'd just taken. Behind us, bellowing like a bear, was the fearsome Coach McPherson, a mountain of a man if there ever was one. Naturally, he was chasing me and Dingus because we had stolen the baby goat. Well, not so much stolen so much as rescued it, since it was our school mascot. See, me and Dingus went to Billy the Kid Junior High on the other end of town, and the seniors at Pat Garrett High thought it would be funny to steal our goat as a prank. Even though we didn't have a lot of what you'd call school spirit, me and Dingus made up our minds that we would be the ones to rescue the goat. But anyways, the point is I was peddling for dear life down the hallway when the janitor pushed his cleaning cart right in my way and suddenly—

Actually, on second thought, maybe this isn't the best part to start my story at. I was kinda worried that if I started it right at the beginning it might be too boring. But, come to think of it, there's just too many things I'm leaving out. So let me back up to the morning when I was still at home and had just gotten up.

The day had started out pretty normal except for my aunt and uncle, who I live with, were in the kitchen arguing. My uncle just put in a new washer and my aunt didn't think it matched the old dryer next to it. Something about one being a different shade of white than the other. People their age worried about the strangest things.

If all I had to worry about was going to work, a few bills to pay here and there, and having domestic arguments about the color of the appliances, I'd have it made. Old people always say life's easy and carefree when you're young, but I think they forget what it's like to be fourteen and in junior high. Going there every day's like going out into the jungle, except instead of trying not to get eaten, your main goal is to look cool in front of girls and keep up your social reputation in general. At seven hours a day, five days a week, that can get kind of stressful after a while.

I ruffled my hair in front of the bathroom mirror with a towel to get it to fall just right. Doing the shag look takes more work, but it's worth it. More girls notice me with my hair long than when it was short it seems like. I'm kinda what you might call a throwback when it comes to my looks because I don't look like anybody in my family except Dorado. Dorado looks quite a bit like me in the face except for he's lighter complected and has reddish hair.

My skin's got a darker tint and I've got pitch-black hair. That's why I said I'm considered a throwback, because I take after our mother, who was Hispanic, and Dorado doesn't. The most interesting trait me and my brother share are our eyes, though, because they're sorta different colors. Or, what I mean to say is, where most people would usually just say they have blue or brown eyes, me and Dorado both have green eyes with a weird, gold-brown ring right around the pupil. There's some fancy name for it, heterocro-something, but I can never remember the rest. Me and him are the only ones in the whole family to have it, though, apart from our dad. Or so I hear at least.

I guess I forgot to mention something else that's kinda important, too. I don't have my real parents anymore, hence why I live with my aunt and uncle. My mom died a little after I was born so I don't remember her like Dorado does. Same for my real dad, Hondo, but only because he took off right after she died and hasn't been seen since. Most people in the family seem to think Hondo's dead except for Dorado, who still believes for some reason that he's not. I don't care, though. You can't miss someone that you don't remember as far as I'm concerned.

My Aunt Patty adopted me and Dorado right after my dad left when I was still a baby, so she's basically my mom. Me and Dorado get along real good with her husband, Rod, at least, which is unusual where stepdads are concerned—or step-uncle in this case, I guess. A little over a year ago, Aunt Patty and him had their first baby, which they named Roddy. It made me feel weird in a way since before that I was used to me and Dorado being their only kids. But, other than that initial weirdness, I like Roddy pretty good. He's sort of like a little brother same as I could consider my aunt and uncle my mom and dad. I think I might enjoy him when he gets to be a little older. Right now Roddy mostly just screamed and wetted himself a lot.

From the bathroom I heard the screen door screech open and slam shut. Once I heard Rod cuss under his breath, I knew my Nana had just hobbled in. Nana lives in a dilapidated old trailer right on our front lawn, which I guess I should mention too.

"Patricia!" she called to my aunt. "Patricia, I need a lighter for my smoke. I know you hid it somewhere in here."

"Why don't you go out back and rub two sticks together like in the old days," Rod yelled from the floor, still hooking up the washer. I can't blame Rod for not liking her since she's his mother-in-law, and from what I understand, son-in-laws are supposed to be irked by their mother-in-laws.

"Mother, the doctors told you that you had to quit smoking. It's not good for you," Aunt Patty shouted from the back of the house as I walked into the kitchen to get something to eat.

"Aw, what the hell do they know? I been smoking since before them sonsabitches was born," Nana said in between coughs. "You'd think an old lady could enjoy her last days in peace, but noooooo."

"I don't have time for this," Aunt Patty muttered as she brushed past me in the kitchen and Nana staggered behind her. Aunt Patty turned to me. "Pancho, don't forget we're taking Roddy to the pediatrician in Albuquerque this afternoon, so we won't be here when you get home from school. But Dorado is supposed to pick you up, right?"

"Yeah, he is," I said with a mouthful of toast.

Dorado moved out three years ago when he graduated high school and hadn't been home in quite a while, so I was pretty excited when he called last night to let us know he was visiting. That, and he could help me and Dingus with our little scheme we were cooking up regarding Pat Garrett High.

Last night, once I got Dorado on the phone and Aunt Patty was out of earshot, I had asked him if he could do me a favor and pick me up tomorrow from Pat Garrett High when school let out.

"I thought you were still in Billy the Kid Junior High this year, Pancho?" he said.

"I am. But tomorrow I need you to pick me up from Pat Garrett High. Got it?"

There was a pause for a second, then he said, "You little scoundrel. I don't know what kind of horrible act you and Dingus are about to perpetrate, but whatever it is, I'm proud of you."

I laughed. That's why I loved Dorado more than anybody else. Heck, sometimes I figured even if I still had my real mom and dad, I might love him the most. No matter what, he always had my back. "Thanks, man. Oh, and one more thing. Don't wait for me in the main parking lot. Maybe park out behind the football field, okay?"

Like I said earlier, some of the kids from Pat Garrett High had kidnapped our school mascot/pet, which is a billy goat. You probably don't know this unless you live out in the country, but a young billy goat is called a kid, hence Billy the Kid. Get it? Like I said before, me and Dingus didn't have a great deal of school spirit. And, we weren't what you'd call animal activists either. We were just bored, and getting the goat back sounded like a fun challenge.

Anyways, with Dorado set to be our getaway driver, the plan was all set for tomorrow for me and Dingus to skip school in the afternoon, get on over to Pat Garrett High, and rescue the goat. We figured once our school learned what we did we might not even get in trouble. But, on the other hand, if we did get in trouble, that would just make us even more popular among our own class, so we won either way.

Even though I was excited about it that morning, I was still nervous, too. A little part of me was even thinking of chickening out of it when Uncle Rod broke into my thoughts. "I don't see why your aunt's so intent on getting the old woman to stop smoking. If it were up to me, I'd let her smoke three packs a day."

Rod finished tightening a water line on the washer, cussed at it one more time for good measure, and added, "Actually, maybe we could take her to the vet and have her put down."

I choked on my toast laughing. "You're terrible, old man," I said. I guess we have a warped sense of humor, but we don't really mean it. At least not most of the time.

I walked to the front door and could see the bus coming down the road kicking up a cloud of dust. I picked up my backpack and went out the screen door letting it slam behind me. We're a happy family and all, but we don't fuss about saying hello and goodbye like most people do.

The bus doors came screeching open. Man, I hate the smell of a school bus; they always stink like old crayons or something. I walked on to the back and sat down by my friend Misael. I can't pronounce Misael though, and neither can anybody else, so we just call him Missile. He looked like he was studying for his history test. We usually studied or did homework on the bus on the way to school. We sure weren't gonna waste our time doing it at home.

"Hey, do you remember the name of that cattle baron we were talkin' about in class last week? The one Professor Mendez said fought in the Lincoln County War?" Missile asked, frustrated.

"Not really." The only thing I remembered about class last week was when Rita Aramijo bent over to pick up her pencil at the pencil sharpener after she dropped it.

"Aww, wait. I remember now. It was Chisum, like the John Wayne movie," Missile said, finally looking up from his book.

"Dang. I shoulda' remembered that," I said. That movie was probably the only reason he remembered who Chisum was.

"I guess I better study, too," I said and got my book out of my backpack and tried my best to remember all the key names and stuff like that. I always end up doing stuff right at the last minute, and it usually works out okay, except today I was super preoccupied about me and Dingus's goat scheme.

The bus screeched to a stop, and everybody got up. Sometimes it cracks me up because all the kids walking and bumping into each other making a ruckus sort of reminds me of cattle being herded through the livestock gates. I see a lot of that living in New Mexico.

I stepped off the bus and looked around. It was a usual morning on the school grounds. Two girls were talking as loud as they could at each other about who had been saying what and who hadn't, the kicker kids were trying to chew some chaw and see to it that everybody saw 'em doing it except for the teachers on duty, the brainy kids were looking over some math homework with their pocket calculators, and the jocks were seeing who could outdo each other with their putdowns and acting like they were going to fight even though everybody knew they weren't. I'm not sure which group me and Missile fit into, but probably something in between the kickers and the jocks.

"Hey, Pancho!" I heard someone shout.

I looked around for who was calling me and saw Dingus making his way through the crowd. Dingus is one of the funniest kids I ever seen, and you'd never know we were related to look at us. Whereas I'm dark-haired and dark-complected, he looks like an albino by comparison. Plus, he looks more like he should be in the 4th Grade instead of the 9th being a really short, towheaded kid. But don't be fooled by his appearance; that kid's a force to be reckoned with. He's the craziest person I know, and believe me when I say I know some pretty crazy people. He can make fun of anyone or anything faster than anybody I know. He's not mean though, just mischievous.

Dingus was getting closer and he was still shouting at me. "Pancho! You ready for this afternoon, man?"

I'd been so caught up in studying for that dumb test that I'd nearly forgot about what was really important: our big scheme. I looked around; too many people were within earshot. "Whoa, calm down, man. Let's go over where there's not so many people," I said as Dingus skidded up in front of me. There seemed to be a good spot in the corner of the school that nobody was using so we started to walk over there.

"Missile?" I said, turning to our friend.

"No way! I'm staying out of this one," he said, eyeing me determinedly.

About three weeks ago, Missile had gotten into big trouble and negotiated with his parents he wouldn't get into trouble ever again, which technically to him meant not until after Christmas. Me and Dingus, however, felt we could pull our scheme off without getting caught. Plus, I had someone on the inside to help us.

"Hey, so did you talk to Becky one more time just to be sure?" Dingus asked me.

Becky was my girlfriend who went to Pat Garrett High. She was a year older than me, but just barely, and told me exactly where the goat was being kept. She was also the one to get me and Dingus the cheerleader uniforms.

"Yeah, man. She says she checked again yesterday, and the goat's still being kept in a pen outside of the football team's fieldhouse. Like I said, if we can get in there before practice starts around 2:00, we should be golden."

"You sure you can trust her, though? She might be a turncoat," Dingus said.

Damn if that kid didn't get the wildest ideas in his head sometimes. "She's my girlfriend, of course I can trust her. You been watching too many movies, Dingus."

"All I can say, Pancho, is I seen plenty a James Bond movie where he only thinks he can trust the girl, and then she turns out to be a double agent. Then—bam!—before you know it, Blofeld's dangling him over piranha infested waters or Goldfinger's got a laser shooting between his legs or—"

I cut him off because he would go on and on if I didn't. "This is just school, man, not secret agent stuff. Besides, Becky ain't got any more school spirit than you or me got. She just wants to see that poor little helpless goat go free."

"Well, alright. You have the uniforms on you?" he asked.

I unzipped my backpack to show him that I did. "I just hope they're my size," he said as he peered in at the skirts.

Now, did Dingus and I really need to dress up like cheerleaders and such to steal the goat? I reckon not. But Dingus loved elaborate plans like that. And he did have a point. Somebody might recognize us as boys, but as girls, maybe not.

"You bring a wig?" I asked.

"Yeah, my brother's wife had one laying around in her closet, so I snatched it," he said, pulling out a golden blonde wig from his backpack that matched his own hair.

"Awesome, man. It's your color and everything," I said. Since my hair was long enough, all I'd have to do was tie some of those scrunchie things in my hair on both sides to make me look like Pippi Longstocking.

"Alright, one more time. We'll meet up here again at lunch and slip away while nobody notices," Dingus began repeating the plan, probably for his own amusement more than anyone else's since I knew it pretty good by now. "I did a dry run yesterday, and with both of us on my bike, it'll take us about thirty minutes or so to get from one end of town to the other, which should be just enough time to slip in at the end of their lunch break unnoticed. And then, we spring that poor creature out of goat jail. Agreed?"

"Agreed," I said as the bell rang, signaling that it was time for us all to go inside.

"Okay, until noon, Pancho," Dingus said and looked down, pressing a button on his watch. I don't think it actually did anything, but he pressed it.

Me and Dingus were always up to something and getting in trouble. We had a reputation that way. I guess I kind of have a bad reputation around town in general thanks to my family—and I don't mean because of Dingus and Dorado. Even though those two are pretty wild, I get my rep from my dad's twin brother who he named me after. See, my Uncle Pancho was regarded as a ne'er-do-well by the residents of Fort Sumner, while my dad, Hondo, was the town sheriff. I hear people called Pancho the bad twin and my dad the good twin. People probably would have forgotten who my Uncle Pancho even was except for that at the same time he disappeared, so did Billy the Kid's tombstone. Since they both disappeared at the same time, people just figured that Pancho must have stolen it. Anyways, that's why some people thought I was so wild—because I was named after my wild uncle. That was dumb if you asked me. Me and Dingus were always getting in trouble because it was fun, plain and simple.

Just like last week, we had to stay for two hours after school in detention. Two whole hours gone! Ordinarily I might have been able to let that slide, but that day after school, Christopher Teeter, one of the dumbest, wildest kids at Billy the Kid Junior High, was going to imitate some stunt on his bike in the dirt pits that he'd seen on a TV. Well, when we missed Chris's performance at the pits Friday and saw him this Monday with crutches and a cast, we knew we'd missed something wonderful.

I don't know if what me and Dingus did was worthy of two hours of punishment, but we had just gotten out of Home Economics. It's a girly class where you sew and knit and bake stuff, but truth be told, I secretly enjoy it. That month the teacher was making us take home baby dolls—those fake battery-operated ones that cry—for the weekend to show you how hard it is to be a parent or whatever.

I had taken mine home the weekend before. Dang thing woke me up at all hours of the night. I decided that if my old man never had to wake up in the middle of the night with me then I dang sure wasn't doing it for no fake baby, so Saturday and Sunday I made it a little bed in my dresser drawers and shut it up in there and it stayed real quiet the whole rest of the weekend. I'm still waiting to see my grade. Anyways, last Friday just happened to be Dingus's turn to take it home, only after Home Economics me and Dingus also had Woodshop Class… and well, one thing led to another and I'm sure you can imagine.

To be honest, if I were an adult, I wouldn't have allowed Dingus to take Woodshop Class to begin with, but as far as I was concerned, that was their fault. I should've known better than to participate, but dang it, stuff like that only happens once. Anyhow, the point is even though that fake baby might have had a chance meeting with the skill-saw, I still didn't think it justified two whole hours of Friday after-school detention. In our own minds, us skipping school this afternoon to do something fun would make up for the two hours they'd stolen from us last Friday.

Anyway, anticipating our scheme for the afternoon made it hard to concentrate on my classes that morning, especially the first one, A.R. A.R. stands for accelerated reader and you have to read so many books a semester. I hate the books we usually have to read for that class. They're always wanting you to read one of those girly books about kids living in the frontier days and all the hardships they went through and all that. They try to make it exciting but they still just end up being boring if you ask me. Teachers seem to think reading is the most wonderful thing you can do, but the way I see it, you can learn just as much from TV.

Dingus at least makes things interesting; every now and again he'll spiral around in his chair and scribble all over the page I'm pretending to read with an ink-pen and then swivel back around again before the teacher notices.

Then, in 2nd Period, I get to sit next to Missile and we make fun of the announcements where students read the news over the P.A. system. I wouldn't make fun of them except I can tell they're being forced to read something the teachers wrote for them because it's really corny. If it was written by one of us it'd all be about who was with who, and who was thinking about getting with who, and so on. I do like the announcements, though, because it takes a chunk out of having to do busy work like word searches and junk like that. We've had to cut down on our remarks at the "newscasters" though, because our math teacher, Mr. Harrison, has threatened us with more demerits, so now we only let out with the really good stuff that's actually worth a demerit.

Right before lunch was New Mexico History. I might actually like that class except for our teacher, Professor Mendez, really had it in for me. I guess it's because my brother Dorado was a real pain when Mendez had him, so now he doesn't like me, which I don't think is fair one bit which goes to show teachers can be just as petty as kids.

The Professor had a gaunt face, with these big alert eyes gleaming with intelligence that reminded me of a hawk. Most of us didn't think the Professor was really a professor though, because we figured if he was he'd be teaching at a university instead of a middle school.

Lately we'd been learning about Billy the Kid and the Lincoln County War. Everybody in Fort Sumner knows the tale of Billy the Kid. How he was born in the slums of New York and killed his first man at seventeen. How Billy became a sort of vigilante hero fighting for the poor citizens of Lincoln County, and how he ran up here to Fort Sumner where he got killed by Sheriff Pat Garrett. Some people said Garrett and the Kid used to be good friends before they became enemies. Others even said Garrett let the Kid get away the night he supposedly shot him and buried an empty coffin containing a few bags of sand to fake his death. In the 1940s, a man named Tumbleweed Williams came forth claiming to be Billy, but he couldn't ever prove that he actually was. Not long after that, the tombstone from Billy the

Kid's grave mysteriously disappeared. Like I said earlier, most people think my dad's twin brother did it since he went missing right after. Our dad used to tell Dorado that Uncle Pancho stole it because it had a treasure map hidden inside, but it was just a bedtime story to cover up the fact that his brother was a thief.

I believed the stories for a while when Dorado told me them, but I eventually wised up. Dorado never did though. He still wants to believe our old man was telling him the truth, but I know better. Aunt Patty figures Hondo went off looking for Uncle Pancho somewhere and got killed, but maybe that's just a bedtime story, too. I figured he just didn't want to have to raise two kids on his own and left because of that.

I try not to think about it in general, but right now it's kind of hard not to. The whole town is all stirred up because about a month or two ago they found the tombstone out in a field in Texas somewhere. (That's another reason I don't think Uncle Pancho actually stole it. If he had, he would've broken it open to get to that dumb treasure map, or whatever.) The mayor made a big deal about it coming home to the real grave, and now that it's back they even put a steel cage around it. This weekend, on Halloween, they're even going to host an event called the Tombstone Race where participants have to run a race holding a 50-pound replica of the tombstone. There was even talk of the tombstone being placed in a museum in Santa Fe. That's what the professor was talking about now.

"As it's a very topical subject with the return of the tombstone to Fort Sumner, along with that tacky tombstone race being held this weekend before they ship it off to Santa Fe, we'll resume our discussion on Billy the Kid and the Lincoln County War," he began.

The Professor looked around the room. "First off, how many of you think Pat Garrett shot Billy?" About half the class raised their hands and I made it a point to be one of them. I didn't wanna be counted among the crazies who think he didn't get shot. Mendez seemed pleased and then asked, "Now, how many of you think Garrett let Billy get away?" The other half of the class raised their hands.

"50/50, I see. How interesting. So half of you believe that a respected lawman like Garrett risked losing out on a $500 reward just to let the Kid go because he was really a good person deep down? And then nearly 70 years later, an old man, obviously desperate for attention and wanting to make his mark on the world before he dies, comes forward claiming to be Billy the Kid?" The people who had raised their hands slowly started to take them back down. They looked embarrassed, which pleased the professor. Mendez enjoyed making people feel stupid. I think it was one of his primary goals in life.

"And the other half of you believes that a sheriff shot an outlaw for reward money. Of these two scenarios, which seems the most plausible to you?"

A girl raised her hand to answer and Mendez said, "That was a rhetorical question, put your hand down." He leaned back on his desk and crossed his arms to finish his point. "Has it ever occurred to most of you that you believe the Tumbleweed Williams story only because people have a tendency to want to believe in the more interesting story? Well, I've got news for you. The less interesting story is almost always the one which is true."

He stood back up and walked to the chalkboard. "That is why in this class, we will discuss such fairy tales no further and instead stick to the hard facts of Billy the Kid and the Lincoln County War."

He wrote the words Lincoln County War across the chalkboard. "The Lincoln County War was fought mostly over land and cattle. On one side were Billy the Kid and the poor peoples of Lincoln, and on the other the rich illustrious Santa Fe Ring—a so-called group of corrupt politicians and lawyers that supposedly ruled the entire territory of New Mexico in secret. However, who is to say which side was really the good and which was really the bad? History teaches us a lesson in perspective—

I couldn't resist cutting him off. That business about the Santa Fe Ring had always tickled me. "But Professor, are you saying the Santa Fe Ring really existed? I mean, don't it sound sort of like something from a really lame James Bond movie?"

A few people in the class snickered. The professor turned around from his chalkboard to look at me, but instead of looking angry, he looked kinda pleased that I had challenged him, which was never a good sign. "Oh no, Pancho, make no mistake, they existed, some people say as recently as ten years ago. Which brings me back to my point before I was so rudely interrupted."

He leaned back against his desk again. "Who is to say who the real hero of the Lincoln County War really was? Today, to your youthful anti-establishment generation, it is Billy the Kid. But not one hundred years ago. One hundred years ago the Kid was a ruthless killer, in it for himself as much as he was for the so-called poor peoples of Lincoln standing in the way of progress in the Old West. Some people might even say our state would have been better off today had no one stood up to oppose the Ring."

I knew this would have consequences, but I couldn't resist. I can't seem to keep my mouth shut for anything when I think of something funny to say. "Professor," I began real sincere like, "are you part of the Ring?"

The class laughed and for a second he looked at me like he'd like to kill me. But then his lips parted into another one of those thin smiles and I knew I'd really done it.

"Very funny, Pancho. In fact, I think it's so funny that tonight, I'd like all of you," he pointed his finger around the room to let us know he meant the whole class, "to complete a two-page report on the legend of Billy the Kid, the Lincoln County War, and the Santa Fe Ring."

No sooner than the words left his mouth we let out a collective groan and Missile, who sits behind me, hit me with his notebook. "Nice going, Pancho," he whispered. Then a girl spoke up and said, "Aw, come on, Professor. Why don't you just make Pancho write the report? It's his fault!"

Almost everyone yelled, "Yeah!" and a few people threw paper wads at me, which I guess I deserved.

Mendez shushed the class and then looked at me to answer her question, "No, because just as Billy the Kid's actions affected those around him, so too do your classmate Pancho's. You see, like the Kid, our friend Pancho is what you might call a juvenile delinquent, and we all know where that got Billy the Kid. As I always say, those who do not learn from history," he smiled and paused for a second, "are always doomed to repeat it." Just as he said those last words the bell rang. "Class dismissed."

I couldn't help but shiver as I stood up.

"That's just great, Pancho. Now we all have to write reports!" Missile said as we walked out.

"I'm sorry, man. I just couldn't help myself."

"You and that mouth of yours, man. Geez."

As we walked down the bustling hallway, I suddenly realized that it was lunchtime. I had been so caught up arguing with Mendez that I forgot it was zero hour for me and Dingus. "Oh, crap!" I said. "I'm supposed to meet Dingus outside. You sure you don't want to come? It'll be fun."

Missile held up his hands. "Like I said, I want no part of this."

"Okay, but you're gonna be sorry you missed out," I said as I ran off.

I didn't even grab any lunch—there wasn't enough time, and time was of the essence. I ran outside to rendezvous with Dingus and hop onto his bike. I didn't realize it then, but the trouble we were about to get into at Pat Garrett High was nothing like the trouble I would get into later that night.

II.
FISTFULL
OF DEMERITS

Two hours and a few mistakes later, there me and Dingus were barreling down the hallways of Pat Garrett High with the baby billy goat. Things had gone mostly to plan except for it took us longer to get to Pat Garrett High than we planned, change into the cheerleader outfits, psyche ourselves up once the reality of the situation set in, and so on. By the time we were ready to snatch the goat, football practice was already in session. Or, in other words, we got caught. That's why Coach McPherson, members of the football team, and a few disgruntled cheerleaders in towels were currently chasing us down the hallway. (Since we couldn't make our escape through the football field like we planned, we'd had to double back to the school and in the process might have accidentally gone through the cheerleader's fieldhouse as they were changing.)

As we sped through the halls creating a ruckus on the bike, I could see kids peeking out from open classroom doors to see what all the fuss was about. It was about fifteen minutes before school would get out, so the halls were clear at least, but my legs were starting to burn from all the peddling I'd been doing. If I slowed down at all, Coach McPherson and his army of jocks and cheerleaders would catch us in an instant.

"How the hell did you get me into this, Dingus? You said this would be easy!" I yelled.

"Rescuing him was easy!" he yelled back. "I never said getting away would be! That's your department, which means Dorado better be outside waiting for us!"

"Oh, keep your dress on! He'll be there. I hope," I whispered that last part to myself as we rounded a corner—a corner I had expected would lead us to freedom and a nearby exit. Instead, I saw trouble. Up ahead was a wet, freshly mopped floor with the janitor and his pushcart right in the way. There wasn't much room to get around him and the cart both in the hall.

"Stop those kids!" Coach McPherson yelled to the man, and time seemed to start going in slow motion. The janitor's eyes lit up as they locked with my own, but I kept on going right at him.

"Alto!" the janitor cried out, raising his mop in the air as though to strike us down with it. My mind immediately went to a Steve McQueen movie where he slid down sideways on a motorcycle and went skidding across the ground a considerable distance. I may not have been as cool as Steve McQueen, and I was on Dingus's bike instead of a motorcycle, but in that moment, it seemed to be my only option. I pivoted my weight all to one side, bringing the bike into a slide. Me, Dingus, and I think even the goat all screamed as we tipped over just as the janitor took his swing. The bike met the slick wet floor and went sliding, and it was all I could do to look behind me to see the wet mop make contact with Coach McPherson's face, bringing him down hard. Not just him, but all the other players and cheerleaders collapsed into a heap like a bad car pileup on the highway.

It felt like me and Dingus must have slid forever across the slick floor before we finally came to a stop. There was no time to gawk at the accident, even though I sure wanted to. I righted myself from the floor, struggling to stand on the slick surface. Dingus looked up at me pitifully, offering me the baby goat.

"Here, take him. You're stronger than me, Pancho. You've always been stronger," he said weakly, like he was dying.

Dingus hiked up his leg after I took the goat, revealing a bad scrape on his knee as though it were a mortal wound. "I'm finished. You'll have to complete the mission without me."

"You have a scratch," I said, irritated he was acting like a drama queen. I extended my hand to help him up. He shooed it away.

"It's no good, Pancho. I'll only hold you back."

I looked at Coach McPherson and the others all starting to get up. Coach caught my eye and shouted, "Stay where you are, Dumez!"

"Dang it, Dingus! I ain't got time for your bullshit. Get up already!" I hissed at him.

He grabbed me by the collar. "Listen to me, Pancho. I want you to have children, a life… all the things I'll never have. Now go! Go now! Save yourself!" Dingus cried out dramatically.

"Oh for shit sakes!" I swatted his hand away and took off with the goat down the hall. Dingus liked to pretend life was like a movie sometimes, and this was just one of those moments. If he wanted to get caught, that was on him. I was getting the hell out of there.

I ran about fifteen yards and rounded another corner down a different hall. Believe it or not, aside from Dingus getting left behind, things hadn't gone completely off the rails. Truth be told, getting out through the football field had only been our Plan A. We also had a Plan B—B as in Becky Garrett. If things went south, which they had, I was supposed to find her in the west wing of the school, where she'd take us to a "safe room" as Dingus had called it. Now it was just a matter of finding her in the west wing. "Becky," I hissed in a whisper. "Becky!"

I was proceeding cautiously along the wall when an arm suddenly reached out and pulled me into a stairway. It was the arm of a doe-eyed, dark, curly-haired beauty. It was Becky.

"Why if it isn't the noted desperado, Pancho Dumez," she said.

"I was wondering where you were." I leaned in and pecked her on the lips real quick.

"Come on. They won't look for us up here," she said in kind of a whisper and led me up the stairway to the second story. I could hear Coach McPherson and the mob making a ruckus, too, but I don't think they coulda seen me go up the stairs since they hadn't gotten around the corner yet.

"Where's Dingus?" she asked as we ran up the stairs.

"He didn't make it. Told me to save myself."

"Oh geez," was all she said. She knew Dingus pretty good, too, and like me, wasn't too worried about him. Dingus was like a cat. He always landed on his feet and I'd seen him get out of worse situations than this.

At the top of the stairway, Becky stopped and looked both ways down the hall. She put her finger to her lips, signaling me to be quiet. The little billy let out a baby goat bleat right then and we both laughed. She grabbed my hand and we ran into a room just across the hall. She shut the door.

"We should be safe in here. It's the laundry room," she said.

"I see that," I said looking around. It was noisy, too, since a load was in one of the washers, which was good in case Billy got to bleating again. Becky was making all over him just like I figured she would. She loves animals.

"Hey, who are you more happy to see, me or the goat?" I said as she took him from my arms.

She looked at me with those googly eyes girls make whenever they really want something. "Pancho, do me a favor. Don't take him back to Billy the Kid Junior High. Set him free?"

"Are you kidding? That little goat has it made being a school mascot. Thanks for letting me borrow your uniform by the way. I think it looks better on you, though," I said as I began to take it off. By now people would be looking for a guy dressed as a cheerleader, and I needed to change my appearance.

"You know, they say Billy the Kid hid out as a woman once to evade the law," Becky said nonchalantly as she continued to pet the goat.

"Did you bring me something else to wear?" I asked as I finally managed to slip out of the uniform. I wasn't embarrassed for Becky to see me in my boxers. It wasn't any different than if she saw me in a pair of swim trunks down at the slough.

"Yeah, I brought you some football pads and a helmet to hide your face on the way out of here."

Dang. Me and Dingus shoulda just dressed up as football players and it woulda been a lot easier. Something told me that Dingus probably realized that, too, but had intentionally chosen the cheerleader outfits because it would make for a better story.

"How much time you think I got?" I asked her as I tossed the skirt and top on the floor.

"I'd say another six minutes before the bell rings and you can blend in with the other kids when school lets out."

That seemed like a good plan. Schools were always chaotic when the last bell rang, so I didn't worry myself with getting dressed right away. I walked over to Becky, who was still petting the goat. "Why don't you just keep him?"

She gave me a mocking look then grinned. "In case you've forgotten, I'm the sheriff's kid. I can't exactly steal a goat and get away with it."

"Oh, I haven't forgotten. Believe me." The fact that she was Sheriff Garrett's kid was one of main attractions in my nightmares—and that was way before he ever tried to kill me.

"And on that note, is your dad working tonight?" I asked hopefully.

She smiled deviously. "He is."

"Well, I was thinking I could come over and we could work on our costumes for the Halloween dance tomorrow night?"

She laughed and gave me a look. "As if that's your main objective."

"What?" I grinned. "I just want to make sure they're top-notch."

She laughed, not buying my B.S. "I'll think about it."

I was about to do some pleading when all of a sudden there was a loud bang on the other side of the door.

"Open up, Dumez!" McPherson bellowed. "We know you're in there. Your little friend told us everything!"

"They made me talk, Pancho!" Dingus shouted. "I didn't want to but—"

Somebody, probably one of the football players, cut Dingus off.

"You got to the count of ten to open this door on your own before we use the keys!" McPherson shouted.

"Ten!"

"How do we get out of here?" I asked.

"Nine!"

"The window, it's the only way," Becky said.

"Eight!"

I ran over and opened up the window. It wasn't that far of a drop. Plus there was a nice fat bush to cushion me and the goat's fall. "It's not that far down. He'll be fine," I said referring to the little goat, who couldn't have weighed more than ten or fifteen pounds.

"Seven!"

I dropped the little goat. He bleated all the way down the short ten-foot drop into the bushes. He was fine.

"Six!"

"I'll see you tonight?" I said as I was crawling out the window.

"Five!"

"Hold on. I'm coming!" Becky yelled to the door. Then, to me, she said, "Okay, yes. You can come over tonight. Now go!"

"Four!"

"One more kiss?" I asked, pointing to my cheek with my free hand.

"Three! Two!"

Becky pushed me out the window then promptly shut it.

"One!" I heard Coach call out as I hit the bushes. It knocked the wind out of me, but at least I didn't land on the goat, who was already attempting to eat the bush next to us.

"There's nobody in here but me," I heard Becky say real irritated to Coach.

"I'll be the judge of that. Now where is he?" he said. I started to get up and brush myself off. Just as I scooped up the little goat, Coach McPherson opened up the window.

"I knew it!" he hissed to himself. Then he shouted at me, "Give us the goat, Dumez, and me and my team won't pound you into the ground."

"I guess I've only got one thing to say for myself," I said, looking up at him.

"Oh yeah? What's that?" he said.

"I'm really glad I went out for track instead of football," I said and bolted. It wouldn't take long for some of the faster guys to get downstairs and start chasing me, so I ran as fast as I could for the football field. Sure enough, it wasn't two seconds before I heard the double doors of the school bust open. From out of them came some of the players and eventually Coach himself.

I decided to quit wasting my time looking behind me and focus on what was ahead of me. I scanned the dirt road running parallel to the field for Dorado's car. Sure enough, I could see his red-orange 73 Camaro in the clearing between two old oak trees. God bless my brother, he never let me down. It also struck me that maybe I should have given him more details other than a time and a place, as I'm sure he'd be wondering why I was running through a football field in my underwear carrying a goat while being pursued by the football team and angry cheerleaders in towels.

As I got closer, it didn't sound like the car was running. I squinted and could see why. He wasn't alone. Dorado had brought along his on-again-off-again girlfriend Rosalita, and it looked like they were killing time making out.

"Dorado! Dorado! Start the car!" I screamed at the top of my lungs, still running as fast as I could with the little goat. Even though he wasn't heavy, he still threw off my balance a little bit having to hold him to my chest.

I was coming in so hot and panicked that I didn't think to start slowing myself down as I came up to the car. "Dorado!" I yelled as I plastered myself across the passenger window, bringing myself to a stop. Rosalita spun around and screamed. Then the baby goat bleated real loud, and she screamed again.

"Pancho?" Dorado looked at me as though he almost didn't recognize me, and I realized I never undid my pigtails.

"Start the car! Quick!" I said as I opened the passenger side door, tossed the goat in the backseat, and crawled in after him.

"Dorado, what the hell is going on?" Rosalita shrieked. He didn't get a chance to answer because about then Dingus came roaring up to the car on his bike. He was even whiter than normal due to his near brush with death back in the halls.

"Pancho, why are you naked? And why is Dingus in drag?" Dorado asked, but I was more focused on Dingus as he barreled into the backseat with me.

"You sold me out, man! And here you were worried about Becky being a turncoat," I yelled.

"I'm sorry, Pancho. They broke me, man. Threatened to make me wear Pete Patterson's jock strap on my head if I didn't talk! What the heck was I supposed to do?"

"What is that thing?" Rosalita asked in reference to the poor baby goat.

Dorado had finally started the car and had put it in reverse. "It better not shit on the backseat," he said glancing at us as he was backing up.

"It's our school mascot," I answered Rosalita breathlessly. "They stole it," I pointed to the angry mob that was just about to be upon us, "and we rescued it."

Dorado had backed up to where he was facing the road now, but he still wasn't going, and they were getting closer by the second.

"Dorado, man, what are you waiting for?" Dingus asked in a panic.

"This," he said with an ornery grin and peeled out so hard that he kicked up a flurry of dirt all over Coach, the players, and even the poor cheerleaders.

As we sped onto the open road Dingus and I high-fived over how awesome the moment was while Rosalita was hitting Dorado on the shoulder as she yelled at him. Part of it was in Spanish, but the English parts that I could make out went something like this: "What the hell was that? I thought you said this was our time to be alone? Not so you could pick up your brother and his friends!"

Dorado shrugged and gave her a meek smile. "I like to multitask. Excuse me for being efficient."

"Oh whatever, you *baboso*!"

Dorado and I still aren't sure what *baboso* means but we know enough to know it's not good. I can't say I care for Rosalita. She's smoking hot, don't get me wrong, but she's kind of scary. When she starts yelling at Dorado or me in Spanish it's like a verbal tornado or something. One time, once she finished yelling at us in the living room at the house, I think I actually saw the sofa cushions in different spots. Actually, the most Spanish I've ever learned is from listening to her yell at Dorado. They're always breaking up and getting back together again.

It had been a while since I'd seen my brother, and I caught myself staring at him. He didn't have any new scars on his face, either from racing or getting into fights, so that was good at least. Dorado looks sort of like a bigger, older version of me, only he's got a lighter complexion and his hair's a strange reddish copper color. He always has an expression etched onto his face that could only be described as a look of restrained orneriness, like he's got something really horrible to say and he's either trying his best to hold it back, or he's too excited because he's about to say it anyway. He's crazy about cars, and I really mean crazy. He gets the same slack-jawed look on his face whenever he sees a car he really likes or a hot long-legged blonde walking down the street, as if he's putting all of his mental energy into picturing what's underneath their hood.

The most impressive thing about my brother is his reflexes, which are like lightning. Dorado grew up like a lot of kids around here wanting to be Billy the Kid. Only, unlike a lot of people, Dorado actually is a good shot. I even saw him shoot a tin can in midair twice one time for target practice, and I ain't never seen anybody else be able to do that. I guess that's what makes him such a good driver, too, he's able to react quick. Last I knew, he was racing cars down in Mexico; that's why I was so surprised to see him back home. Actually, I was a little uneasy about it even though I was happy to see him. So was Rosalita, apparently.

"All I know, Dorado, is you've been down in Mexico all summer doing God knows what with God knows who and I can't even get five minutes alone with you! You didn't even come down here just to see me like you said, did you?"

She had a point. I wasn't sure why Dorado was here either. I kinda hoped that maybe it was for my birthday, but something in my gut told me it was more than just a visit to see us. "Yeah man, not that I'm not stoked that you're here and all but...why are you here?" I asked.

"Is it because you lost that race in Mexico and all your sponsors?" Dingus blurted out. Dingus ain't exactly one for finesse, but I have to admit, I'm glad he asked.

"No," Dorado answered defensively. "It is not because I lost my sponsors. Where did you hear that?"

"Cade," Dingus answered, referring to his older brother, which made sense since Cade had been down in Mexico with Dorado for a while.

"You lost your sponsors? When were you going to tell me this?" Rosalita said and hit him again.

Dorado shot Dingus a look. "Thank you for that." Then to Rosalita, he said, "I was gonna tell you, baby."

"So, does this mean you're out of a job?"

"Not out of a job, just in between jobs."

"Wait, so you found a job here?" I asked, confused. I thought between jobs meant you had another one lined up.

"You could say that. Sort of," he answered.

Then all of a sudden Rosalita screamed again. The goat was chewing on her hair. "Bad Billy," I said and pulled him back and a chunk of her hair came with him.

"Okay, that is it! Stop the car, Dorado, I am getting out!" she screamed and was already trying to pry open the door even though we must've been going forty miles an hour.

Dorado swiftly pulled over. "Baby, don't do that," he pleaded with her as she got out.

"No, I am walking home! I can tell when I'm not wanted," she shouted, slamming the door.

"That's not true. In fact, later tonight we'll do something special," Dorado pleaded.

"Later tonight we'll do something special?" she repeated his words with her hands on her hips. "See, you just admitted that you do want me to leave right now. Why don't you just say so, Dorado!"

Boy, girls sure did have a funny way of interpreting things we said. If I didn't know anything else about them, I knew that at least.

"You just said yourself you were going to walk home!" Dorado responded. That is what she said, and she didn't really live that far from where we'd pulled over, either, so I didn't see what the big deal was.

Dorado unbuckled and scooted over to the passenger side, sticking his torso out the passenger window. Dorado pushed a finger to her lips. "Rosy, baby, honey. You know I love you. You're the only girl for me. And tonight, we will do something special. I promise."

He lowered his voice, but I could still hear him. "It's just I haven't seen the kid here either in several months and it's gonna be his birthday. But, like I said, later tonight we'll go out and do something special, okay?" he gently grabbed her by the waist and looked up at her with pleading eyes.

"Oh, I can't stay mad at you." She leaned down to kiss him again and I looked away.

Once they were finally done with their goodbye, Dorado slid back over into the driver's seat and put the car into gear again. Once Rosalita was a safe distance away, Dorado shouted, "Just don't wait up too late, okay? I have a little job I've gotta do and I don't actually know when I'll be done."

"What!" she screeched as Dorado peeled out.

"I love you, too!" he shouted over the roar of the engine, and I'm pretty sure I heard Rosalita scream out, "We're finished, Dorado! Finished!"

I guess Dorado heard it too because he just shrugged and said, "Eh, we were overdue for our routine breakup anyway."

"Weren't you guys already broken up when you were down in Mexico?" I asked, confused.

"Oh, we were. That was us getting back together when you and Dingus barged in on us. And now we're broken up again," he said as though it were a simple matter.

It was true, though. Dorado and Rosalita broke up every other week it seemed like. I asked him why once, and he said something about it keeping the fire in the relationship alive.

For the rest of the drive, he told me and Dingus stories about his summer down in Mexico. I couldn't tell if all of them were true or not, or if he was just making them up for the benefit of me and Dingus, but they were good stories. I also wondered if he was telling them to us to avoid any more questions about why he was back in town. I figured I'd lay off of him about that until we were alone. After we dropped Dingus off at his brother Cade's ranch, Dorado took me back home so I could finally get some clothes back on.

Our house sits kinda on the outskirts of town and isn't much, just two bedrooms, a kitchen, living room, and one bathroom, but it's the only home I've ever known. We don't have much in terms of a yard, but we do have a patch of grass in the back. Out front it's mostly just dirt and engine parts from Rod's various projects. Rod always has lots of different projects he's working on to Aunt Patty's horror.

Rumor has it my aunt used to be a neat freak, but she gave up on that when I started walking and Dorado was seven years old and already running wild. Roddy is lucky he had me and Dorado to break Aunt Patty's spirit where cleanliness is concerned since he gets away with murder. He can dirty the house in a million different ways and never get yelled at. If I even did half the stuff that kid does on a daily basis, Aunt Patty would've dropped me off in the middle of a vacant field a long time ago.

The real *piece de résistance* of our place is Nana's dilapidated old trailer which sits practically in the front yard. She never wanted to move to an old folk's home, so we moved her out here to keep an eye on her. I could see her peeping out at us through the blinds as we drove up. I was hoping we could get inside before she saw me and the goat and asked a million questions.

I got out of the car and let the goat out, walking kinda fast hoping that we'd make it inside before Nana managed to hobble outside. We had almost made it when she shouted, "Hey! Don't pretend like you don't see me!"

Dorado gave me a shocked look and whispered, "Nana's still alive? You told me she died?"

I just shrugged. "She got better."

"Hi Nana, good to see you," Dorado said once she hobbled up next to us.

I was hoping she was rushing over to see him, but apparently not. "Pancho, where are your clothes? Aw, never mind. At your age I don't want to know. I just got a call from your school saying you was truant this afternoon."

Boy, I was glad Aunt Patty wasn't here. She was harder to dupe. "It's okay, Nana. Dorado just came by to pick me up early. That's all."

"Aw hell, Patricia leaves for one day and you turn into a dad-gummed hooligan. It's too much stress for a helpless, pitiful old woman. And what the heck is that?" Nana pointed to Little Billy.

"A goat," I said.

"Well, I know it's a goat. But what's it doing here? It's not gonna live here, is it? I don't want this place turning into a pigsty."

About that time a pig over at our neighbor's place literally started squealing. "I don't think you'll have to worry about that, Nana," I said and spread out my hands, motioning to all of Rod's car parts, dead engines, and her trailer.

She was still studying Little Billy. "Sure, it's all fun and games now, but what about when it grows up and I get gored in the ass? Then what? And you, when did you blow into town?" she said, finally acknowledging her other grandson.

"Just this afternoon, Nana," Dorado answered.

"You get thrown outta the circus already? It's not like being some kinda rodeo clown is that hard, is it?" Nana said. She was always mixed up for some reason about what Dorado did.

Dorado sighed. "We've been over this. I'm not a rodeo clown. I'm a race car driver. I race cars."

Nana threw her hands up. "Aw heck, it's all the same. You're both just like your father and your uncle—adrenaline junkies, and we all know where that got them," Nana said and looked up at the sky, crossing herself. "God rest their souls. I gave those boys good homes and they both up and run off on me. See there, now you're goin' and makin' me cry."

"Sorry, Nana," I said and did start to feel a little bad, even if I hadn't brought them up. "Hey, I'm gonna go inside and get some clothes on while you catch up with Nana," I said to Dorado. When I headed in Little Billy came in with me even though I didn't mean for him to. I'm sure that having a baby goat loose in your house probably wasn't a good idea, but right then I was too tired and hungry to care.

I ran to my room and changed into some dark colored jeans and an old white T-shirt. Then I went into the kitchen to look for something to eat since I missed lunch and was starving. I looked down at the counter. Aunt Patty had written me a note.

Pancho,

Please put on a load of whites in the new washer and do the breakfast dishes in the sink while we're gone. Be back late tonight—Patty

Dang. I should have never told Aunt Patty I had learned how to do laundry in Home Economics, now she was asking me to do it whenever she couldn't. But Dorado had told me a long time ago that if you mess stuff up enough women will quit asking you to do things, so I always make sure to accidentally drop in a wrong color with the whites. The only problem is so far Aunt Patty hasn't gotten too mad and I have several pairs of pink boxer shorts that used to be white.

Aunt Patty already had the whites set out for me to wash; she just didn't want to leave the new washer unattended I reckoned. That might have been a good idea. As soon as I put them in to wash, it made all kinds of racket our old one didn't ever make.

"What the heck is that noise?" Dorado had just walked in and was opening the fridge.

"New washer. I don't think Rod hooked it up right," I said as I sat down at the kitchen table.

"I feel like I'm in the hull of an ocean freighter," he said regarding the noise as he rooted around in the fridge. A second later he surprised me and drew out two beer cans instead of one. He slammed one down on the kitchen table, slid it over to me, and then started chugging his own. He wiped off his mouth and looked at me disdainfully. "Well, what are you waiting for?"

"Patty'll kill me if she finds out I drank one of Rod's beers."

"Oh, just drink it. I'll tell her I did it," he said as he poured some beer into a little water dish I'd gotten out for Little Billy, who took to lapping it up immediately.

I took my first swig. I like beer even though my Aunt Patty doesn't know I've ever tried it before. Aunt Patty hates it, but Rod and Dorado love it. I snuck into the kitchen one night when I was 12 to try one myself, figuring that I'd love it too. I nearly spat the first time I tasted it, but got to liking it after a while. Aunt Patty and Rod never found out since they blamed Dorado when they found one missing, and apparently he thought that he'd drunken it too, since he seemed like he was lying when denying it.

"So...you in town for Halloween or something this weekend?" I finally asked—'or something' meaning my birthday. I was born the day after Halloween, on a Spanish holiday they call Day of the Dead, which is kind of ironic, I guess. It's this weird celebration, kinda like Halloween, where people dress up like skeletons to honor the dead and stuff. But nobody really celebrates it much outside of the Southwest, and truth be told, my family didn't celebrate it either. Besides, like I said, November 1st was my birthday. Last year was the first birthday of mine that Dorado had ever missed, and I was hoping that maybe this year we could make up for it and do something crazy on Halloween night.

"Halloween's this weekend?" Dorado responded absentmindedly.

"Are you kidding?" I shot him a look.

After a second, he seemed to read my mind and held up a finger. "I did not forget about it being your birthday, okay. I just forgot about Halloween; there's a difference." He took another swig of beer.

I couldn't believe that he'd forget it was going to be Halloween. It was only one of his favorite days out of the whole year. People sure got weird as they got older. I was never going to quit enjoying Halloween.

"Well, are you here for my birthday then, or what?" I finally came out and asked.

He looked at his beer can. "Eh, can we not talk about that?"

My hunch from earlier was right. He did have an ulterior motive for coming here that had nothing to do with me. "Why are you acting so weird, man? You never used to keep secrets from me. What gives?"

"Panch,' ever heard the old expression that what you don't know can't hurt you?"

I couldn't believe what he was saying. Me and Dorado were always a team, watching each other's backs so we didn't get in trouble between Aunt Patty and Rod. We never even tattled on each other when we were young, we always backed each other up.

"Come on, man. And besides, how many secrets have I helped you keep from Aunt Patty and Rod all these years?" I argued.

"This is different. It's not like me sneaking in through the window past curfew and you telling Aunt Patty we were chasing a raccoon out of our room."

I stared at him and crossed my arms. If I stared at him long enough without saying anything, I figured he'd start to feel guilty and cave.

He was looking down at the table and fiddling with an old pocket watch that used to belong to our dad. Finally, he said, "Fine. But you're not gonna like it."

"I won't get mad, man. Come on."

"Remember how when you were little and I told you all those cool stories about Uncle Pancho stealing Billy the Kid's tombstone because he thought there was a treasure map inside?"

"You thought those stories were cool."

"Oh come on, so did you."

"Yeah, until I got old enough to realize dad told you those stories to cover up the fact that Uncle Pancho was just a worthless thief. Not to mention dad used tracking him down as an excuse to leave us." I never quite got why Dorado was so hung up on our dad. We apparently didn't mean anything to him, so as far as I was concerned, he wasn't going to mean anything to me. Dorado felt differently, but maybe that's because he could actually remember him.

"It's not like that, Pancho."

"How would you know? You were six years old when he left."

"I just know. And tonight I'm gonna find out for sure."

"What are you…" I stopped in midsentence. It finally hit me what Dorado meant. "The tombstone," I blurted out.

He gave me a knowing smile.

I stood up and leaned over the table. "No, don't tell me. Don't tell me that the very thing that destroyed our family resurfaces and the first thing you plan to do is go and repeat history by stealing it."

"Not steal it. Break it open," he said as though that made it sound better.

"Is that really supposed to make me feel better? And besides, if there was a treasure map inside, then why didn't Uncle Pancho break it open himself?" I said and walked over to the counter.

"I don't know. Maybe somebody killed him before he got the chance? Maybe he lost it? Besides, you can't discount where they found the tombstone either."

I leaned back against the counter. "They found it in a field in Texas, what's so special about that?"

"They found it in a field in Granbury, Texas," Dorado said as though that should mean something. I just stared at him blankly. He sighed. "Granbury, Texas, the town where Billy "Tumbleweed" Williams had a heart attack in 1950. Don't tell me you don't know who that is."

"Yeah, your old buddy Professor Mendez gave us all a lecture on him today. Williams was just another crazy loon who told fairy tales like dad."

"One, don't even say the name Professor Mendez around me, and two, you can't be that skeptical. This means something. Trust me."

Little Billy let out a bleat, breaking the silence. He had lapped up all his beer. Dorado sighed. "Here, destroy the evidence," he said and dropped the metal can in his dish, which Billy started chewing on. I'd seen goats eat cans before, so I reckoned he'd do it.

"You do know Sumner has put an iron gate around the tombstone since it's been returned, right?" I asked.

"Yeah, and they're already talking about putting it on display in a museum in Santa Fe, hence why I'm about to go see Cade on the ranch to borrow his welder. Speaking of which, you wanna come with? To the ranch, I mean."

"Sure. I made plans with Becky anyway. I can walk to her place from Cade's."

"You're still going out with Becky?" He acted like he was surprised, but I couldn't blame him.

"Yeah."

"And does her dad know—"

"No," I stated matter-of-factly. Our family had a complex relationship with Xander Garrett. When our dad used to be the sheriff of Fort Sumner, Xander had been his deputy. Now Xander was the sheriff. Not only that, he was a direct descendant of Pat Garrett, which kind of made him a big deal.

"Good, guy gives me the creeps. And you don't have to walk. I can drop you off after I get done at Cade's. Cool?" he said.

"Yeah, cool."

He looked at me kinda awkward. "Are we though… cool, I mean?"

"Look man, if this is something you have to do, I'll respect it. I just don't want you to get in trouble, that's all."

"And I won't. Trust me. I got a good feeling about this." He grinned and started to walk towards the front door. "Now hurry up and get ready."

I ran into the bathroom to look my hair over one more time. It looked good enough. I went into the kitchen and refilled Billy's water dish—with water this time—and then put it outside and him along with it. Him chewing up the house all afternoon would send Aunt Patty into orbit when she got home. I tried to think of what else I needed to do before I left. I couldn't seem to think of anything else that needed to be done. For a split second, I thought of that stupid report I was supposed to write for Mendez. "Screw it," I said and grabbed a jacket just in case it got cold later. I wasn't gonna let some stupid report get in the way of me spending time with Becky and my brother. I burst out of the house and locked the door behind me, ready to go.

Nana was griping at Dorado again outside of her trailer. She was holding something strange in her hand that looked like it was made of tin foil. "That crazy aunt of yours gave me this new silver rolling paper, only I can't get it lit," she said.

Dorado took it from her hand. "Nana, this isn't silver rolling papers. It's a nicotine patch. You're supposed to stick it on your arm, not roll it up and smoke it."

"Stick it on my arm? What the hell kind of idea is that?" she said with disgust.

Dorado unrolled it. "What is this you have in here anyways? Tree bark?" He shook his head and handed it back to her when he saw me. "Uh, ready to roll Panch'?"

"Sure," I said.

"Alright, Nana, I'll talk to you later, okay? Don't burn the house down," he said and we walked towards the car.

We both got into the Camaro while she sat down on the front steps of her trailer, ranting about how she got "no respect". She was trying to light her patch, only Little Billy came up next to her and grabbed it in his mouth. She was still chasing him around trying to get it back as I watched them get smaller and smaller in the rearview mirror.

I doubt there are many people out there who can pick a precise moment in their lives when everything changed. I can see now that mine was when I got into the car with Dorado to go to Cade's. As I glanced back at the house I'd grown up in, I didn't realize the next time I saw it, I'd feel like a completely different person.

III.

THE FAT AND
THE FURIOUS

"So you're telling me after all these years you're still a believer in all of Uncle Pancho's B.S.? Personally, I always felt the guy was a little off," our cousin Cade said from under Dorado's Camaro. He was underneath it, draining the oil so he could change it, while Dorado was shooting at some tin cans for target practice.

Dorado and Cade made a good pair because Cade liked to work on cars just as much as Dorado liked to drive them. Cade, who as I said before is Dingus's older brother, is about six years older than Dorado, so to me he almost seems more like an uncle than a cousin. He's slightly overweight—not exactly fat, but close—and has longish, curly brown hair with a mustache. He's high-strung like Dingus and always sounds like he's yelling when he talks. To make it worse he has this terrible country accent that makes him sound more like he's from Texas than New Mexico.

He looks a lot older than 27 too, but I think that's because he did a tour in the jungles of Vietnam as a helicopter pilot for the army. Right now he has a little ranch on the outskirts of town with a few horses and sheep and stuff. Actually, his property looks more like a ranch for dilapidated old cars up on blocks since he has quite a few of those, too. We had gotten to his place about twenty minutes ago and right away he started to work on the Camaro while Dorado did a little target practice and explained his scheme. Only, like me, Cade wasn't exactly buying the whole thing about Uncle Pancho and the tombstone.

Dorado finished picking off another row of tin cans, then replied to Cade's comment about Uncle Pancho being off his rocker. "Weren't you only like one when he disappeared?"

"Hey, even a one-year-old can tell when someone's a little off," Cade said and rolled out from under the Camaro. He picked up the orange-colored oil drain pan and carried it over to an old table saw. "Speakin' a which, you know I can't concentrate with gunfire in the background. Takes me back to the days of fightin' Charlie in 'nam."

Charlie, as in "communist Charlie" just in case you don't know, is what Vietnam vets called enemy soldiers. On one of his missions in 'nam Cade had survived a pretty gnarly explosion in his vicinity. Not only did it make him hard of hearing, hence why he yells when he talks most of the time, but it also made him pretty wary of loud, sudden noises. But, if you ask me, Cade was a little crazy even before he went off to 'nam.

"Okay, after this last round, I'm done," Dorado said and started to reload his gun.

"Alright, Dingus, I got the bolt back in the oil pan. You can pour the new quarts in. I wanna stay down here and see if there's a leak," Cade said to his brother as he rolled back under the car.

Dingus gave me and Dorado a look that said "watch this" and walked over to the table saw. Instead of grabbing the new oil, he grabbed Cade's cold bottle of beer.

"Sorry I couldn't hear you. You said the oil in the orange pan, right?" Dingus said, referring to the piping hot oil that had just been drained. Right as Cade shouted, "No!" Dingus started pouring the cold beer down in between the radiator and the engine where it would drip down all over Cade. "Sorry I'm missing. It sure is heavy in this big barrel."

Me and Dorado put our hands over our mouths and did our best not to laugh out loud as Cade began to scream, thinking the cold beer was searing hot oil. Cade flew out from under the car as Dorado and I finally lost it.

He was dancing around the car screaming, "Oh Lord, I'm blind! I'm blind!"

Dingus held up the empty beer bottle and raised an eyebrow. "Oh really, you're blind?"

The realization of what had just happened finally dawned on Cade, who was rubbing the beer out of his eyes. "You little shit, get over here!" he yelled and then tried to swat Dingus with his hat, but he was too fast and was already across the yard.

"Don't let him fool you. He knows what he's doin'," he said turning back around to me and Dorado. "He's trying to get me to cuss so he can make a killing off of that…that fluffin' swear jar Missy set up." Cade pointed to a large glass jar full of quarters and dollar bills that sat on a bench outside the house that his wife Missy had set up. A piece of paper with the words "Swear Jar" was taped to it, only the 'e' in swear was backwards.

"Last week little sucker threw a roll of lit firecrackers through the bathroom window when I was in there and made five bucks off of me." He looked towards Dingus, who was sulking away in the distance and shouted, "But now I'm learnin' to beat the little fluffer at his own fluffin' game!"

Cade sighed and finished wiping the beer off of him with a rag. "No, my friend, I'll overhaul your car here, but anything illegal, count me out." Cade started to pour the new oil into the engine. "Me and the Fort Sumner PD ain't exactly in good standing ever since that incident I had at the Police charity golf tournament two weeks ago."

Dorado looked at me and I shrugged. Just like Dingus, Cade was always in some sort of trouble. "And I'm still trying to pay off that new tow truck over there," Cade added as he rolled back under the Camaro to see if there was a leak or not.

Dorado leaned in close over the front fender. "Well, you do realize if we break inside that cage and crack open that tombstone, the map inside leads to more than a billion dollars in gold."

Immediately he rolled back from under the car. "Wait, you mean there's money in this thing?"

"Yes, Cade, just like in your swear jar." Dorado sounded disgusted. I could believe that Cade missed a major detail like that, though. He is pretty dense. "What do you think Uncle Pancho stole it for?"

"Well heck, I just always thought he stole it because he was bored. But yeah, if there's money to be made, I'm in!" Cade was already up unlocking his tool shed to get out his welder. I don't think I'd ever seen Cade move so fast.

"Is Pancho going too?" he asked from inside the shed.

"No," Dorado said, beating me to it.

"I'm going to Becky's," I said.

"Heh, and here I thought I was in trouble with the law," Cade said as he hauled his welder out and started rolling it over to his truck.

"Yeah, well he still doesn't know, and you'd better keep it that way," I said as I helped him and Dorado load the welder up in the back of the truck. Dorado slammed the tailgate shut and snapped his fingers. "Keys."

Cade tossed them to him. Dorado always liked to drive, no matter what we were in and Cade had always let him.

"Shotgun!" Cade called, but I didn't care.

"Don't call shotgun for your own vehicle. It's embarrassing," Dorado snapped.

I slid into the backseat and laid my head back. Becky's house wasn't super far from here, I could've even walked but figured I might as well let them take me and save some time.

Dorado started up the truck and we headed back towards town. I looked out the window to watch the scenery. Technically we live in the desert, but it's not like the ones you see in the movies. There aren't any saguaro cactus, just yucca and some other types. And the ground isn't always just dry dirt either; a lot of it's covered in weeds and prairie grass. Fort Sumner is only desert on its outskirts, though. Within the town, things are pretty green. There's a lot of farmland surrounded by cottonwood trees and irrigation ditches.

About five minutes had passed since we left and I hadn't tried to keep up with Dorado and Cade's far-out conversations and was lost in my own thoughts. Car rides did that to me. Aunt Patty told me once that to get me to go to sleep when I was a baby sometimes she'd take me out on long car drives. That and lots of Triaminic.

I looked back out at the scenery passing by through the window. A couple of white trash bags had snagged onto some Yucca cactus, waving like ghosts in the late afternoon wind. I guess ghosts came to mind since Halloween was coming up. This was going to be the first year I didn't go Trick or Treating, I had decided. It would be weird not to, but then again, it felt kind of weird last year when I did go. I didn't know it last year that it would be the last time I ever Trick or Treated, but after some mean old lady refused to give me any candy because I was "too tall" that kind of ruined it for me. Dingus fit in just fine being as short as he was. He had tried to convince me to go this year and said I could go as a ghost and walk on my knees to hide my height, but I figured I'd spend this Halloween with Becky since it sounded more fun. Actually, it might be kind of neat to be the one handing out candy instead of the one taking it.

We'd get to dress up at least for the dance Friday night, but it wouldn't be the same as Trick or Treating. That's kind of what adults did on Halloween, I guess, dress up for parties and stuff. I wasn't sure if I was happy to be growing up or sad to be leaving other stuff behind.

All of a sudden, I started to get a funny feeling about the night. Maybe it was the way the sun hung close to the horizon, looking more like the moon obscured behind the blowing dirt. Then again, I've gotten a bad feeling about stuff before and gotten myself all worried and worked up and then the thing I was so worried about never happened. Maybe tonight would be like that.

It's not like Dorado hadn't gotten in trouble before. When he lived at home he was always in all kinds of trouble at school, and who knows what he'd been up to racing down in Mexico. I know Aunt Patty worried something awful about him down there. But this business with the tombstone was something else. I didn't know whether the stories about my uncle stealing it were true or not, since nobody ever proved that he did it. Twelve years later, my dad took off looking for him and neither had been seen since. I guess that's why I was so worried about my brother getting mixed up in it. Truthfully, Dorado was almost more like my dad than anyone, even though I'd sure never tell him that. Rod was great and all, but Aunt Patty and him didn't get married until I was about ten. Plus, Dorado was always the one to teach me stuff. As much as I love Aunt Patty and everybody else, if anything happened to Dorado, I'd feel kind of alone in the world. Maybe that was a dumb way to feel, but without our real parents, I always kind of felt like it was just me and him against the world.

The wailing of a police siren cut into my thoughts and I felt myself become saturated with sheer dread. It wasn't because it was a police siren, I'd been pulled over with Dorado plenty of times. It was who might be driving that scared me. Dorado cussed and pulled over. I was afraid to turn around and look. Maybe it wouldn't be Xander. But I also knew he was out on patrol tonight, hence why Becky was letting me come over. I turned to look, and sure enough, there he was getting out of his patrol car. Xander is tall and stocky with a black handlebar mustache. I don't know what color his hair is; he doesn't really have any and keeps what he does have clean-shaven. He hardly ever takes off his black-cowboy hat though, so you'd never know anyways.

"Dang it, Dorado! Why can't you ever go the speed limit? And do you see who it is?"

"Yes, I see who it is and I'm sorry," he hissed.

Even though Xander kind of likes us, that doesn't mean I want him to know I'm with Becky. He bent down and peered into the car. "Well, well, well. If ain't the Dumez Boys."

"Sheriff Garrett," Dorado said with a hint of nervousness in his voice I'm sure only I could detect. "How's it going?"

"What are you doing back in town, Dumez? Last I heard, you were down in Mexico racing cars. Mostly losing."

"Eh, I just came back to see the family. Ya know, hang out and stuff."

"Well, I couldn't help but notice you boys sure were haulin' ass. If I didn't know better, I'd think you were up to something." He paused for a second, then added. "You're not up to something, are you?"

"Aw hell no," Cade answered. "Pancho here's got a hot date with—

I pretended to cough and kicked the seat. "The doctor. I think I'm getting sick."

Xander gave me a look. "Goin' to the doc's, huh? And what's with that welder you got in the back?"

"Oh that, we're just takin' it to the repair shop, that's all," Cade responded nervously.

Xander looked off at the setting sun. "Taking Pancho to the doctor and your welder to the repair shop this late?"

"Yes sir, that's the reason I was speeding and all," Dorado said.

Xander looked at his watch, "Well, it is almost five o'clock. I reckon I better let you boys go so you can get your rat killin' done."

"Thanks Sheriff," Dorado said to be polite. "Really appreciate it."

"Don't mention it. You boys are practically family I known you so long. Your old man was a good boss to me back in the day. Good friend, too." He drummed his fingers along the window seal and said, "Like I said, you boys get goin'—just not too fast, ya hear?"

Dorado pretended to laugh and said, "Yes, sir."

Xander raised up from the window. "Be seein' you," he said, tipping his hat at me as he backed away.

I shivered and let out a cuss once he was out of earshot. Xander always creeps me out.

"Alright, glad that's over," Dorado said as Xander got back in his squad car.

"Well, does that settle it for you?" I asked as Xander drove past us.

They both looked at me like I was an idiot.

"Settle what?" Dorado asked.

"Well you can't go and open up the cage now that Xander's seen you with a welder! Plus, it's going to be Halloween soon; not exactly the best time of year to be in a cemetery."

Before Dorado could respond, Cade held up a finger to butt in. "First of all, Pancho, Halloween is the perfect time of year to break into a cemetery. Ain't you ever seen a movie before? And sencont, I done told Xander we was taken my welder to a repair shop. It's what's called an alibi. Look it up in the dictionary some time."

As surprised as I was that Cade knew what an alibi was, or even how to use a dictionary for that matter, I was even more surprised that Dorado wouldn't back down.

He looked at me with a resigned expression. "Panch', we're doing this tonight. I have to."

He turned back around and started the truck. "Now, let's get you to your girlfriend's."

We spent the rest of the ride in silence. I doubted he'd tell me what was up even if I asked him the whole way over, so I decided not to. We got to Becky's house along Pecan Drive near the outskirts of town right at twilight. It's a pink two-story with a nice green yard and trees out front. She was alone because her parents were divorced and her mom had moved to Texas, but Becky wanted to stay here in Sumner.

"You sure your buddy the sheriff won't be stopping by tonight?" Dorado asked as he pulled up to the gravel driveway.

I started to get out. "Yeah, Becky knows his schedule pretty well. Besides, I'm not the one about to desecrate a national treasure. You're the one that needs to watch out." I slammed the door shut.

Dorado got out and grabbed me by the shoulder as I started to walk away. "Come on, man, I thought we were over this?"

I turned around and shrugged. I wasn't sure what to say. "Just be careful, alright?" I tried not to sound worried so he wouldn't make fun of me, but I couldn't seem to hide it tonight.

He punched me on the shoulder softly and grinned. "Come on, Panch'. It's me we're talking about. You know I'll be fine."

"Yo, Dorado, let's go!" Cade hollered from the truck.

He turned to look at Cade and then back at me. "Like I said. Don't get caught." He pointed at me and ran back to the truck.

"You too," I said as he got back in and shut the door.

As I watched them drive off, I could hear Becky's screen door creak open. I turned around and there she was standing in the doorway with her arms crossed. She was already wearing her costume for the dance tomorrow night. I'm pretty sure she was trying to be Black Widow from Marvel Comics since she was dressed in all black. All she needed was a red wig to hide her dark curly hair. Becky's mixed like me. She's mostly white, but Pat Garrett's wife, which would be her great grandma, was Hispanic. Her skin was like mine, not real dark, but not real white either. And she had these wild green eyes that somehow managed to look innocent and mischievous at the same time.

Seeing her made me feel better automatically. I think I love Becky but I'm not sure. Aunt Patty says I'm too young to know what love is, but then again old people always say you're too young to know what a lot of things are even though you do.

"Hey sexy. You get into trouble for aiding and abetting the enemy this afternoon?" I asked, referring to Coach McPherson.

"Um, no. McPherson is terrified of my dad, so I don't have to worry about him. That's at least one perk to being the sheriff's daughter."

I laughed. "He pulled us over on the way here by the way. Don't worry, I didn't tell him where I was going, though."

I leaned in to kiss her and after a second she pulled away, half laughing, half gagging. "Ugh, I can still smell it on you!"

She meant the goat. I guess I had gotten used to the smell. "I'm sorry, I didn't have time to shower after."

She laughed and walked back into the house. "As if you would have anyways. And why aren't you wearing a costume?" She crinkled my jacket collar in her hand as I followed her.

"I was thinking of just going to the dance as myself, the noted desperado Pancho Dumez."

"You are not going as yourself. Hold on," she said and started to walk back to her room.

"Hey, what'd you tell your dad about the dance?" I shouted.

"I didn't tell him yet, but I'll just say me and the girls are going together alone."

She came back with an eye patch. "Here, put this on."

I took it. "Who does this make me? A pirate?"

"No, Nick Fury. You know… head of S.H.I.E.L.D. and all that?"

"I'm the guy in the relationship and here you are the comic book nerd," I said.

She looked me over. "Now you just need a trench coat or something. I'll be right back. Besides, you should just be happy I'm not one of those girls that insists we wear matching costumes for Halloween," she said as she ran back to her room.

"Ha, you mean like when Cade's wife made them dress up like Raggedy Anne and Andy together?" I opened her fridge and started to look around.

"Ugh, don't remind me," Becky said. Becky was kind of mean, but I liked that about her.

"Hey, you got anything to eat in here? I kinda missed dinner," I hollered.

"Yes," she sounded almost irritated and gave me one of those looks as she came back into the kitchen. "Just don't raid the fridge too hard. Dad would never believe I ate all the leftover steak so go easy."

Actually that was pretty smart. "Okay," I said and grabbed a little piece of steak wrapped in tinfoil. I didn't bother to get a knife and fork and just started biting chunks out of it.

"Ugh, Pancho, why can't you use a fork like a normal person?"

"I'm being considerate. This way you don't have to feel obligated to wash any dishes when I'm done."

She just rolled her eyes at me and turned around to look through her pantry. "So, what's Dorado doing in town?"

I stopped chewing. I had hoped she wouldn't ask. "Ever heard the old expression what you don't know can't hurt you?"

She turned from the pantry and gave me a look and I knew I'd cave. I can't keep a secret from Becky to save my life.

***

"So, has your dad ever said whether he believes all that stuff or not? I mean Pat Garrett faking the Kid's death so they could hide a treasure map?" I asked.

Me and Becky were lying on our stomachs on the floor eating candy in front of the TV. *Billy the Kid versus Dracula* was on. I know, it's crazy, but they actually made a movie about the Kid battling Dracula back in the 1960s. Right now it was on the part where the poor old man playing Dracula could barely pick up the damsel in distress and carry her off. It was pretty funny. We weren't really watching it that intently, though. For the past half hour or so we'd been talking about the whole thing with Dorado and the tombstone.

"Not really. I think he thinks all that stuff about Garrett helping out the Kid was just a bunch of B.S."

"Well, there's one thing we have in common."

I was hoping that would end the conversation and we could switch over to something more important: making out. But, just as I leaned in close to kiss the side of her face, she said, "The only thing I don't understand is why you're not out there with your brother."

I sighed and dropped my head to the carpet. "Because it's stupid. If my stupid uncle hadn't of stolen the stupid tombstone, then my stupid dad wouldn't have gone off looking for him, and now my stupid brother wouldn't be out committing a potential felony." I raised my head up and looked down at all the candy wrappers on the carpet. I started to twist one between my fingers.

"Why don't we go and check on him then?" When I didn't say anything she rocked into my shoulder and added, "Come on. You're worried and you know you want to."

"Yeah, but if we get caught then you'll be there with us."

"Umm…have you forgotten who my dad is?"

"Yeah, hence why I don't want to get caught with you. And you know what they say about Billy the Kid's grave at midnight, the very hour at which he was shot by Garrett's gun."

"You're not going to scare me out of it, stupid." She hit me on the shoulder. "And besides, you do know that it's my family history, too. Actually, it's more my family history than yours since my great-grandfather supposedly shot the Kid… or not." She cocked an eyebrow at me and I knew we were going. "And this is a good night for graveyard hopping."

"Okay," I said, giving in. Becky could get me to do almost anything.

I really did want to go check on Dorado, too. And as much as I hated to admit it, I was curious what would happen when he broke that tombstone open.

I looked over at a spotlight Xander had laying in the corner. I also kind of wanted to get even with Dorado. "Hey, does that spotlight work?"

"Yeah, I think so. Why?"

I just smiled and decided not to tell her. "Ha, you'll have to wait and see until we get to the cemetery."

She smiled and leaned in to kiss me and then leapt up off the floor. "Come on, it'll be a night you'll never forget."

Now I wished that she was wrong, but boy was she right.

IV.
HELL'S
HALF ACRE

I love wandering around at night. I know it's dangerous sometimes, but I can't help it. Something about the night air gives me extra energy it seems like. Whenever I'd stay over at Missile or somebody's house for the night, we'd usually sneak out and then go walking around different neighborhoods, maybe sometimes knock on a door or two then run off, pee on some random stranger's lawn, mysteriously re-arrange the yard decorations, stuff like that. It's not necessarily that you want to go out and do something bad; it's just fun. I don't know why.

Tonight was an especially good night. The wind was blowing lightly and I could smell somebody burning trash, which is actually a good smell believe it or not. I was having so much fun running around and making Becky laugh that I had gotten over my uneasy feeling from earlier. I didn't even care that technically I was way past curfew with Aunt Patty and Rod, assuming they were back from Albuquerque. But maybe I could say I went out with Dorado and it was his fault the next morning.

Right now we were following an old irrigation ditch—there are lots of those in Fort Sumner—near the Pecos River to get to Billy the Kid Road. I knew we were getting close when I saw a row of old cottonwood trees, then not long after that we saw the big wooden sign with the paint peeling off it proclaiming, "See Billy the Kid's Real Grave." About ten minutes later, I could see the adobe walls of the old cemetery and the museum they built next to it. Technically, this area was all part of what you'd call Old Fort Sumner where the soldiers used to be posted. Nothing of the old military post remained, not even the house where Pat Garrett allegedly shot the Kid, which had gotten torn down a long time ago. Now the only remnant of the old days was the cemetery where they buried the Kid. I scanned around for Cade's truck and eventually spotted it, parked out in a field a ways behind the graveyard.

I'd been to the museum before a few times. Actually I thought it was pretty neat. It's a cool old western looking building. I liked the way it smelled inside, like old wood. The museum had been built just outside of the cemetery sometime in the 1940s. The cemetery was about two blocks square encased entirely inside an adobe wall just a little taller than me. A few towering elm trees on the outside made the place even more shadowy and dark than it would've been already. Actually, for a graveyard there weren't that many graves in it. Just the Kid's, a famous land baron named Lucien Maxwell, and less than a dozen others. If it weren't for the Kid, the whole place would've probably been forgotten about.

It's technically called the Old Military Cemetery, but most of the old timers call it Hell's Half Acre for all the people buried there that died violent deaths. I knew an old man who told me he saw Billy's ghost once. Said he saw the Kid come trotting up on a horse just outside the cemetery at 11:30, the very hour he met his demise at. That's about what time it was now.

I stood in front of the museum door. "Ever been in here?"

"Eh, when I was a little girl. But not recently."

I had a sneaking hunch it wouldn't be too hard to get in. Fort Sumner is a very trusting town. I kneeled down and peeled back the welcome mat. Sure enough, there was a key. I picked it up and held it in front of Becky. "Let's check it out."

"You're really determined to add to that rap sheet, aren't you?"

"I don't think it's breaking and entering when you have a key."

No sooner than I had walked inside I bumped into something. I took out my lighter to light up the room a little. It was a mannequin I had bumped into. It had a crooked mustache and a sheriff's badge. I realized it was Pat Garrett, and the mustache was falling off since I ran into it.

"Well, excuse us, sir. It looks like your mustache has become crooked," Becky giggled and straightened it.

"Becky, that's no way to talk to your great grandfather," I mocked.

"Oh, why yes, he is the terror of evil-doers across the land," she said in a mock-southern accent and then grew serious. "It's creepy. I can actually see the resemblance between him and my dad."

"I wish my grandpappy was somebody famous," I said.

She laughed and we kept looking around the museum. They had all kinds of crazy stuff in it. I stopped to inspect a newspaper up on the wall about the theft of the tombstone.

Becky came up beside me. "So how does this whole treasure-map-hidden-inside-of-a-tombstone-thing even work? I mean, you can't exactly hide something inside of solid stone."

"Well, it's all pretty stupid if you ask me, kinda like a conspiracy theory. Supposedly the guy who made the tombstone chiseled out a hidden compartment in it somewhere." I paused for a second. I was embarrassed I even knew about the next part. "And see, the thing is that would have taken days to do, which means he had to know Billy was going to die several days in advance."

"Which goes to show that Garrett and the Kid knew they were going to fake his death, right?"

"Exactly. See how dumb it all sounds?"

"Well, at least tonight maybe you'll finally find out, right?" She grinned mischievously and started poking me in the ribs. "Admit it, you're dying to know."

"I'm dying to get this over with," I said and tried to get her to stop poking my ribs. "Come on, let's go."

***

Like I said, the museum was built right next to the old graveyard, so we didn't have to walk far at all. There was only one way in and one way out of the cemetery, and we didn't want to risk Dorado and Cade seeing us, so we kept close to the adobe wall on the outside to try and listen in. The wind had picked up a little, so I had to lean in close to try and hear anything. I couldn't hear much, so I grabbed the wall and hoisted myself up far enough that I could see over it. It was just like I remembered, a big patch of desert land with a few old crosses and weathered tombstones. In the middle, with a concrete walkway leading up to it, was the Kid's grave. The only thing different about it was the big metal cage they'd built around it. I squinted and could see the cage door swinging open, so they had gotten inside for sure. Plus, Cade's blowtorch wasn't even out there, so they must've already loaded it back up in the truck. For a second, I was worried that I'd missed them when I heard a funny noise, sort of like digging. Just then Becky hoisted herself up beside me.

"What the heck are they doing? I thought they were just going to grab the tombstone?" she whispered.

"I think... I think they're digging." I slung my leg real slow like over the wall and then gently lowered myself down. Then I helped Becky down so she wouldn't make much noise.

I had looked around real good earlier, plus, nobody lived real close to the cemetery or I wouldn't do what I was about to. "Give me that spotlight. Time to teach these fools a lesson," I whispered to Becky.

I switched it on, and once the light hit the grave, I shouted, "Cade and Dorado Dumez! Come out with your hands up... and your pants down!" Both their heads popped up from the ground. Me and Becky started to laugh uncontrollably. Dorado had his arm over his eyes, blinded by the light trying to figure out who it was. Cade just stared right into the light with his mouth hanging open.

"Wait a minute," Dorado muttered as he hoisted himself out of the grave. "Pancho! What are you doing here?"

Cade was right behind him. "Dad gone it, Pancho! I coulda killed you!" Cade yelled and threw down his shovel as though it was some kind of deadly weapon. "And you're darn lucky I didn't."

I laughed and pointed at them. "You thought we were the cops! Admit it."

"I did not think you were the cops," Dorado said, embarrassed as he walked towards us.

"Well, not the cops, but I do have the sheriff's daughter here," I said.

"I can see that," he said and grinned at Becky.

"Hi Dorado," Becky cooed innocently.

"You guys shouldn't be here. I told you to stay away," Dorado said. I ignored him and walked over to the cage to take a look. Just like I thought, they had been digging, but why?

I spun around. "You're not just stealing the tombstone; you're opening the grave!"

"Yes, Pancho, we're doing some digging. Very astute of you to notice," Cade retorted. I ignored him and looked at my brother.

"Why didn't you just grab the tombstone and run? What are you lingering around for?"

"Because I want to know if the story about faking the Kid's death is true or not, and there's only one way to find out."

I looked at Becky. She didn't even seem upset. "Wait, don't tell me you're okay with this?" I said.

"What? It's not like I'm a bad person for being curious whether a legend that involves *my* ancestor is true or not. Like Dorado said, there's only one way to find out."

Dorado smirked at me snidely. "I knew I liked this girl."

"Fine," I hissed and grabbed a shovel. I walked over to the grave and got right to digging.

"What are you doing?" Dorado asked, irritated.

"What's it look like? I'm speeding this up since you idiots don't have sense enough to get out of here before you get caught."

Dorado jumped in and started shoveling alongside me. "Hey, you're the one who turned a spotlight on us."

"There was nobody around," I hissed. "But that doesn't mean somebody might not drive by any minute. Somebody like Xander. You'll get busted for grave robbing and I'll get busted for—"

"For what?" Becky looked down at me from above the burial plot, hands on her hips.

"Nothing," I grinned and tossed out another shovel full of dirt. When I went to dig out another chunk of earth my shovel struck something hard. Me and Dorado stopped. It was the casket, had to be.

"Well, what are you waiting for?" Becky leered over the grave intently.

Dorado looked at me. Now that the moment of truth was at hand, it seemed like even he was chickening out. "Well, you're the one who wanted to do this, Dorado. Have at it."

"Well, I mean…" Dorado stalled.

"Come on!" Cade hissed. "It's like y'all never opened up a grave before."

Cade jumped down and lodged his shovel under the casket door and pried it open.

I braced myself for the sight of an ugly corpse, only that's not what was inside.

"I don't believe it," I said. Inside the coffin were three large bank bags. There wasn't a body in sight.

"It's true," Becky said. "Pat Garrett didn't kill him."

"Well, there's some new information for my history class report," I said.

"You think we should bust 'em open. Just in case there's gold or something inside?" Cade asked about the bags.

Dorado smiled. "Let's see." He used his shovel to pierce one open. For a second it did look like gold came pouring out of it, but pretty quick I realized it wasn't and so did everybody else.

"Sand," Dorado said disappointedly. "But still, if that part of the legend was true…"

"The tombstone," I said as my brother's eyes met mine.

I wasn't sure if I was more excited or scared. On the one hand, it would mean our dad and uncle had been right, which was great… I guess. And on the other hand, them being right was kind of scary in some ways.

We both walked over to the tombstone while Becky and Cade followed. I had never actually seen it before since it had been missing since before I was born. It wasn't too tall, but it was fairly thick. It was rectangular, with a pointed top kinda like a triangle instead of rounded like other tombstones. It didn't give his real name, William H. Bonney, and just called him Billy the Kid. The inscription read, "THE BOY BANDIT KING, HE DIED AS HE LIVED."

I kneeled down to help Dorado pick it up. All of a sudden, I heard something land in a tree close by and make a squawk. A hawk had touched down in one of the big trees outside the cemetery. Even though it sounds crazy, I really felt like it was looking at us. I could tell Dorado thought it was weird, too. Before we could do anything else, we heard another noise… like a distant rumble. The *thwack thwack thwack* kept getting closer.

"Shit. They weren't supposed to be here for another hour," Dorado muttered to himself.

"Who?" I asked, but he ignored me, staring up into the sky. The trees started to rustle and it wasn't just the wind anymore, not by a long shot. A helicopter was flying overhead. It was flying low and getting nearer by the second. A bright spotlight shined down on the cemetery, like it was looking for a spot to land. That was when Cade went into an all-out panic.

"It's them, isn't it?" he yelled, pointing at the light in the sky. As crazy as Cade was, at first I figured he thought it was a UFO, but then he said, "If I'd have knowed this had anything to do with Mexico, I wouldn't a come tonight, Dorado!"

Cade grabbed his hat to keep it from blowing off his head and ran for his truck. I looked at Dorado, only he wasn't running and he didn't exactly look surprised, just remorseful.

"Who's 'them'?" I shouted to Dorado as the noise of the helicopter became louder and louder.

He didn't answer my question, just grabbed me by the shoulders and shouted, "You and Becky need to get out of here, now!"

"But what about you! Why aren't you going?"

"There's no time to explain." His eyes trailed off and I could barely hear Cade's truck starting through the noise. I looked to where Dorado was looking and could see Cade already driving away!

"Cade!" He yelled before he realized it was futile. "Dammit, he's already gone. You two need to hide, fast." He pointed towards the gate that led outside the cemetery.

"Not until you tell me what's going on."

"I wasn't doing this just for me, Pancho. I got into some trouble and owe some people some money."

"Who?"

He looked ashamed. "A Mexican Drug Cartel. Which is exactly why you two need to leave."

I couldn't believe it, but before I could say anything else Becky tugged at my arm. "Pancho, let's go!"

I didn't know what to do and the chopper was starting to land, kicking up a violent torrent of dust and wind. Dorado nodded at me and had a sad look on his face like this could be the last time I ever saw him. I gave in and ran with Becky outside the cemetery just as the helicopter was landing. Once we were out a ways, I stopped.

"Pancho, what are you doing?"

I shook my head. "I'm not leaving him. He's my brother, he's practically all I've got."

She gave me a pained look. "Just stay out of sight!" I yelled and took off running back into the cemetery.

I heard her yell my name once more and then I was back in the cemetery walls, her voice lost in the torrent of wind and dirt stirred up by the massive blades. It was like being in the middle of a tornado with the deafening noise and dirt. I covered my face in my arm and coughed.

Dorado saw me. "I told you to go!" he yelled and pointed at the gate. When I didn't move, he shoved me towards it, but I pushed his hands away. "No! We lost our stupid dad to this thing, I'm not gonna lose you too!"

He looked at me shamefully as though he hadn't thought of it from my perspective. There was no time to say anything now. The chopper was idling down. I looked up and squinted, my eyes braving the dirt which was just starting to settle. The helicopter wasn't like the ones I saw the newscasters from Albuquerque use. It was bigger, like a military chopper. It was painted black and had a big 'Q' on the side, only the Q was made of a coiled snake. The chopper's name was printed on the side in cursive. It looked like it read *Heart of the Sky*. The doors opened and out jumped four armed men which formed an escort for the two men that followed.

The first was dressed in a white suit, complete with a white panama hat which he held firmly to his head in the whipping wind. He sported a neatly trimmed mustache and had an heir of authority about him, like he was used to giving out commands. He carried a cane and seemed to walk different from the rest.

"Do me a favor and don't stare at his left leg," Dorado said to me nervously.

"Why?"

"Because he doesn't have one."

Dorado didn't need to worry about me staring at the first guy because he looked totally normal compared to the man next to him. He looked like a scarecrow come to life. Even his skin looked ancient and weathered, as though it'd been blasted by the sand and the sun. He wore a black duster with an old beat-up, black cowboy hat that almost looked more like something a witch would wear. His hair was long and in it hung the rattle of a rattlesnake. As if to complete the look, he also had an eye patch over his left eye and an arm that ended in a metal hook instead of a hand. He was older, 60 maybe, and had long gray hair and his neck was covered with a scarf. He might have been Native American, but I couldn't tell what tribe.

"Never mind what I said about not staring at him. Don't stare at the other guy," Dorado said.

"Please tell me that's a Halloween costume," I said, but something told me it wasn't. I looked at Dorado. "Who the hell did you get mixed up with?"

He kept staring ahead. "Just keep quiet and let me do all the talking. I know how to handle them... I think."

Somehow the air seemed to get colder as they got closer and the wind started to pick up, almost like it was accompanying them. Me and Dorado just kept where we were leaning up against the adobe wall of the cemetery.

Dorado nodded to the man in white. "Dr. Villegas, glad you could make it. And I see you brought a friend."

"You said that you would be alone. Who is this?" Dr. Villegas motioned to me.

"Well, I needed a little help after all," he said and motioned towards the cage around the grave. "But it's okay, he's my brother."

Villegas gave me a funny look, almost like he recognized me from somewhere, then said, "I suppose I can see the family resemblance."

I know Dorado told me to keep my mouth shut, but I just couldn't. "Nice friends you got here, Dorado. How exactly did you all meet?"

Dorado shot me a look, but I didn't care. It was his fault for keeping me in the dark.

"Oh, make no mistake, we're not friends," the man called Dr. Villegas answered. You could tell English wasn't his first language because he had an accent, but at the same time he sounded eloquent when he spoke. "You could say we're business associates of your brother's. We made an arrangement for him to throw a few races for us in Mexico."

So Dorado had been throwing races for the Mexican mob? I knew he could be a scoundrel, but this was a whole new level.

"Unfortunately, on the one occasion we asked Dorado to win a race for us, it turned out he was better at losing." Villegas frowned at Dorado.

Dorado shrugged and flashed a sheepish grin. "And here I thought you paid off all the other drivers to lose, classic misunderstanding."

"So you did all this for some lousy cash?" I looked at my brother.

"You mean you didn't tell your own brother the specifics of our little arrangement?" Villegas said, amused, while Dorado looked helpless. "Very well, when your brother failed to win his last race, and I lost a sizeable amount of money, I had an inspired thought. You see..." Villegas held out his hand and looked at me. I realized he wanted my name.

"Pancho," I answered.

"Pancho." He nodded as though the name suited me even though most people usually didn't. "Named after your uncle, I presume?"

A chill ran down my spine and the hairs on the back of my neck stood up. It was rare that I ever met anyone who actually knew my uncle. All my life Uncle Pancho had been sort of a myth to me, but now myth was becoming reality. Villegas must've seen my eyes widen because he said, "Oh yes. I met your Uncle Pancho after he fled the States to come to my country. I didn't really think anything of him until one day comes along this man," Villegas put his hand on the shoulder of the strange man next to him, "looking for him because of a wild tale that your Uncle Pancho knew the location of a fabulous treasure map hidden inside the tombstone of Billy the Kid. I wouldn't have believed it myself, but if you saw the trouble those two caused fighting over it, you would be a believer too. Long story short, when the smoke cleared, your uncle disappeared, and I had a new enforcer."

Villegas patted him on the back and smiled. I don't think the man liked it, but on Villegas went with his story. "We thought we would never find the map, then one day, what a coincidence, I meet Pancho's nephew Dorado here and strike up a deal with him. I agree to tell him everything I know about his uncle and in return, he wins or loses a few races for me. Now, when he failed to win his last race as promised, lo and behold, I see a story on the news about Billy the Kid's famous tombstone finally returning to Fort Sumner. And it seemed to my friend and I here to be the perfect way for him to repay his debt."

"And you are?" Dorado asked the strange old man.

"Oh, I'm sorry, I forgot that you two had never actually met," Villegas answered again. "Seven McCaw is what you would have called a bounty hunter in the Old West."

"But I prefer the term professional killer," the man finally spoke, tipping his hat up with his hook as he did. His voice was rough and gravelly.

"Don't you think that's a little overkill, what with the eye patch and everything?" Dorado blurted out with grotesque fascination.

"Ah, kids say the darndest things, don't they, Seven? Why don't you tell the boy how you lost your eye?" Villegas chuckled as though it was a funny story.

"Let me guess," Dorado began again, determined to show he wasn't intimidated. "Did you actually get the Official Red Ryder Carbine-Action Two-Hundred-Shot Range Model Air Rifle for Christmas when you were a kid?"

McCaw grumbled and then threw a knife in between Dorado's thighs so quickly I barely noticed it until I saw it wobbling in the adobe wall. Dorado was silent for a moment and then looked up from between his legs and said coolly with a hint of irritation, "Well, clearly you're not a BB gun connoisseur."

"You'll have to forgive me for missing," McCaw said emphasizing the last word. "My aim isn't as good as it used to be. But in the end, it was worth it. You see, I gave my eye to Itza-chu."

"Itza-chu?" Dorado and I both said.

McCaw smiled and looked at the hawk up in the tree. He whistled and it flew down, perching on his arm. "This is Itza-chu." The way he said the bird's name it sounded as though it was the only thing he loved. Then he pointed to his missing eye. "Now, I can see what she sees." The hawk looked at us when he said the words with an almost human intelligence and cocked its head.

"Well," Dorado said, thoroughly freaked out, "this has all been…great. But I know you didn't fly all this way to regale me with tales about you and your pets. Shall we." He walked from the wall and motioned his hand towards the burial plot.

Villegas and his men didn't move. Instead, he just laughed, clapped his hands together, and then pointed at Dorado. "You Americans are so presumptuous. I love it." He motioned to his men who walked behind us, and before I knew it, they butted me and Dorado behind the legs with their guns, bringing us to our knees.

"Whoa, what is this?" my brother shouted.

Villegas stepped in front of him. "Let's get one thing straight, you are not in control of this situation. In fact, before we do this, map or no map, you still owe me compensation for not living up to your original bargain. I lost a lot of money on that last race you know."

"What are you talking about? You're going to make more money off of that map than you ever would have off of that race," Dorado said nervously.

"True, but I am still a staunch businessman." Villegas nodded to his men. They hauled my brother over to another tombstone and slammed his left hand down on top of it. I started to stand and the guard behind me reminded me it was a good idea not to by butting me in the back with his rifle.

"What are you doing?" I shouted.

"Teaching him a lesson that it's always best to honor your promises." Villegas nodded at McCaw. He waved his hand and the hawk flew away as he walked towards Dorado. "The little finger, or the big one?" he asked Villegas.

"The little one. It's tradition after all."

My brother looked wild and terrified as McCaw drew out a knife and raised it above Dorado's hand. "You can't be serious," he said.

It was all like a lucid nightmare, only when the worst was about to happen, I didn't wake up. McCaw slammed down the knife and cut the tip of Dorado's pinky finger clean off. His head jerked back and he let out a terrible yell. The guard released him as he fell to the ground clutching his hand.

"*Yubitsume.* It's a little something I learned from the Yakuza when one of their men doesn't make good on a promise and fails his master. Only they have the decency to cut off their own finger." Villegas tossed Dorado a handkerchief.

I was too shocked and scared to say anything. Dorado wrapped his hand in the cloth and stood back up.

"Don't look so mortified. It's not like you lost an arm," McCaw said.

"Or a leg," Villegas added and pulled up his pant leg while his men all laughed at his remark. I caught a quick glimpse of his fake leg. It looked like it was made of gold and had a snake wrapped around it. I got the chills again.

Villegas began walking towards the grave. "Now to see if the most important part is true." He motioned to the tombstone. "And this will depend upon your life." One of his men knocked Dorado back to his knees and aimed the gun at his head.

But then Villegas looked at me. "No, on second thought, make it his brother's."

Before I could even take in what was happening, Dorado's face went white as a sheet. "Wait. No. Please no. Me, point the gun at me, not him. He had nothing to do with this!"

"Then you can let that be another lesson," Villegas said.

I heard the click of a safety being released and then something hard pressed into the back of my skull. I started sweating and locked my eyes on McCaw and one of his lackeys as they walked over to the tombstone. My life was about to depend on whether or not a stupid fairy tale about a treasure map in a tombstone was real or not.

The man bent down and picked it up. He looked to McCaw for permission. He nodded and the man slammed it violently to the concrete walkway below. It broke in half. McCaw pushed away the top portion of the tombstone, separating it from the bottom. My heart sank. It was solid all the way through. McCaw looked at Villegas and shook his head. I felt like I was going to be sick.

Villegas looked at me and said, "Kill him," without even a hint of emotion in his voice.

"No!" Dorado screamed and lunged forward before a guard caught him.

It felt like I had a horrible fever and was about to pass out from it as I waited for the inevitable. I probably wouldn't even know when it happened. Maybe it already had? Maybe I was already dead and I was just a ghost watching it all happen?

But then McCaw spoke. "Wait."

My heart was pounding harder than it ever had in my entire life. Everyone turned to look at McCaw in shock. He was kneeled down inspecting the tombstone.

He held up a chunk of it in his hand. "This thing's brand new. Looks like it was made yesterday. No cracks, no weathering."

"So?" Villegas looked confused.

"It's a fake," McCaw said.

Villegas immediately turned to look at Dorado. "Wait, I know what you're thinking but we both know I'm not nearly clever enough to procure a fake like that."

"Fortunately for you, I know," Villegas said.

"And the grave!" Dorado yelled desperately. "Look in the grave. It's empty. That proves something. You know it does."

Villegas looked to McCaw for confirmation. He said, "The empty grave does prove at least one thing: Garrett didn't kill the Kid just as the legend says. And I'd wager to bet that whoever produced the fake tombstone also has the real one."

"Look, I swear to you I will find that map. I'll do...anything, just don't hurt my brother," Dorado pleaded.

Villegas looked at the man behind me and I finally felt the gun pull away from my head. Villegas seemed to be deep in thought and then finally said, "You and your brother have until the Day of the Dead, Monday morning, to find the real tombstone that holds the map."

Monday morning, that would be my birthday. How ironic that the day that I was born would also now be the day that I died if we didn't find the damn tombstone. Day of the Dead, indeed.

"After the real tombstone is in my possession, I will consider our debt settled," Villegas continued. "And, if I'm feeling really generous, I'll even still tell you the truth about your uncle."

Villegas and McCaw walked back towards the helicopter. Before he got in, Villegas turned to Dorado and said, "One more thing, if you take this time to run instead of getting me what I asked for... Well, let's just say that if I can't find you, I will find your family."

Dorado shook his head. "I will find you that map. You have my word."

Villegas laughed. "As if that's worth anything." He tossed a card on the ground in front of Dorado, still on his knees. Dorado picked it up and then stood. I looked at the card. It was a phone number.

"Call that number when you have what I want," Villegas said.

"And don't worry, I'll be keeping my eye on you." McCaw smiled and stepped into the chopper as the blades began to really get going. He shut the door and the chopper took off. Within moments they were gone.

Dorado started to teeter like he was going to fall over, so I steadied him back towards the adobe wall and we sat down against it.

"I'm sorry, bro. I'm sorry, Panch,'" Dorado kept repeating. I wrapped the handkerchief around what was left of his pinky finger tight.

"What did he mean…the truth about our uncle?"

He clutched the rag to his bleeding hand tight as he spoke. "They came to me while I was racing in Mexico. Villegas said he knew who our uncle was. He said if I'd throw a race for him, he'd give me proof that he might still be alive. So I threw the race for him like he asked. I was favored to win, so he made some good money off of his bets when I lost. When I went to collect my end of the bargain, he gave me this." He dug an old photo from his pocket with his good hand and handed it to me.

A chill coursed through my body and the hairs on my neck stood up. It looked like Uncle Pancho, only older. "You sure that's him and not just someone who looks like him?"

Dorado shook his head and drew out our dad's old pocket watch he always carried with him. I knew what he was doing. It had a photo of my dad and his brother in it. Dorado opened it so I could compare it with the photo that Villegas gave him.

The old photo showed Hondo and Pancho when they were in their 20s. The new photo looked like it showed a man in his 50s walking down the street. I couldn't deny it anymore. It was him.

"Okay, now I believe you. That's Uncle Pancho."

Dorado shook his head. "No, I think it's dad." I gave him a look, but he cut me off before I could say anything else. "Don't ask me why, it's just a hunch."

"Well, considering they were identical, you could be right." I slunk my head back into the wall and handed the photo and the watch back to him. Truthfully, I didn't know how I felt about the photo—whether I was happy or sad.

"He said if I won the next race he'd tell me where I could find him. Only thing is if I didn't win, he said I'd owe him big… and then I lost."

"Why didn't you tell me?"

"Because I didn't want to get your hopes up." He looked at me sadly.

"I wouldn't have gotten my hopes up, Dorado, because I don't care." I knew a part of me was lying, but I didn't know if Dorado did. He looked disappointed. "I mean I don't care if we find dad or our uncle if it means losing you, stupid. Can't you figure that out?"

"You're right, Pancho. I'm sorry. But you're wrong about our dad, he didn't leave us for no reason. I knew him. He wouldn't do that." He laid his head against the wall and stared off into space.

"How are we going to find the real tombstone?" I finally asked him.

"I think I know a man who can help."

"Who?"

"Remember Old Man Baca? He was a friend of our dad's."

I had only met him once, but I remembered him. "Yeah, that old Indian. He lives on the reservation down south."

Before we could finish our conversation, I heard footsteps coming. We both looked over our shoulders. "Becky!" I jumped up and embraced her. She looked over my shoulder at my brother. "Dorado, what happened?"

He forced a smile. "Oh, just a little run-in with a Mexican Drug Cartel. I wouldn't recommend it."

She kneeled down next to him and looked at his hand. "We need to get you to a doctor."

"No doctors. The bleeding will stop eventually," he said.

"Okay, but you guys need to get out of here," Becky said. "A helicopter landing in the middle of a cemetery is bound to get the police department's attention."

"You're right," I said.

I helped Dorado get up.

"Where are we headed?" I asked him.

"Back to Cade's. We're going to need a car."

***

After about an hour and a lot of walking, we were finally getting in to Cade's place. From a distance I could see him digging a hole in between two cottonwoods a ways off from his house.

"What's he doing?" Becky asked.

"Digging a latrine," I sighed. Whenever Cade's PTSD gets really bad he reverts back to his 'nam state of mind. Typically when one made camp for the night they would dig a latrine which was what I assumed he was doing right now.

At the sound of our voices Cade's head darted in our direction. He looked like a prairie dog peeking out of its hole.

"Halt! Who goes there!" he yelled and then I heard a shotgun getting loaded.

"It's Dorado, don't shoot, you idiot!" my brother shouted.

"Dorado?" Cade said. I could tell he was starting to come around now. He looked at the shotgun in his hands curiously like he forgot he was even holding it, sat it down, and then climbed out of his hole.

"Whoa!" Cade was dumbfounded at the sight of Dorado's bloodied hand, which he now clutched in his own. "Don't tell me you made another deal with—"

"I had to," Dorado interrupted him.

Cade took off his hat and hit Dorado with it. "What are you doing making deals with them again? Besides, don't you know we got mafias here in America you could deal with instead?"

I wasn't sure if Cade was upset about Dorado being mixed up with the cartel or that he was exporting jobs to another country. Just then, a figure in a pink bathrobe came shuffling out of the darkness. It was Cade's wife, Missy.

"Cade, what the hell are you doing?" she hissed in a low whisper.

"Dad gone it, woman! I told you to leave me alone tonight! And keep your voice down!" he yelled back super loud.

She threw her hands down, cussed at him, and then marched back to the house. I guess the swear jar didn't apply to her. I can't say I was thrilled about Missy overhearing our conversation, so I was glad Cade sent her away. I don't think she ever particularly liked us to begin with.

"Don't worry. I told her if anyone asks, I was home all night. I never left," Cade said decisively.

"What about us?" Dorado looked incredulous.

"Ha! Y'all idiots is on your own! Now how the hell did you get involved with the Mexican mob again?"

I looked at Dorado. We didn't have time for this. "Short version," I said to him.

"Okay, cliff notes version. You know how they asked me to throw some races for them last summer and I did, then they asked me to win a race and I lost, yada, yada… Now I owe them tons of money; thought I'd use the map in the tombstone to pay them back, only it was a fake," he said breathlessly.

"The map?" Cade asked.

"No, the tombstone. Try to keep up."

Cade looked like he was trying to solve a really hard math problem. I grabbed him by the shirt collar. "We need to get out of town and fast, man." He was the only one who could offer us some transportation. Before he could say anything, Becky asked, "Where are you going?"

"There's a man in Mescalero that can help us," Dorado said.

"You're goin' to hide out with the Indjians?" Cade asked in disbelief. "I got me a security bunker nobody knows about we can all hide out in right here! And you're darn lucky I even invited you."

It was true, Cade actually did have a bunker he had dug out and built a long time ago. He thought nobody knew about it but me and Dingus had found it practically right after he dug it out and built it. I'd rather go on the run than hideout with Cade in his smelly bunker, that was for sure.

"I'm not going there to hide out. I'm going to go see Delbert Baca. He was the last person to see our dad alive," Dorado answered.

I turned to Becky. "Guess that means no dance tomorrow night," I said, feeling pretty bummed.

"How about I go with you guys?" Becky put her hand on my shoulder.

I thought of what the cartel said about killing our family if they didn't get the map. "No, it's better nobody knows you're with me right now. That cartel said if we didn't come through they'd come after our family next. And if they know we're together…"

"Then let my dad help," she said. "Like I said, this is our family history as much as it yours."

"No, don't tell your dad. It's not worth you getting in trouble. Plus, I don't think he could help us." I could tell I wasn't getting through to her, so I just said, "You'd only be putting him in an awkward position anyways. Think about it." Truthfully, I didn't trust her dad, but I didn't have the heart to tell her that.

Dorado backed me up. "It's true, Becks. If you went on the run with us or told your dad what happened I'm pretty sure it would just make things worse. Listen, the minute we find out any new information we'll call you, alright?"

I looked at her pleadingly. "I promise."

"Alright, I won't tell him. But I still think it's a bad idea."

Dorado grinned. "Well, in case you haven't noticed, bad ideas are our specialty." He looked at Cade. "I'll need my car back."

"Your car? That's impossible. I got it torn apart right now!"

"I gotta get outta here, man. Don't you have something you can loan me?" Dorado pleaded.

Cade sighed. "Alright, you can take Ol' Bessie."

Ol' Bessie was an El Camino that Cade bought right before he went off to 'nam and still had. It was kind of beaten up, but we sure couldn't drive Cade's truck that Xander pulled us over in earlier and risk getting recognized.

"Thanks man," Dorado said. "I'll take care of her just like she was my own car."

"You don't take care of your own car! I take care of it," Cade shouted as he went to get the keys.

***

We finally got on the road about thirty minutes later. First, Cade had taken Dorado down into the bunker where he kept some emergency medical supplies. He managed to get Dorado's half-finger cleaned and bandaged up proper and then gave him some painkillers to help him get through the next few days. There was no time to go to the hospital, plus we were worried about keeping a low profile. Cade said Dorado would be fine and went on to remind us about the time he accidentally cut his toe off with a shovel until we reminded him that we needed to hit the road.

We dropped Becky off on her block and then headed south towards Mescalero. I decided to try and let the car lull me to sleep, but I didn't feel peaceful and sleepy like I usually did on a car ride. How could I after what just happened? I just pressed the side of my face against the cool glass and looked at all the other headlights passing us by in the night. I wanted to be back home. I didn't care about how mad Aunt Patty would be at me that I stayed out all night. I didn't care about the fact I never wrote my report like I was supposed to. I didn't care what the school did to me for all the trouble with the goat. It seemed like all that stuff happened off in a whole other world that didn't even matter anymore.

Like I said, the day had started out pretty normal, but it sure didn't end that way.

V.
MESCALERO

FRIDAY, OCTOBER 29, 1976

When I woke up the next morning, the first thing I could smell was hot leather and dust. It's weird to wake up in a strange place, and Cade's smelly old El Camino was pretty strange. I opened my eyes and immediately shut them again. It was daytime now and already pretty hot, meaning it wasn't early morning. My arm was sticking to the leather upholstery, too, as I lifted it up to shield my eyes and look around. Last night Dorado had taken us off the highway to a secluded spot in the desert where no cops would see us and we could sleep.

I glanced at my brother. He looked exhausted, and from the way his eyes were darting around under the lids he was having some dream, or more likely a nightmare about last night. I looked down at his bloody bandaged hand and my stomach did a loop. It was an ugly reminder of the night before.

I reached over and gently shook him. "Hey."

"What!" Dorado violently sprang awake and gripped the steering wheel tight, looking quickly to his left and right until he saw me. Still only half-awake, he seemed to mumble something I couldn't make out.

"Hey, it's okay, man. Whatever it was, it was a dream," I said.

He took in a few deep breaths and then looked at his bandaged hand. "Well, that was a dream," he said. "But not this." He wiggled his fingers and then laid his head back to catch his breath. We both just sat there and stared at the hula ornament Cade kept on the dash for a while. It was hard to wake up. I yawned. "What time is it?"

He pulled out the pocket watch and flipped it open. "Dammit, it's past noon already." I guess all the stress would be enough to knock someone out until noon. He started up the car and then drove us back to the main highway and headed south for Roswell. You have to pass through there before you can get to Mescalero, where the Indian Reservation is.

My stomach grumbled. I was starving; the little bit of leftover steak I ate last night long gone. All of a sudden, I thought of Aunt Patty. I'd never stayed out all night without coming home before.

"What about Aunt Patty?" I asked.

"What about her?"

"Hello. I didn't come home last night. She's probably worried out of her mind."

"Oh, yeah," he said as though he hadn't thought about it. "Sorry, I guess being out on my own I forgot all about having to worry about Aunt Patty and curfews and all that."

I stopped to think about that for a second. "Living on your own, what's that like? Is it pretty cool?"

"Yeah, you eat what you want, sleep when you want, come home, or not, when you want." He grinned. "But that doesn't mean I don't get homesick sometimes. Truthfully, I'd love to go back to when I was your age. No matter what you might think now, it's pretty nice to live at home. A lot less worries, trust me."

I thought that was nuts. You couldn't do anything at my age. "I'll be glad when I'm out on my own. Aunt Patty hardly lets me do anything."

"Aw, give her a break. She's not so bad."

I couldn't believe the words coming out of his mouth. First forgetting it was going to be Halloween, and now defending Aunt Patty. I hoped I wouldn't start thinking like that when I got older. Besides, Dorado was always getting in trouble with Aunt Patty. "What about that time you stayed out all night when you were a senior? She tore into you and yelled at you worse than Rosalita ever did."

He laughed. "That's pretty hard to do in English, too."

"What are we gonna tell her? I mean, we have to call her, right?"

He could tell I was too scared to call her myself and grinned. "Don't worry, I'll call her for you. We'll stop at a gas station when we're in Roswell." He drummed his fingers along the steering wheel. "I'll say… I took you on a surprise trip with me… for your birthday."

For a second, I let myself pretend that's what we were really doing and not going on the run with our lives hanging in the balance. I almost laughed. "The sad thing is it's sort of not a lie. Only instead of it being a trip to celebrate my birthday, I guess it's more of a trip to make sure that we don't die on my birthday."

We drove along the highway some more. I started thinking about the photo. "I guess you're right. In that photo it could be our father or our uncle."

"Yeah, basically."

That was the bad part about my dad having a twin. I heard Nana could never tell them apart either. Sometimes Uncle Pancho would grow a mustache to make himself look different from Hondo. But I hear most of the time they liked it that nobody could tell them apart. I wondered for a second what it would be like to have a twin.

"So…how do you know when it was taken? Maybe it's an old photo from a long time ago?" I asked.

Dorado took the photo back out. "No, whichever one it is, they look older. And see that car? That's a 1975 Vega. The picture is only a year old at most. One of them is still alive… or at least they were a year ago."

About then the engine made some funny noises and the car shook. Dorado hit the steering wheel and the hula girl fell off the dash. "Just great! Cade loves to work on everyone's cars but his own," he said as steam started to come out from under the hood.

We pulled over into an old Sun Country on the outskirts of Roswell. I knew it had to be Roswell because I started to see some alien and UFO signs. Since we were in another county, we weren't too worried about anyone recognizing us. Plus, who knew if what happened last night had even made the news yet? I doubted it. New Mexico was the land of mañana (that means tomorrow in Spanish). It probably wouldn't be reported until tonight.

Dorado parked along the side of the building and handed me five bucks. "Get us something to eat while I look this thing over."

I walked inside and headed for the bathroom. I hate convenience store bathrooms. I feel dirtier when I come out of one than when I go in. I gave my face a good once over in the spotty bathroom mirror. You could tell I didn't get a real good night's sleep, but I looked passable and my hair hadn't gotten too messed up the way I slept on it. I still got some water and ran it through the unruly parts to tamp them down and washed my face off a little. That felt real good. I used a paper towel to open the door handle since I figured it was dirty and walked back outside into the store.

Luckily they had a grill going, so I got a breakfast burrito for me and Dorado. I wouldn't eat any of their nasty pre-packaged sweet rolls if my life depended on it. That much sugar this early in the morning would make me sick for sure. I went up front to pay. Above the cash register they had a TV mounted on the wall. The news out of Albuquerque was already playing, which meant it must've been close to one o'clock.

"$4.74," the old man behind the counter said.

I dug into my back pocket. Just then the newscaster said something about Fort Sumner.

"This morning Sheriff Xander Garrett and his men were in for the surprise of their lives when they got a call from the owners of the Old Fort Sumner Museum who said that the grave of Billy the Kid had been vandalized."

Xander was on screen being interviewed at the site. "We got a call first thing this morning. Said somebody had been in there and broken into the cage."

"The De Baca County Sheriff's Department already says they think they know why it happened," the newscaster continued.

"We think it was just a Halloween prank. And when we find out who did it, we won't go easy on them," Xander said, and I breathed a sigh of relief. They didn't know it was us.

I hoped maybe the report was over, but then the newscaster said, "Other residents have their own theories about what happened."

They cut to an old lady with curlers in her hair. "I seen a bright light fly over my house at midnight and then land right over there in the graveyard."

"What do you think it was?" the off-screen reporter asked.

"It was tham aliens, I know it. My sister lives in Roswell. Those things come down all the time over there and we're not that far away."

Something fishy was going on, though. The newscaster hadn't said a word about the tombstone being broken in half yet. Then it got weirder. They showed the grave, which had been filled back in, and the tombstone was still there, intact. For a second, I thought maybe it was old footage from earlier, but then the newscaster said, "And as for the famous tombstone which was just recently returned home, it still sits safely at the gravesite unharmed. Perhaps even the pranksters couldn't bring themselves to steal it after it had finally been returned home after twenty-five years. This is Marisa Melendez with Action Eight News."

My mouth dropped open and the clerk noticed.

"A crying shame ain't it?" he said.

"Yeah," I said absentmindedly. My mind was racing with possibilities since whoever had placed the fake there earlier had apparently already replaced it with another.

"Damn kids drive me nuts. Ain't good for nothing anymore but to degenerate society." The clerk started to hand me my change. "Oh, I don't mean you, though. I'm sure you're a very nice young man."

"Oh, yes sir," I said, flashing him a fake smile and taking the change.

I walked outside. Dorado was on a payphone talking to Aunt Patty just like he had promised to. I could tell it was Aunt Patty because of the way he was holding the phone far away from his ear. That meant she was yelling. I couldn't hear exactly what she was saying, but I did pick out the words "goat" and "shit" at one point, so I guess Little Billy was still there. "Like I said, I'm sorry I never called you and Rod," Dorado pleaded, "but I'll have him back by the end of the weekend, I promise. I mean, aren't you glad we're spending some quality time together?"

If Aunt Patty only knew the "quality time" of which he spoke.

"Look, I gotta go. I'll call you when we get to Capitan, okay?" She started yelling again and he just hung up the phone.

"You told her we're going to Capitan?"

"Yeah, said we were going to go camping." He started walking back to the El Camino.

"So Aunt Patty didn't say anything about the news?"

"The news?" he turned to look at me.

"Yeah, it's all over the news already."

"Wait, did they—"

I knew what he was going to ask, so I said, "No, don't worry. They didn't identify us."

I looked at Old Bessie. "What about the car?"

"I think she gave us her last hurrah." He patted the hood.

"Great. So now we have to hitchhike." I leaned against the fender and handed Dorado his burrito and then started eating my own.

In between gulps, he told me, "I already took care of it. See that guy over there? He recognized me from the racing circuit and wants to give us a ride."

A Texan even goofier than Cade waved at us. He was wearing shorts and a baseball cap. His shirt had a Cowboys star on it. He was cleaning the windows on one of those giant wooden paneled station wagons with his wife and kids—about four of them from what I could tell. Great, a road trip with the Brady Bunch, I thought to myself.

"Is he actually going to Mescalero, though?"

"Ruidoso, so close enough." It made sense; people were always passing through Roswell on the way to the mountains.

We threw our burrito wrappers in the trash and started to walk towards him. "Did he ask about your hand?" It was pretty noticeable. I didn't see how anyone could not ask.

"Yeah," he said nonchalantly.

"Well, what'd you tell him?" Dorado could come up with some pretty big whoppers sometimes, so I was curious what he told him.

He shrugged. "The truth, a Mexican Drug Cartel cut it off. He thought it was the funniest thing he ever heard."

I sighed and shook my head. I guess sometimes you could tell the truth, and if it was wild enough people would think it was a joke.

"You actually told him that? What if he turns you in or something?"

"Like I said, he's a fan. We can trust him. I'm pretty good at reading people, I swear."

I grinned at him and held up my pinky finger. "Pinky swear?"

He gave me a dirty look.

"Too soon?" I put my hand down.

Before he could clobber me, we were to the Texan's station wagon. His face lit up the moment he saw Dorado. "Oh my lands, the folks back home will never believe I got to give Dorado Dumez a ride."

It was weird to think my brother had fans, but apparently, he actually did.

"You don't mind if my little brother tags along, do you?" Dorado asked.

"Lands no, son, we always got room for one more." Before I could even try to be polite and introduce myself, he started yammering on again. "Kids, this here's a famous race car driver and his brother. Say hello." We looked into the backseat to see four little kids between the ages of four and ten I'd say. They all just stared at us blankly. They were too young and shy to say anything and the oldest was reading a book.

"Oh well, they'll warm up to you eventually. Go on and get inside. Kids, make room," the man said.

We piled into the backseat as the man—I think his name was Jerry—introduced us to his wife and kids, but I'm really bad at remembering names, even when I just heard them. We made pointless small talk for the first half-hour, like him asking me if I played football and such, and when I said no, he took that as an opportunity to tell us about all of his high school football glories. Nobody else in the family could get a word in edgewise. The good thing about people like that is you don't really have to listen to what they're saying because before you know it, they'll have changed the topic to something else. Right now he was going on about how they had a cabin near Ruidoso they were going to visit.

He and his wife had started talking about something else so Dorado and I could finally carry on a conversation of our own. Obviously, it wasn't something we wanted Jerry and his wife to hear. The kids, on the other hand, were too little to care, and the oldest one had never looked up from her book.

"Hey man, I didn't get a chance to tell you earlier, but there's something fishy going on about the tombstone."

"It's broken as far they know, right? What about it?"

I shook my head. "Not exactly. On the newscast they acted like all that happened was that the grave was dug up. They didn't say a word about the tombstone being broken. In fact, somebody already replaced it with another one."

"This keeps getting weirder and weirder."

Before we could discuss it further, one of the little kids was crawling over the backseat and staring intently at Dorado's hand. I guess he just now noticed. Dorado looked at him and smiled. "A one-eyed man with a hook sliced it off. Neat, huh?"

"Wow," the little kid silently mouthed and then slowly slinked back behind us. When he got older, he'd probably think that was a made-up story.

We were driving through the Hondo Valley. That's where the town of Lincoln itself was located, the place where all of the trouble with the Lincoln County War actually occurred. The road was even called the Billy the Kid Scenic Byway.

The Hondo Valley is beautiful. If you didn't know any better, you wouldn't even think you were in New Mexico with all of the brooks, streams, and pine trees. All of the leaves had turned either gold or red, but soon the cold front would come in and they'd all be gone.

It would've been a really nice trip except for towards the end they all decided to have a sing-along. I don't know about you, but I ain't much for sing-alongs, and after an hour of one, I'm about ready to go on a killing spree. But once we passed Fox Cave, it seemed like we were in Mescalero in no time.

Even though it's called the Mescalero Apache Indian Reservation, it still looks like anywhere else in New Mexico with houses and mobile homes. I had only been there once before when I was eight. I had been pretty disappointed. I thought since it was called an Indian Reservation there would be teepees and people with those feathered headdresses. During the 4th of July they throw a Coming of Age Ceremony where they pitch tepees on the hill and live like they did in the old days. Otherwise, they're just as modern as anybody else.

Jerry and his family dropped us off just outside of town. Dorado tried to give him some gas money but he wouldn't take it and insisted Dorado give him his autograph instead, so he signed an old napkin for them and we went on our way. I decided then and there I'd never ask a celebrity for their autograph, especially if all I had was a dirty old napkin.

From there we walked towards St. Joseph's. I guess last night while I was asleep Dorado stopped in at a payphone and found Baca in the phone book and called him. He told Dorado to meet him at St. Joseph's, an old church atop a hill, in the afternoon. St. Joseph's was an imposing bricked structure with an old flare to it.

We walked into the church. The interior was brick just like the outside. The giant stained-glass cross shone brightly in the afternoon sun. There wasn't hardly anybody in there except for a few old ladies up front lighting candles. One gave us a suspicious look. It seemed like there was something you were supposed to do when you entered a Catholic Church like kneel and cross yourself but I didn't remember for sure. We don't do all that stuff in our church.

We scanned the pews. I didn't see any old men anywhere.

"You're late," a voice said behind us. "I've been waiting here for an hour."

Dorado and I both turned around to see an old man in his late 70s with his arms crossed. He had long gray hair and had a serape draped over his shoulders.

"You haven't seen us since we were little kids. How did you know it was us?" I asked.

"Because I can see Pancho and Hondo in you both." He pointed at Dorado and said very seriously, "You in the spirit," and then to me, "and you in the flesh."

"Really?" Dorado said, amazed.

"No." Baca looked at him like he was a moron. "You're just the only two white boys to walk into this church in years, dummy."

"Oh," Dorado said, embarrassed, and I felt kinda dumb right along with him.

"But that is how you expect us people to talk, isn't it?" Baca grinned and then went to sit down in one of the pews and said, "I saw the local news already. So tell me, how bad is it?"

Dorado held up his bandaged hand. "About this bad."

***

Baca was studying the photo that Dr. Villegas had given Dorado. We had told him everything that had happened at the cemetery the night before and left nothing out.

"Can you tell which one it is?" Dorado asked.

He kept on studying the photo and finally said, "No, I'm sorry, but I can't. I knew your father well, but not well enough to tell him apart from Pancho."

"Do you at least have any idea why the tombstone was a fake, or who would've put it there?" I asked.

Baca pointed to his temple. "Use your head. Once the tombstone was recovered it probably would've been given to someone within the city government, right?" We both nodded and he continued. "Therefore, they would've also been the ones to make the decoy and place the fake tombstone in the cemetery to keep the real one to themselves. I'd say what you two have is Santa Fe Ring trouble, and the worst part is by destroying their decoy, you've alerted them to your presence."

"The Santa Fe Ring? I thought that was just a myth," I blurted.

He smiled. "Sounds like it. But no, they exist all right. Unfortunately, the Ring will be the least of your problems so long as you have McCaw after you."

"You know McCaw?" I asked.

"Yes, he was once an Apache."

"I don't understand. How can he not be an Apache anymore?" Dorado asked.

"We excommunicated him as you white people would say. For witchcraft."

I thought of what McCaw had said about being able to see things through the eyes of his hawk. "Witchcraft? You guys really believe in that?"

Baca looked at us as though there was something we didn't know. "Brujos are very real. Don't underestimate them. That's how I got this scar."

Baca lifted up his shirt to show us what I assumed was a knife wound across his stomach.

"No way," Dorado said.

"Oh yes way. Hurt like hell, too. Unfortunately, I didn't find out McCaw was a brujo until it was too late. Last I saw of him, he was following your father into Mexico."

"How did our dad and Uncle Pancho become involved in all of this?"

"I fear that is too long of a tale to tell right now, so I'll give you the cliff notes version. Are you both familiar with the man Tumbleweed Williams?"

We both nodded, and he continued.

"As you know, Williams' visit to New Mexico was highly publicized, and he even met with the governor. This would have been about 1950, the same time that your father was serving as Sheriff of Fort Sumner."

We both nodded.

"Well, your uncle Pancho had always had a fascination with Billy the Kid, so when he found out about Williams, he decided he had to meet him. To do so, he took advantage of being Hondo's twin. One day he stole one of Hondo's extra uniforms and his badge and took off for Santa Fe where Williams was meeting the governor."

"So he impersonated our dad?" Dorado asked with a grin. "That guy really was a scoundrel."

"That's right. By pretending to be the Sheriff of Fort Sumner he was granted an audience with Williams as well. Apparently, Williams told him the story about the tombstone, and you know what happened next."

"But what about our dad?" I asked. "How did he get involved?"

"Once your father found out what Pancho had done, he too sought out Williams. But he was too late. Williams had died of a heart attack, and Pancho had fled to Mexico. However, Hondo did obtain a letter written by Williams to Pancho before he died. The letter told of a hidden canyon of gold, known by many as the Lost Adams. As it turned out, back in the early 1880s, the Kid actually met Old Man Adams, and he revealed the location of the gold to him. With the help of Adams and a local priest, Billy found the canyon. All three men took their share of the gold they found, but soon after, Old Man Adams died. When this happened, Billy and the priest decided to bury Adams with some of the gold along with a map to the Lost Adams Canyon. More than anything, the map itself is what the Ring now seeks."

"Wait, but I thought the tombstone had a map to the gold in it? But now you're saying that the map to the canyon is buried with Old Man Adams and the gold?" Dorado said.

"That's one thing you boys will have to learn about history. When stories get passed down year after year, they get twisted and misconstrued. Even though what's inside the Kid's tombstone leads to the gold, it isn't a map itself. All we know is that it was called the *Ojo del Oro*, or the Eye of the Gold, which somehow reveals the location of Adams' grave."

"But how?" I asked.

"We won't know until one day when somebody opens it." He shrugged. "Anyhow, the priest that made the Ojo del Oro was killed by the Santa Fe Ring, who was also after the Lost Adams Canyon. Billy went to his friend, the sheriff Pat Garrett, for help, and together he and the Kid both agreed that so long as the Ring was out there, the canyon should remain hidden. So Garrett and the Kid agreed to fake his death and then hide the Ojo del Oro in the one place the Ring would never imagine to look."

"His tombstone," Dorado and me said at the same time.

"Exactly. But there's a catch." Baca got a funny look on his face as though he had something he needed to say but didn't know how exactly. "Ever seen one of those terrible infomercials on TV where the annoying sales guy says, 'But wait, there's more!'?"

"Yeah," we both said at once, puzzled.

"Well, there's more," he sighed. "It's not as simple as just getting the tombstone and cracking it open like an egg, because the Eye will only reveal the location of the buried gold at a certain place at a certain time. Not only that, once the location of Adams' grave is revealed, you'll need a special key to access it." Before we could ask what he meant, he held up his hands and said, "Don't ask me how because I don't know. All I know is that the location of the key is in the letter that Williams gave to your father."

"Whoa, so last night had that actually been the real tombstone…" Dorado's words trailed off as he realized what might have happened when Villegas discovered he didn't actually have everything he needed to find the gold, not to mention that they probably would have broken the Eye inside.

Before Dorado could ask what to do next, Baca held up a finger and added, "Lucky for you, your father left this with me before he set off for Mexico." Baca held up a tiny key. "I brought it with me when you called because I had a hunch you'd need it."

I reached out and took it when he handed it to me. "What is it?"

"The key to your father's safety deposit box which contains the letter by Williams, which will tell you everything else that you need to know," Baca answered.

"Why didn't he just tell you where to find it?" I asked as I stuffed the key down in my pocket tight so I didn't lose it.

"I don't know what's in the letter because I don't want to know what's in the letter. I just pay the rent on the damn box as a favor to your old man."

"Which bank—" Dorado started to ask, but Baca answered before he could even finish the question.

"The First National Bank in Santa Fe. And that's all I know."

A thought occurred to me that didn't make sense. "Wait, if our Uncle Pancho had the tombstone, and our dad knew the location of the key, then why didn't they team up to get the gold?"

I could tell by the look on Baca's face that he regretted me asking the question. "Your father's relationship with his brother was a strained one, and as I am partly to blame for that..." he shook his head as though he didn't want to continue talking. "Like I said, you had better get going. Santa Fe is a ways away from here." He stood up.

Dorado stopped him. "Wait, there's something you're not telling us. What about our dad and our uncle?"

"You need to understand something. I am only helping you because I owe a debt to your father. He came to me because the legend of the gold is an Apache one. Only we Apache believe the gold should remain hidden. After some time, I convinced your father of this as well. Truthfully, if he knew you were hunting the gold to find him, he would be greatly saddened."

"Why? What's so dangerous about finding a little gold?"

"Like I said. You had better get going." He began to walk away.

"No, tell us why."

Baca turned stern. "You should thank me. If I told you why then you would be held accountable for your actions."

"We're already in trouble with the law," Dorado said, puzzled.

"I didn't mean the law." Baca glanced at a cross on the wall before turning towards the altar at the front. I looked at the cross. I think I knew what he meant, but it didn't make any sense to me. Why would God care if we found some gold? Maybe Baca was just a crazy old man.

Before he reached the altar, he turned back to look at us one more time. "I know it's too late for you to turn back now, but I want you to remember something, my sons. Once you come face to face with a legend, it will either make you a legend along with it, or you will not live to tell about it at all. Neither of those are a good thing." And with that, he turned and sat down to pray. It was clear that was all we were going to get out of him.

"Crazy old man," Dorado muttered.

"How are we gonna get to Santa Fe?" I asked. We were so focused on getting here we didn't know what we'd actually do after we saw Baca.

"I guess we can start by calling Cade and just hope he picks up," he said and smiled grimly. We walked towards the church's exit to leave. As soon as Dorado opened the door, Xander and several men were on the other side to greet him with a gun barrel to the face.

VI.
RUN, MAN, RUN!

"Isn't this a little bit out of your jurisdiction?" Dorado said with Xander's gun barrel partly up his nose.

"I suppose." Xander grinned. "But when someone vandalizes a monument like the Kid's grave, well, people get upset."

"How did you know…" I stopped myself as soon as I realized I was admitting to our guilt by asking the question.

"How did I know it was you two? Well, I only saw you idiots hauling around a blow torch last night. Plus, you left something behind, didn't you, Dorado?" Xander clutched Dorado's bandaged hand and then one of his men held up Dorado's severed fingertip where he could see it.

"I have been looking everywhere for that thing," Dorado said.

Xander glanced in my direction. I was still inside the church, so he said, "Pancho, get out here where I can see you better or I'll blow big brother's nose, if you get my drift."

"Well, I lost half a finger last night. Why not a nose today?" Dorado sighed.

I slowly walked out of the church as my mind raced. How did he find us? Did Becky tell him where we went? If not Becky, then who? Would he actually pull the trigger on my brother or was it a bluff? He wasn't in uniform, that much I could tell and for some reason I got the impression the three guys he had with him weren't part of the police force.

Xander lowered his gun. "You two want to tell me what you're doing down here hiding with the Indians?"

"Actually, what I want to know is how did you find us?" Dorado said.

Xander gave him a dirty look and replied, "A little birdie told me."

So Becky had told him. I guess she was just trying to help, but it was still frustrating. Finally it dawned on me why Xander was so angry. Thanks to me, I had put Becky in some serious danger last night.

"Look, I'm really sorry I didn't tell you about dating your daughter. And I'm sorry I took her with me to the graveyard. I had no idea a Mexican Drug Cartel would get involved and cut off my brother's finger."

He kept his steely gaze on me considering every word I said.

"Hey, and that tombstone was a fake, so it's not like we broke the real one," I added.

He looked at me like I was an idiot. "I know, son. I helped put it there."

Dorado was shocked. "You're the one who placed that fake. So you're part of the—"

Xander cut him off. "Santa Fe Ring. And no, kid, I don't much care for the name. And now thanks to you, apparently we've got competition to get the Ojo del Oro with a Mexican Drug cartel."

"Oh, don't worry. They don't know about the Eye yet. Wait, how do you know about the Eye?" I asked. Dorado shot me a look that said I was saying too much.

"Heh, the real question is, how do you? The Indian tell you?" Xander replied.

"No such luck," Dorado said. "In fact, he's not even here today."

"That's bull. You know it, and I know it. Now let's go in there and see him together."

Xander switched his attention from Dorado to me and pressed the gun into my back. He grabbed my jacket collar and walked me back inside the church. Baca was gone. All that remained was his old serape slung across the vacant pew.

Xander noticed too. "What the hell!" his echo bellowed through the whole church and an old Indian woman turned around from her candle and glared at him as though he were the devil.

He hauled me out of the church by my jacket collar. "Where did he go?"

"We don't know! Look, I'll tell you everything he said. Just don't point the gun at my brother again," Dorado said.

Xander tipped his hat up with his gun. "Okay, but not here. We're going to go somewhere nice and private to have a long talk. You boys ever been to Perdition?"

Me and Dorado looked at each other. "Perdition?"

Xander just laughed. "You boys are in for a treat then."

He grabbed me by the shoulder and hauled me to a nearby truck, which I assumed was his off-duty vehicle, while one of his goons did the same to Dorado.

Xander got into the driver's seat while two of his men cuffed us. Then they helped us into the back of the truck and made me sit on one of the rear wheel wells with Dorado next to me. They sat across from us and I noticed each had a gun on his belt. I didn't recognize them from around town, which pretty much confirmed my suspicions that they weren't his off-duty men. I looked inside the cab and was surprised to see a couple of hound dogs, trackers obviously, riding inside with the other two men. So the dogs get to stay inside while we ride in the back, I thought. Xander started the engine and we headed south down one of the back dirt roads. There are a lot of unpaved roads in this part of New Mexico.

Dorado was giving the guards a hard time. "So, the Santa Fe Ring, cool name. What do you guys do mostly, build forts out of sofa cushions, things like that?" They stared at him blankly. "Do you guys have like a super-secret cool handshake… anything like that?"

I was too caught up thinking about Becky to laugh. "I can't believe she lied to me," I said to Dorado. It was all I could think about. "She swore she wouldn't tell him."

"Well, that's women, bro."

"Yeah, but I thought Becky was different."

"I know, man, that's what we all say."

I wished the truck ride wasn't so rough. Jostling around hurt the crick in my neck that had been going away up until now. We started heading up an old mountain road twisting and turning around various bends. My conversation with Dorado wasn't going anywhere, so I looked down at the road passing underneath us.

"Don't think about jumping," one of the guards said. "You'd break every bone in your body."

I sure as heck wasn't thinking about that. Anybody over 21 assumes if you're 14 then you must be the dumbest kid alive. I was trying to think of ways to get out of there, but it wouldn't be by jumping out of a moving truck and almost breaking my neck.

I was wrong.

A few seconds later, Dorado very quietly said to me, "Pancho, remember all that crap you always used to give me about Rosalita?"

What the heck did that have to do with anything? "Yeah."

"How she's too jealous and paranoid? How whenever I disappear, she thinks I'm cheating on her and she tracks me down? No matter where?"

"Yeah…" I still didn't get it.

"Well, all that's about to pay off in a big way." He nodded at the road passing behind us.

I looked and couldn't believe what I saw. Rosalita's red and white Ford truck was following us up the steep road.

"How the hell did she find us?" I said in amazement. I'd seen Rosalita track Dorado down to movies, baseball games, and even a funeral once, but this took it to the next level.

He shook his head. "I don't know. The girl truly has a gift."

The two men watching us finally took notice of the old Ford roaring up the road to get next to us and began to get fidgety.

"Who is this? A friend of yours?" one of them asked.

Dorado grinned as her truck got closer and closer. "Oh, not just a friend. That would be my jealous Latina girlfriend. I don't know if you boys have ever had one before, but you do not want to make them angry. Trust me."

Rosalita pulled up beside us on the guards' side to the right and started yelling at Dorado immediately. "Dorado, you *baboso*! You never called me last night. Where were you? Who were you with?"

I thought Dorado might say, "Thank God you're here!" Or, maybe, "Rosie, get out of here. It's not safe for you!" But no, that's not what he said. Instead, he looked at her angrily and yelled, "Get out of here, you crazy bitch! I don't want to see you!"

"What the hell's going on?" I heard Xander yell from the driver's seat.

He started to speed up, but Rosalita kept pace in her truck.

"What the hell are you doing?" I asked Dorado as she worked to catch back up to Xander.

"Trust me," he whispered where only I could hear it.

Rosie pulled back up next to us. "Who were you with, you pig! I know you were with another woman!"

"You really want to know who I was with?"

"Yes!"

"Are you sure?"

"Tell me, you *baboso*!"

Dorado measured his words carefully. "I was with your sister."

Rosalita's face became red and everyone froze. It was as if an atomic bomb had just detonated and we were all sitting there helplessly watching the mushroom cloud about to come and envelop us. There was literally nothing worse that one could say to one's Mexican girlfriend.

"Get ready to jump," Dorado whispered to me, and I knew what he was thinking.

Rosalita screamed like a Spartan soldier going into battle and swerved her truck towards Xander's to sideswipe us.

"Now!" Dorado and I stood up. I struggled like a surfer riding the waves to hold my footing. When the two trucks impacted it knocked our two guards over and we jumped over them sideways like we were doing a pole vault, landing hard in the back of Rosie's truck bed. My back smarted pretty bad from the impact. Xander retaliated by swiping back into her and she swerved off the road and cut into the grass. I could still hear Xander yelling from his truck and could tell they were going to follow us.

I tried to sit back up.

Rosalita was already yelling again. "How could you? You pig!" Through the open back window she was reaching around to smack Dorado.

"I wasn't with your sister last night, you idiot. She lives three hundred miles away!" he managed to get out as she swatted him. "And is that really what you should be worried about right now?"

"How the hell did you find us!" I asked her.

"I went to your cousin's house and had a little chat with his wife!" she yelled and I knew she meant Missy.

Xander's truck was catching up to us. It had a better motor than Rosie's old truck, which, if I remember correctly, already had about 250,000 miles on it.

"Go back and get them!" Xander was yelling to one of his men. The guy with the gun holster was standing up, poised to jump when they got close enough. Rosie swerved hard to the left and the plastic bed liner in the back of her piece-of-crap truck slid a little bit. It felt loose to the point of being unstable. We hit another bump and the plastic bed raised up underneath us. It was becoming clearer and clearer to me that it was a size too small.

"This bedding is way too loose!" I shouted to Dorado.

"I know, I put it in!" he shouted back.

"You're a horrible boyfriend!" I yelled at him.

"I know! I know!"

I raised my head again to look and see where Xander was. "Pancho, keep your head down!" Dorado yelled.

No matter how fast Rosie pushed the old truck, Xander's kept pace. He was right next to us, and before she could swerve away, the guy jumped and landed hard in the back of the bed. As he did, the plastic bed lining came loose even worse. He smiled at us and pulled out his gun. He was going to force us to stop. Maybe it was stupid, but I knew they wanted us alive, not dead, and I was about to kick him in the stomach. Only Dorado beat me to it with his longer legs. The man dropped the gun over the side while his body toppled backwards. His impact knocked the tailgate down, but he didn't fall out. He grasped the railing with his hands and began climbing back towards me.

Dang it! I wished I had my hands free. Like this I was helpless. I brought my knees up to my chest and brought my cuffed hands underneath my butt. I still couldn't get them past my legs. I pointed my toes forward and just barely managed to slip the cuffs past my shoes. It hurt, but my hands were at least in front of me again.

I looked at Dorado. "Just do like I did!"

Dorado tried but couldn't. His legs were too long.

Suddenly, the gunman grabbed my ankle. He had managed to crawl back up the truck bed. Just then we hit another bump and the bed slipped again. I could tell because the truck's cab window now seemed further away and the guy clinging to my leg looked even more terrified. Rosie was pushing the truck harder as we went uphill. Inch by inch, the bed slipped.

"Uh, Rosie!" Dorado shouted. "You're going too fast!"

She misheard and yelled back, "Faster! Are you crazy!" Then she gunned it.

"No!" we both yelled, but it was too late.

She was swerving around a steep bend as the bed slipped even further. With my hands cuffed it was hard to hold onto anything but the bed itself. As she rounded another bend, me, Dorado, the guard, and the plastic bed liner went flying out of the end of the truck. With a thud that knocked the breath out of me, we slid off of the side of the dirt road and down the hill, only it seemed more like a mountain to me with its steep incline. Before I had a chance to get my bearings, I could feel the bed sliding down the hill, its smooth bottom picking up more and more momentum.

The other guy wasn't interested in fighting us anymore—we were all passengers on the same wild ride. I peered above the walls of the bed liner, watching the dirt whoosh by in the air as we quickly slid across the ground. Before we knew it, we had slid so far down the hill we were going to go right across another part of the dirt road that snaked around it. I hoped the flat road would slow us down. Then I saw a truck coming and hoped that it wouldn't. No, it wasn't a truck. It was the same station wagon that had given us a ride earlier. I could see the family inside all bobbing their heads in unison, singing another song. I tensed up, dreading the impact, but thank God they sped right past us as we went sailing behind them. They were so caught up in their singalong I don't think they even saw us. We hit the flat dirt road but kept on flying, narrowly avoiding becoming roadkill from a car behind them that honked at us as we went by.

Me, Dorado, and even the guard looked at each other and laughed. We were off of the beaten path again and sliding down the hill, picking up momentum. When would it end? Up ahead, I saw something that might end our trip: a rock. A really big rock. I was running on pure instinct, not really even thinking about it as I braced myself sideways, pushing my arms and legs against the sides of the bed to wedge myself in place.

We hit the rock hard, flipping the bed into the air. My stomach did a loopty-loop as the view above me changed from sky to dirt, to sky, and back again. We hit the ground with a hard thud.

"Pancho!" Dorado yelled as he fell out. Then I heard the other guy scream and he was gone, too. I was the only one on this wild ride now and peeked my head up above the bed. It was like being on a mad toboggan ride, only on the dirt.

I felt another hard thud and went flying out of the bed. Landing on my side, I began my long descent down the hill.

I think I cussed every time I rolled over. I just hoped I didn't roll over a cactus. Gasping, I managed to see a tree just ahead of me. It was a fairly young tree and had grown sideways along the hill, so its branches weren't too far off the ground. I got ready, and as I skidded underneath it, I managed to grab a branch at just the right moment. Wouldn't you know it—out of all the healthy branches on that tree I grabbed a dead one that snapped right off. I hadn't even grabbed it long enough to slow my momentum and I kept right on going down the hill.

I had an idea, though. As I slid across my belly with the branch still in my hands, I raised up my arms and plunged the stick firmly into the steep decline. It dragged through the soft dirt and finally sunk in deep enough to stop after a few feet. I couldn't believe it. As I slowed my breathing, I realized my feet weren't touching anything, just hanging in space.

I let my eyes slowly look down. Below my waist there was nothing. The branch had sunk into place in the earth just in time. I sighed. "Thank God."

I started to pull myself up on the branch. Brittle old thing snapped and I was free-falling, only this time I didn't know when I was going to hit the ground. It seemed like I yelled for an eternity before I hit dirt again. It was another decline, so as I rolled, it took off some of the impact. I don't know if I got knocked out or not, but it felt like I was waking up after I finished rolling.

Something was poking me. "You think he's dead?"

It sounded like a little kid. I lifted my head from the grass and saw two young boys in overalls looking at me. "Aw, man, he's not dead," the other boy said, disappointed.

I groaned and sat up. "Where am I?"

"You're in Bent," the little boy said and used his stick to point to an old rotten sign. Sure enough, the sign read "WELCOME TO BENT-POPULATION 145"—only the 145 was crossed out and someone had spray-painted a 12 on it. All I could remember was that Bent was a little town west of Mescalero somewhere.

"Dang, man, we heard you screaming all the way down the hill," the other boy said. Then he saw my handcuffs and asked, "Are you a criminal?"

I must've looked like a dang juvenile detention escapee with those handcuffs on. The boys seemed to think that was neat, though, so I just played into it.

"Yeah," I said. "How'd you like to help me get away?"

They looked at each other and nodded their heads.

First thing I wanted was to get out of those cuffs. I looked around the town, if you could call it that. There was only one paved road, and so far all I could see was a gas station, a food mart, and a few abandoned buildings. One of them looked like it used to be a school.

"Alright, well, you think we could get these handcuffs off of me?" I asked.

"Yeah, I saw a TV show once where a guy couldn't get the cuffs off, so they had to saw his hand off," the taller boy said matter-of-factly.

"I'll go get daddy's hatchet!" the other boy said, running off to what I assumed was his home.

"Well, I don't think we'll have to do that," I said, "but we can use the hatchet to cut the chains."

The other boy came running back from his house with a decent-sized hatchet. I went over and spread the chains as wide as I could across an old tree stump. The taller boy took the hatchet.

"No cutting off my hands," I said sternly. "Cut the chain right here in the middle."

"Alright," he sighed and raised the hatchet so high I thought he'd topple backwards with it.

I prayed he didn't miss. I couldn't believe I was at the mercy of what looked like two eight-year-olds. I closed my eyes and kept praying. When I heard the ax hit the tree stump, I jumped and noticed my hands were free. He had hit the chain dead on.

"Whoo, good job, man," I said, wiping my forehead.

"You think those are looking for you?" the other boy asked.

"What?" I asked and then heard two dogs barking. Probably those hounds from the truck. Xander was getting his money's worth out of them. They were close, too. I would have to hide in the foliage somewhere. I couldn't run, they'd see me in the open spaces that stretched ahead outside of Bent.

Then I remembered something I'd seen Paul Newman do in *Cool Hand Luke.* "Get me some red pepper!" I yelled. "Anything powdery and hot you can find."

They both ran into the house this time, and within moments were back with a couple of shakers. One had regular black pepper in it. That wouldn't do much good, but the other was full of red chili powder.

"Alright, now if you guys want to see something neat, just sit over there," I said, pointing to the gas station. "And if they ask where I went, tell 'em thataway," and I pointed north.

I walked out onto the dirt road and sprinkled the red powder. I made quite a trail of it. It blended in well enough with the reddish dirt. I tossed the empty shaker out of sight and hopped back into the bushes by the hillside where I had fallen.

About two minutes later, I heard the dogs barking and knew from the sound they were close. I peeked out of the bushes. The dogs had their noses glued to the ground, working overtime. Xander was talking to the two boys. They didn't exactly point north like I'd told them, but they at least pointed the opposite direction from where I was.

Just then was when the dogs started to get into a sneezing fit. The little kids busted out laughing and I was trying not to laugh myself. Those dogs wouldn't be sniffing anywhere near that ground again.

I felt something funny tickle across the back of my legs as I lay in the grass. I looked behind me. A snake about two feet long was slithering across them. I can handle spiders, scorpions, lizards… just about any sort of creepy crawlies except for snakes. Snakes made me lose my cool. My head went light and before I knew what I was doing, I jumped out of the bushes and cussed loud enough they could probably hear me all the way up in Santa Fe. I was looking behind me and brushing myself off when I saw Xander looking at me with his crooked grin.

I grinned back and then bolted. I didn't have any kind of plan this time—just to run. I heard Xander yell, "Aim for the legs," and then something that sounded like firecrackers. As the dirt next to my feet started exploding, I realized gunfire doesn't sound like it does in the movies. I looked for the nearest cover and saw the old blue school building that looked like it had been built back in the 1940s. One of the windows was broken out at ground level, so I jumped through it.

My feet landed with a heavy clop. Everything in the school was silent, but I could hear my heartbeat in my head and Xander's yelling outside. Then I heard something else.

Down the hall, I could hear the heavy clop of boots hitting the tiled floor. Someone else was coming. I turned to see a man walking towards me from around the corner. He looked like he just stepped out of a movie or something. He was wearing tan riding pants with dark brown knee-high boots, a white dress shirt with a brown vest over it, and a long brown, leathery-looking duster coat.

He had jet black hair like mine dripping across his ears and face in waves and swirls. He looked like he was in his twenties, and a thick layer of black stubble covered his face, the hair above his lip a little thicker than the rest. We locked eyes. They looked just like mine only in a constant squint, beady and piercing.

It was the weirdest feeling I ever had looking at another person. It was like I already knew him even though I'd never seen him before.

Just then, the hall lit up with sunlight. Xander and his men had burst through the old double doors at the entrance.

"Pancho!" the stranger yelled. He knew my name.

I was stuck between Xander, his men, and the stranger. I didn't have a choice really, but I knew who I would run to.

I looked back to the stranger calling me. I finally realized why he looked familiar. He was me.

VII.
DEATH RIDES A MOTORCYCLE

I couldn't quit staring at the stranger's face even as he dragged me out the back door of the school. It was my own face if I was about six or seven years older, only with skin that was a little darker and more weathered from the sun. Same eyes as mine and Dorado's right down to the gold ring around the pupils, same hair color, same chin and cheekbones. Actually, apart from the beard stubble and the darker complexion, he might as well have been Dorado with long black hair. If Dorado had inherited more Spanish genes from our mother, that's just about what he'd look like.

He jumped onto a black and white Kawasaki motorcycle. "Mach III" was emblazoned on the side. The sound of the engine starting took me out of my stupor. "Would you get on already!" he yelled with a thick Mexican accent, his y's sounding more like j's like Rosalita's did.

I didn't hesitate. Still in shock, I mechanically hopped on and locked my arms around his waist. You don't usually do that with another guy, you let your hands grip the end of the seat behind you, but this guy was going to peel out big time.

He did. The momentum of the wind was whipping my hair in no time. I heard Xander and his men bust through the back school doors which we'd just left behind in the wind. We had passed through all of Bent in an instant. I doubt Xander could've even gotten back into his truck by the time the town was a speck in the distance.

We got onto the main road and headed back east towards Mescalero. A million questions raced through my mind. Did my dad have another son we didn't know about? Or Uncle Pancho? If he wasn't so young I might've even thought I was his son. Was he a long-lost relative from someone I didn't even know about? Or were his looks just one a heck of a coincidence? No, he couldn't be a coincidence, I decided. We looked too much alike. From the way he talked he sounded like he was from deep Mexico, the last place both my dad and Uncle Pancho were seen.

For a while I didn't say anything. It was impossible to talk over the sound of the engine. But, once we got to one of the more forested areas of the road, I shouted, "Can't you pull over yet?" He ignored me. "Hey! I said pull over!"

"Alright, hold your horses," he said and then began grumbling something in Spanish I couldn't understand. We pulled off onto the side of the road, hopped off, and rolled the bike into the forest. I was glad I was in this part of New Mexico now. The forest is a lot easier to hide in than the broad open desert.

We ducked down low for a minute until we heard Xander and his men roar past us, thinking we were still heading east.

He turned to look at me and got up. "Well, we lose them."

"Yes, we did," I said absentmindedly. I got up and studied him some more since we were both standing still. He was studying me just as much as I was studying him. His lips looked as though they were always poised to say something. And while you couldn't tell what he was thinking, you could see the wheels in his head constantly turning, calculating something. Right now he was looking like an idiot twiddling an old toothpick in his mouth. I bit down hard on the straw of grass I was currently chewing on. I do that when I'm nervous. I suddenly realized I was doing exactly what he was doing and then spit it out.

"Who are you?" I finally asked.

He smiled. "Who do you think I am?"

I wanted to give him several good guesses, but I was ticked that he was playing it so coy. "How the hell should I know? I've never seen you before."

"Oh really?" He stroked his chin.

"Okay, I see the resemblance. Who are you, a cousin, uncle?"

"Uncle?" He looked perturbed. "I'm not that old *hermano*." He grinned as though I should know what that meant, but I couldn't remember.

When it didn't register, he gave me a disgusted look. "You mean to tell me you don't even speak Spanish?"

Finally the meaning of the word hit me like a sledgehammer. "Brother." I blurted the word out in shock, but saying it out loud didn't make it seem real. No, it couldn't be. My old man didn't have any other kids, just me and Dorado. He grinned and I shook my head. "No, what's your angle, man? My dad didn't have any other kids, just me and my brother, that's it."

"That's what I said when I learned about you, but here we are. Come on." He walked his bike back towards the road. When I didn't follow, he turned around and looked at me. What can I say? Just because he looked like me and Dorado didn't mean I was going to trust him.

"You coming?"

"I don't even know your name. I don't know anything about you."

"You know we have the same blood, and I saved your life. Isn't that reason enough? Look, you can stay out here in the middle of nowhere if you want. I'm getting something to eat, and then I'm going to slep. And then, I'm going to find the Ojo del Oro."

"How in the hell do you know about that?"

He got on his bike and kick-started it. "All in good time, Mechito. Last chance, are you coming with me?"

I sighed and jumped on the back. It would be getting dark soon. And I had to know how all this had come about. "What the heck does *mechito* mean?"

"You really should learn your Spanish, Mechito. Shame, shame." Before I could ask him anything else, we roared out onto the road, and it would be impossible to talk until we stopped again. All I could keep thinking was, I have another brother.

Since Xander had been headed east, we rode south to a little town called Tularosa. It was sundown by the time we got there, and I was starving. He parked his bike out front of a Mexican Bar and Grill as though this was any other night.

"Are you sure this is a good idea?" I asked.

"To stop and eat? I am hungry. So we stop and we eat."

"No, I mean being out in public like this. I mean what if they're looking for us?"

"They were headed east, and we turned around and headed south. Simple."

He went inside without looking to see if I followed. There was nothing else I could do but go in. I was about to walk inside when I remembered my handcuffs were still on my wrists. I cinched them up my arm till they got tight and were out of sight under the sleeves of my jacket. It was warm inside the bar. Plus, it was Friday night. Or, in other words, the place was packed. When I walked in, all I could hear was mariachi music, the sounds of pool games, and drunk people laughing. It was a big building, with a large sunken area in the center with pool tables and a big bar right in the middle of it. All around the edges of the building was the dining area with tables and stuff.

A big man with a mustache stopped us. "We don't allow minors in here unless they're accompanied by a parent or guardian."

He was talking about me.

"It's alright. He's my little brother. I'm taking him out for his birthday," my newfound brother said, hiding his thick accent best he could. I almost asked him how he knew it was my birthday but stopped myself.

The man looked back and forth between us. There was probably no doubt in his mind that we were related.

"Okay," he nodded and let us through.

When he was out of earshot, I said, "And how do you know it's my birthday?"

He sat down at a round table in the corner. "I didn't. Happy birthday."

I sat down. "Well, it's not actually today, but its—"

I stopped myself. "What the hell? I still don't know your name."

"It's Sean." His head was behind a menu. "How are the enchiladas here, Mechito? Are they authentic? Oh that's right, you wouldn't know."

"Sean?" It didn't sound like a Mexican name to me.

He sighed and put down the menu. "Okay, my full name is Sean Juan Vasco Diego Cuchillo Dorantes y Dumez. Does that make you happy?" He put out his hand for a handshake.

I didn't know if he was making all those names up or not. "Francisco Frances Frank Pancho Patrick Patricio Dumez." I shook his hand, giving him every variation of my name I could think of.

Before I could ask him anything else, a waitress came over. She kept looking at me and at first I worried she recognized me or something, like maybe Xander had put out a wanted poster for me, but then I realized she was comparing me to my brother.

My brother.

I still couldn't get used to that. When she asked Sean what he wanted, he ordered without a hitch, but when she asked me, I just stared at her dumbfounded. It was all a lot to take in. "He'll have the same," Sean ordered for me.

As soon as she left, I tore into him again. "I don't know how things work down in Old Mexico or wherever you're from, but here in New Mexico we don't go out for enchiladas after evading the law."

"How do you know I am from Mexico? I speak the English perfectly."

"Really? You speak 'the English' perfectly." I looked at him and he relented.

"Well, not perfect, but good enough." He quit talking when the waitress came by to give us some water. I hadn't had enough to drink all day and gulped it down. She was a little old now, probably thirty-something, but you could tell she might have been pretty when she was younger. "So, is this your little brother?" she asked, looking at me and smiling as if I were four. She was using me to flirt with him. I guess he was good looking.

This time he didn't hide his accent. "Yes. Taking him out for his," he paused and looked at me before he finished his sentence, "fourteenth birthday."

"Fifteenth," I corrected him. I hate when people still think I'm going to be just fourteen.

"Yes, I mean fifteen. They grow up so fast."

Ugh. The waitress must have stuck around another five minutes showing Sean pictures of her kids until another table called her away. When she left, Sean took a sip of his water. He saw me glaring at him and put it back down. "Alright," he sighed, "let's get this over with. What do you want to know?"

"What do I want to know? You practically drop out of the sky and then tell me you're my long-lost brother. I want to know everything."

He raised an eyebrow. "Everything is a broad topic."

I cut to the chase. "Our old man, is he still alive?"

He looked as though he wasn't sure what to say to that. "No. At least I don't think so."

"But why, I mean why do you not think so?"

"I know he is dead because if he were alive, he would come and find me," he replied as though it was a sore subject, though I guess I couldn't blame him. Even though I didn't know my father, it was still hard to think of him having another family in Mexico.

Something dawned on me. Maybe the stranger sitting across from me was another reason my dad took off. "Heh. Well, that's what me and my brother say. Did you know him very well?"

"No, not really. Your father...our father, he didn't know my mother very well."

I was old enough to figure out what that meant.

He could tell I looked surprised and shrugged his shoulders. "I'm sorry if I ruin your impression of him, but he was human like everyone else, Mechito."

Boy, would Dorado be surprised. He put our old man up on a pedestal. He'd never believe he'd cheated on our mother and had a son with another woman.

"Hey, how old are you anyway?" I was trying to do the math.

"Twenty one."

Billy the Kid was twenty one when they say he died. Odd, but it was the first thought I had. I guess all things considered it was only natural I had the Kid on the brain. But twenty one sounded about right, meaning he was the same age as Dorado.

"But, it's not like we were his secret family in Mexico or anything like that, if that's what you were thinking. Truth be told, I only met him a couple of times. The last time I see him, I was only seven years old."

"In Mexico?"

He nodded.

"Why was that the last time you saw him?" I was pretty sure there was something he was leaving out.

He looked down at the table and started rearranging the salt and pepper shakers. I guess that must've been another sore subject. He leaned back in his chair and sighed. "Can't you ask me something else?"

"I have a right to know."

He looked at me like he was mad that I was making him talk about it. "The last time I see my father, he is talking to a man. A strange man with long hair."

"Did he have an eye patch and was missing a hand?"

Sean looked startled. "Not then, but I know who you talk about. McCaw. You know this man?"

"Yeah, I know him." Now it was my turn to be coy.

"How?" He was intrigued, but I didn't feel like telling him my side of the story yet. As far as I was concerned he owed me some answers.

"I'll tell you my side of the story after you finish telling me yours." I gave him a determined look. "Did McCaw kill our father and his brother?"

"I'm not sure."

"How can you not be sure?"

"I was seven years old," he said, irritated. "Can you remember anything in great detail from when you were seven?"

I couldn't blame him really. I didn't have any real vivid memories of being seven except for the time I got stuck crawling under our porch and saw a snake.

"All I really remember is that the last time I see my father, he is with his brother and McCaw. Then I not see any of them ever again. Now, how do you know this man?" he asked me.

I told him about the night in the cemetery, how Dorado got involved, how we went to see Baca, and what had happened up until the point that he came to my rescue.

Sean looked almost proud and disturbed at the same time. "This brother of yours sounds like a real scoundrel. A Mexican Drug cartel is not something one should take lightly. And, did these men actually come through on their end of the bargain?"

"No, but they did give us a picture…"

"Of what?"

"Either our dad or our uncle. A recent one."

A look of surprise flashed across his face. "Do you have it?"

"No, it's with my brother."

All of a sudden something hit me. "Hey, how did you find me anyway?"

His face took on a guilty expression. "Eh, I hope this does not make you angry, but I have known about you for a while now. When I hear about the tombstone returning to Fort Sumner I went there to check it out. I also paid a visit to the old man Baca in Mescalero. He tell me about you and your brother. I thought about going to see you but wasn't sure what to say. I've been staying with him these past few weeks in Mescalero."

"You have? Why didn't he say anything?"

"You mean when you came to see him today? Out of respect, I assume. He knew I wanted to be the one to tell you, so he honored my request. But he came to get me first thing after you leave. That's when I see you with that damn Sheriff Xander and I follow. And now, here we are."

"Whoa, talk about divine coincidence," I said.

Sean grabbed the pendant at the end of the necklace he wore and kissed it. It looked like a conch shell. Before I could get a really good look at it, he had tucked it back into his shirt. "Indeed. I think I find you today for a reason. And now, you and I together can solve this mystery, no?"

"To be honest, I don't care about the mystery of it all so much as saving my brother from that drug cartel."

"Well, first thing's first, *hermano*. We'll find the Ojo del Oro, and then we'll figure out a plan to rescue your brother from Xander."

"Don't you mean our brother?" I said and grinned.

He grinned back. "Hey, this is all new to me, too. I forget sometimes."

Since he'd been with Baca, there was something I wondered if he knew. "Hey, do you know why Baca is so hung up on the gold being evil or whatever?"

"Eh, not really. I assume he's just a superstitious Indian. Even in all the time I was with him, he would not say much about the lost canyon of gold. Did he tell you how the Ojo del Oro works?"

"Not exactly. He says there's a letter the Kid wrote that will tell us everything we need to know. It's in a safety deposit box in Santa Fe," I answered quickly and surprised myself. I guess I didn't realize until then he had finally won my trust. I was starting to tell him which bank in Santa Fe housed the letter when he surprised me and shushed me, shoving a finger to my lips.

"Wait, don't say anything else!"

I pushed it away, indignant. "Why, who's gonna hear us in here?"

"Those two men over there," he nodded his head.

I turned and looked. Sean threw his head in his hands. "Don't look! Now it's obvious." He began his Spanish muttering as I studied the two guys he was talking about. They looked Native American to me, which was nothing unusual around here, but I had to admit they were keeping a close eye on us.

I turned back to Sean. "But how do you know for sure they're watching us?"

"A Mexican always knows when he's being followed. And those men are following us." Another distressed expression crossed his face. I turned to look again. Sure enough, the two men had stood up. They were all the way across the bar. It would take a while before they got to us.

I began to stand, but Sean pushed me back into my seat. "Wait here while I go find some trouble."

I watched Sean walk over to a rather unattractive Indian woman. Actually, unattractive was putting it nicely. She was the ugliest person at the bar with her broad shoulders and long stringy, coarse black hair. She was talking to an equally huge white man with a curly beard. Sean tapped the white man on the shoulder and said as loud as he could in an exaggerated white country accent, "Excuse me, friend, but that's my woman you're flirting with."

The ugly Indian woman stood up and turned out to be an ugly Indian man. "Did you just call me a woman?" he growled.

A grin spread across Sean's face. "Even better," he muttered to himself—right before the Indian man clobbered him across the head. Sean was knocked backwards into a group of people sitting at the bar. Everyone was deathly silent, waiting for Sean to make his next move. Before he could, the sound of a chair scooting back broke the silence.

A big man, at least a foot taller than Sean and as big around as a mobile home, had just stood up.

"Hold on just a minute! You know the rule in my bar," he said in a gruff voice. Everyone was frozen still as he spoke. He looked down to a shaky guy sitting next to him and nodded his head. I thought maybe the little guy was gonna go and get a gun, but that's not what he did.

The shaky guy got up, nervously walked over to the jukebox, and started to drop some change in. I recognized the song right away. It was "Ballroom Blitz" by The Sweet. The big guy seemed to be waiting for something. I finally realized he was waiting for the song to pick up, and when it got to the part he liked, he smiled and yelled, "Fiiiiight!"

As if on command, the whole bar erupted. Fists were flying, glasses were breaking, and people were yelling. I realized the big stupid guy probably liked the song because he thought they were saying bar-room blitz. I wonder what he'd think if he knew it was really about dancing?

The two guys who had been eyeing us started in on Sean, but he was too quick for them. He ducked down, avoiding the little guy's swing. Then he picked him up at the waist, threw him across his shoulder, and twirled around so that his legs whacked into the bigger one, knocking him over.

Sean threw the little guy down then leaned back against the bar crossing his arms as though he had nothing to fear. That didn't last long. The big Indian man he'd mistaken for a woman earlier came up to him and they started brawling again. Now I couldn't even see Sean anymore. I could only hear his path of destruction underneath the crowd. Most of the guys were still focusing on him. The big guy didn't care who he hit, and I think some of the ones that he did were his friends. They just wanted to fight.

An old man came up next to me. He had wrinkled skin and was missing several teeth. Dirty bum looked like he'd been a barfly for life.

"You ever been in a bar fight before, sonny?" he asked, putting his hand on my shoulder.

"Uh, no," I answered.

"Well, it's never too late." And he punched me in the face.

I got knocked backwards down from the dining area and into the bar and pool hall. It was like one of those rock videos where the guy gets carried around on top of everybody for a minute, but eventually I fell through and hit the floor. The old man was on top of the steps laughing his ass off. Then somebody came up and punched him in the face knocking him over, and it was my turn to laugh. Somebody stepped on my hand and I figured I better get off the floor. I bumped into one of the middle-aged guys a little too hard and he took it the wrong way. So I tried to duck out of his way. No sooner than that had happened, I accidentally knocked into the big fat guy. He didn't have to hit me, though. I bounced backwards off of his stomach like one of those big inflatable bounce houses.

I couldn't get anywhere in this mess. It seemed like every second I was dodging an elbow to the face from people hauling back their arms to hit someone else. One guy's elbow knocked me in the back of the head. It sent me flying into the bar and into this busty lady on the end corner. I didn't mean for my hands to land on her breasts. I was just trying to stop myself, and when they were on 'em, I had to think about it a second before I could take my hands off. Her boyfriend's eyes lit up. He was going to kill me.

He lifted up his beer glass like he was going to smash it into my head. Before I could react, his hand flew backwards—a knife had pinned his sleeve to the wall! I looked in the other direction. Sean smiled at me, and then got punched in the face. I looked back at the angry man. He yanked the knife from his sleeve, and it was on again!

I ran off in the other direction. I didn't know what to do, so I hopped on top of the pool table. About that time one of the brawlers got knocked into the jukebox and the song changed to the Bee Gee's "Stayin' Alive." Some guys even stopped in mid punch to look at the jukebox guy as if to say, "How dare you!" That only lasted for about a second and they went back to brawling to Stayin' Alive. It was a fitting change for me. My assaulter picked up a pool cue and started swinging it at my legs, trying to knock me over, but I managed to jump at just the right time to avoid it. I felt like I was in a disco club dancing around, keeping in rhythm to the song. Actually, I think it kind of helped.

"Listen, I'm sorry! I didn't mean to," I kept saying, but that didn't matter to him.

Since he was right in front of me, I kicked my shoe straight down at one of the red pool balls. I hit it just right and it popped up hitting him in the forehead. He staggered backwards. I saw one of his friends heading for the pool table. I sure wasn't gonna do this all night. I scanned the room, looking for Sean. He was still having it out with the big Indian guy from before. There was a black chandelier above me. I jumped up, grabbed it, and swung over to Sean, dropping beside him.

"What's that cliché you white people love?" he asked.

"Nice of you to drop in?"

"Yeah, that's it. Now take these." He slapped a tiny set of keys into my palm.

"What?" I asked.

"Go and start my bike. I'll be out in just a minute."

I fought my way through the mass of brawling drunks until I made it outside. I ran for the bike, put the key in the ignition, and kick-started it. Sean was right. He wasn't long. He came sailing through the glass window about then. I didn't know if he jumped through or somebody threw him. Either was likely. He got up from the pavement and hopped on the back.

"Aren't you gonna drive?" I asked.

"You're my designated driver. Now step on it!"

That saying's redundant on a motorcycle; you don't have a gas pedal, you have a throttle you work with your hand. But I had driven bikes before—dirt bikes, that is. When I throttled this one, it about did a wheelie, but Sean reached over me and took the throttle.

"Easy, Mechito!" he shouted. He knocked off my other hand and took the brake, too. Now he was driving. "On second thought, I'll get us out of town and then you can take over."

We didn't have to go real fast. There wasn't anyone after us.

"That was crazy, man! What were you thinking?" I yelled over the roar of the engine.

"That's nothing. You should see Juarez on Friday night. The important thing is we got a free meal."

Once we got out of the village, Sean let me take over and throttle it up again. That was pretty fun. It made me forget about all the trouble I was in. We drove north towards a place called Bonito Lake where people like to go camping and found a spot in the forest.

About 30 minutes later, we had a campsite going with a decent-sized fire to keep us warm. "That's going to be a nice shiner by tomorrow," he said as he fiddled with my handcuffs. I realized he meant I had a black eye.

I just groaned my response. I didn't want to have a black eye. I'm fairly uptight about my appearance. Cuts and scars were always cool to show off later, but I don't like to have a big black circle around my eye.

"I didn't know you could pick a lock," I said. He had just finished getting the left handcuff off of me with some kind of special key that he had.

"I can do a little bit of everything," he said as he moved on to my right hand. The cuff clicked off. "Here, you take this," he said, handing me the key. "It'll work on most any pair of cuffs. You probably need it worse than I do."

"Thanks. Is it special?"

"No, just all handcuff keys are usually the same for the sake of convenience," he answered. "Don't say I never gave you anything."

I took the key and put it in my back pocket. Sean started to take off his shirt, which had gotten beer-soaked in the fight. As he pulled it off, it revealed a multitude of tattoos. He wasn't entirely covered in them, but there was still a lot. I don't really like tattoos and don't ever plan on getting one, but I had to admit, they looked pretty cool on Sean.

There were crucifixes, saints, and a bunch of other religious type stuff I recognized. Even the palms of his hands had a crucifix each tattooed on them. On his chest he had some kind of wheel-thingy that I think had something to do with the Aztecs in Mexico, and on his right arm was the New Mexico Zia symbol, but it had an eye in the middle of it just like the one on the dollar bill. It was right on the underside of his bicep.

He wrung out the wet shirt letting the alcohol drip into his mouth. I sighed in disgust. "You want some?" he asked as though that was the polite thing to do.

I shook my head as he opened up a medium-sized satchel hanging from the back of the bike to get another shirt. I glanced inside it. It looked like it was full of knives and explosives!

"You mean I was driving a motorcycle full of knives and dynamite!" I half-yelled.

"Yeah, that's why I didn't want you to crash," he said as if it was nothing. "Actually, the dynamite isn't so bad. It's de nitro you have to worry about."

He noticed my mouth was still open. "What? It comes in handy when you need to… you know, make a big hole in something. I learn it from an old friend of mine."

I studied the contents of the bag a little closer. All I saw was dynamite, not anything that looked like nitroglycerin. "I don't see any nitro in here, just dynamite."

"Aha, I forget to tell you." He pulled out one of the medium-sized knives. "This is a very special knife. You see the hilt?"

I nodded. The only thing that seemed unusual to me was that it was made of clear glass.

"It looks like glass, and it is, but it's full of nitro."

"Wait. How has that not exploded by now?"

"Nitro will explode when you shake it. To shake it, there must be room in the vial for friction. But this one is tight, tight. No room for shaking. It will only detonate upon impact after being thrown."

"Have you ever tried it before?"

He looked at me like I was stupid. "Obviously not or I would no longer have the knife."

"No, I meant like have you had others?"

He shook his head. "This is one of a kind. I'm saving it for a special occasion."

"Like what?"

"Like when we get into a really bad jam."

I laughed. "What do you call the last several hours then?" I asked, referring to our escape from Bent and the barfight.

He snorted. "I call things like that an average Tuesday where I'm from, Mechito."

"Well, you definitely know how to throw a knife," I said while examining the one with the nitro hilt and placing it carefully back in the satchel.

"If I can do it, I bet you can too."

I shrugged. "My brother's a pretty good aim with a gun."

"Ah, but this is more challenging. With the gun you have only to aim. With this, it's not just the aim, but when and how hard you throw it."

"How'd you learn?"

"The same way you will. Just by messing around with it until you get it right," he said and pulled a smaller knife out of his satchel. "Here, this one is balanced, so it's easier to throw for a beginner."

He handed it to me. "That's it?" I said, expecting more advice.

"Here, watch me." He took out his own knife. "It's simple. I hold it by the tip, I pull my arm back, and then I throw." He threw it and hit the trunk of a tall pine tree dead center. "Simple. It's all in the wrist. You'll figure it out."

He patted me on the back and walked away. I took in a deep breath. I always get nervous practicing new stuff in front of people, especially ones I don't know that well. I threw the knife at the tree. It didn't hit anywhere near where I thought it would, but it did stick in the bark at least.

"You see that, you're a natural," he said.

"I didn't even hit the spot I was aiming for," I said, figuring he was just patronizing me.

"Yes, but you managed to get the pointy end into the tree. Usually when beginners throw a knife, the butt hits, not the knife itself. Keep practicing," he said and went to fiddle with something on the bike. "Now, where exactly will we be headed to get the key?" he asked.

"The First National Bank in Santa Fe." I threw the knife again and this time got closer to the middle where I was aiming. "Hey, I almost got it that time."

I walked over to the tree to pluck it out, excited to try again.

"Santa Fe? That is nearly half a state away from here," Sean said.

It was true. We were in Southern New Mexico, and Santa Fe was in Northern New Mexico. "Yeah, that's why we'd better get going soon," I said as I threw the knife. I still didn't hit the middle, but I was closer again.

"Now?" he asked incredulously.

"Yeah," I said, expecting him to get on his bike.

He waved a finger at me as he sat down on the ground. "Hmmm….no. Tonight we sleep, then tomorrow morning we get up and we eat, and then we head for de bank in Santa Fe."

"Are you serious?" I said as I plucked the knife from the tree.

He rolled over on his side. "Goodnight, Mechito."

I sighed and lay down myself. What else could I do? I looked up at the stars. Actually, Sean probably had the right idea. I'd probably fall asleep on the bike and fall off on the way.

"So tell me more about your family, or our family…I guess," Sean asked out of the blue.

"Well, to be honest, I can't remember my real mom since she died when I was a baby, so I've always just had my Aunt Patty. She was single for a while when me and Dorado were growing up until she got married. His name's Roderick and we get along pretty good. Let's see…I told you about Dorado…there's a bunch of hillbilly cousins you probably couldn't stand. There's Nana, our grandma. I think you'd like her. She drinks and smokes so much that you probably couldn't beat her liver to death with a stick at this point. And then there's my little brother/cousin named Roddy that looks like one of those baby cherub angels except for he screams and shits himself all the time."

Sean laughed boisterously at that. "So you and Dorado, you are very close?"

"Yeah, I mean, I never met my dad. And since my aunt didn't get married until a few years ago, Dorado, well, he sort of was my dad growing up." I had to stop and laugh. "It was kind of weird, like having a dad and an older brother all in one. Actually, since you and Dorado are the same age, I bet people would think you were twins."

He didn't say anything. I listened close and could hear his nose whistling. He'd fallen asleep. I guess I was getting sleepy too. It was strange, but I felt like I'd known Sean longer than just a day. Maybe it was because he looked like me. My thoughts began to get trippy just like they always did right before I fell asleep. Every now again I would think, "I have another brother." Every time it felt like a surprise, but a good one. I have another brother, I thought again in amazement, and then drifted off to sleep.

VIII.
ZOZOBRA

Even though I haven't been a whole lot of places in my short life, I still think it's safe to say Santa Fe isn't like any other city in the United States. What other state capital is comprised mostly of old Spanish style adobe buildings and has churches more than 500 years old still in operation?

I knew one thing. I was glad to get off of the back of Sean's motorcycle after five hours. I was antsy, too. The both of us had slept until noon, so now it was 5:30 and I was worried the bank might shut down by 6:00. That was another thing Sean and I had in common, a hard time waking up. Considering I'd fallen down a mountain and gotten into a bar fight yesterday, I'm surprised I didn't sleep even longer than that.

We were in the heart of what's called Old Town, the part of the city that still looks like Colonial New Mexico with its dark tan adobe buildings. The city was unusually packed. Very unusually. The streets were literally teaming with people, some of which looked like tourists.

"What the hell is this?" Sean hissed, and then it hit me.

"Zozobra," I muttered.

"Zo-what?"

"Um, Zozobra, it's like this ancient festival thing where they light a giant man on fire."

Sean looked at me, puzzled.

"The Spanish came up with it. It's a long story," I said.

A long story was putting it mildly. Every Autumn, Santa Fe had a big religious festival to celebrate the Spanish re-conquest of New Mexico back in the 1600s. In 1680, the Native Americans had rebelled, driving the Spanish from New Mexico. Twelve years later, the Spaniards returned and took back Santa Fe, so now every year around this time, they hold a festival several days long. The proceedings are kicked off by the burning of a huge wooden marionette called Zozobra meant to represent the past year's hardships and bad luck, sort of like a Santa Fe version of New Year's Eve. How it worked was people gave letters and documents that they considered to be bad luck to be burned inside of Zozobra—everything from break-up letters to parking tickets, eviction notices, anything. Some people even just wrote down their problem on a single sheet of paper and gave that to be burned in Zozobra. I'm not exactly sure who or what the Zozobra was based on, but some people said the legend of Zozobra was inspired by a mythical golden eyed giant who helped to drive the Spanish from New Mexico during the revolt, hence the puppet's giant stature.

"Well, Mechito, you picked a perfect weekend to go treasure hunting."

"At least we found the bank," I said and pointed across the street.

We both looked at the bank. Even it was made of adobe, but it said First National Bank, so that had to be the one.

"Wow, even the banks here look old," Sean said.

I had to agree. "It almost looks like a church."

Sean began walking towards the bank.

"Wait," I said. "What's your story gonna be?"

"My story?"

"Yeah, your plan. I mean are you just going to strut in there and get it?"

Sean looked at me as though I was stupid. "I'm going to walk in there and tell them I am there to get my father's property. Easy." He turned and began walking back towards the building.

I sighed. "If there's one thing I know, it's never easy," I said, mimicking the funny way he said easy.

"Come on, *hermano*, watch and learn," he said as he stepped through the door.

The bank wasn't crowded at least. Actually, there was no one in there at all except for the people that worked there. I imagined everyone was out to go to the Zozobra burning, which would be happening as soon as the sun set. There was only one teller on duty and one guard sitting in the corner with his arms crossed. He was bald, chewing gum, and staring daggers at us, trying to look tough. Sean leaned onto the counter, oblivious to his staring.

"Good afternoon, sir," the teller said. "The bank will be closing soon. How may I help you?"

"Uh, yes," Sean said, "My father, he had a safety deposit box here. The name on it is Hondo Dumez. I would like to open it." After a moment, he added, "He is dead."

Sean looked back to me and smiled coolly as though to say, "See, I told you so."

"I see," the teller said as though it wasn't necessary to add the dead part. "Let me look that up for you." She went over to a file cabinet and withdrew an old, yellowed file. She flipped through it. I got a little scared when she got a funny look on her face and muttered, "This is odd."

"What is?" Sean asked.

"Oh, I just see here that a Delbert Baca has been the one paying the rental fee for the past fifteen years…" she squinted and traced her finger along the file as my heart rate started to go up. Then she said, "But, the name on the account is Hondo Dumez, you're right."

I let out a sigh of relief and looked at Sean. He looked relieved too.

Just when my heart finally quit racing, the teller asked Sean, "And would you be the heir listed here, Dorado Dumez?"

My heartbeat picked up again and I started to get a sick feeling in my stomach.

"Yes, that is me," Sean lied without even seeming to think about it.

I studied the teller's face. She seemed to believe him, then said, "Okay, I just need to see your I.D. to confirm that it's you, and we can open that right up for you."

My stomach lurched. Why did everything have to be so complicated?

"Oh, that's a problem. See, I lost my driver's license only yesterday. But, as I said before, I am his son. And he is dead," Sean added again.

"And we have the key." I held it up for her to see.

"I'm sorry, sir, but it's company policy that you must have your I.D. on you to open your safety deposit box. But, you can come back as soon as you get a new I.D.," she said and smiled.

"Eh, that is simply not going to work. I need that box tonight," Sean said.

"Well, sir, we'll be closing soon anyways so…"

Sean was muttering to himself in Spanish and drumming his fingers on the countertop as she said it until he finally burst out in English, "Maybe I should rephrase myself! This is a… is a… stick-up!"

"Are you crazy!" I blurted out, then the guard stood up excited as could be to finally have an excuse to use his gun.

It was shaking in his hands as he shouted, "Stand down, son! Hands on your head!"

Sean looked at him with a condescending expression then quickly snatched the gun from his hands. The guard was speechless. "Give me that before you hurt someone," Sean said coyly. "Pancho, cuff him."

I snapped myself out of my shock and walked behind the guard. I took his cuffs and did like Sean said.

The guard couldn't believe any of it. "You mean you didn't even have a gun when you came in here!?" he yelped.

Sean looked at him slyly and tucked the gun into his pants. "I don't need a gun." Sean drew something from his coat pocket. "I have a match." And just like that, Sean stuck it in the guard's nostril and struck it. The guard let out a ticklish sounding laugh/yelp and fainted. Sean took out a stick of dynamite from his coat and then lit the wick.

"Oh my!" the teller exclaimed.

Sean remained cool. "You've got twenty seconds to take me back to that safety deposit box, woman. Seventeen. Sixteen."

The teller grabbed some keys and said, "This way, gentlemen, this way!" and headed for the back.

"Are you crazy!" I hissed at Sean.

"I'd hurry, woman. You heard the man. I'm loco! Six. Five." Sean continued his countdown as the wick got shorter and shorter.

"In here! In here! For Pete's sake put it out." She had just opened the door to a room full of safety deposit boxes. Sean walked in and casually plucked out the wick, which harmlessly burned itself out. The teller and I let out a sigh of relief. He turned to her, "Now, the box."

"Number 394. Would you like some privacy?" she asked sarcastically as she handed him the keys.

"No, this time I think I prefer you stay," Sean said. He tossed me the keys. "Let's see what we got."

I inserted the bank's key, then the key that Baca gave me, into the slot marked 394 and drew out the box. It had all sorts of different stuff in it. An old ring. My dad's sheriff badge. A few photos. One in particular caught my eye.

"Who's this?" Sean asked.

I smiled. "My mother." I took the photo and stashed it in my pocket.

"Is it there? The letter?"

There were several documents in the box and a few more photos, including one of Uncle Pancho with a mustache. We rifled through the box some more. Finally, at the bottom, was an old yellowed letter. That had to be it. I unfolded it. It was a one-page, handwritten letter addressed to Uncle Pancho just like Baca said. I scanned down to the bottom, and it was simply signed "Bill".

"This is it," I said, smiling.

Sean grinned, too. We had done it.

"You did all this for that?" the teller said bemused.

"Yes, now shut up," Sean hissed.

A deep voice in the other room broke the silence. "All right! Everybody down, this is a hold up!"

Sean and I exchanged shocked glances. The teller looked at us.

"He's not with us," Sean said to the teller and shrugged.

"Back here!" the teller screamed.

"What are you doing! That man could be dangerous!" Sean snapped and then stuffed the scarf she was wearing into her mouth to keep her quiet. But it was too late. Into the room came walking two men. The very same men that had followed us to the bar. The taller, older one was pointing a gun at us.

"You?" I said.

"Pancho, you had better come with us," the younger one said.

"Who are you? One of Xander's men? Villegas's?" I asked.

The two glanced at one another as though they'd been figured out. The older one said, "There's not much time to explain. The police will be here any minute, we need to—"

Just then, Sean took him by surprise and charged him, but the man was too slow to shoot. Both of them fell over. "Run, Pancho, run!" Sean shouted. "I'll catch up to you!" I bounded over the two men and ran for the door.

I hated to leave him, but the most important thing was keeping that letter safe. I bolted out onto the sidewalk, now teaming with more people than ever. I looked around for cop cars or any other sign that people were aware that we had just robbed the bank and didn't see any. My adrenaline was racing so hard that before I knew it, I had run two blocks down the sidewalk. I looked behind me. In the distance, I could see Sean running out for the bike while the two men ran after him. After a second, they looked down the block and got their sights set on me. I was so distracted that when I turned back around, I ran right into someone in the crowd. I didn't have time to apologize and started to run again, but the man grabbed me. "Hold it, son."

I looked up and my heart stopped. He was a cop.

"I think I know what you're up to," he said with a funny kind of grin.

"You do?" I said, resigned.

"Yep." Before I could react, he took the letter from my hand.

My mind was racing. Did he know that I was one of the "bank robbers"? Was he part of the Santa Fe Ring?

The cop smiled, then tapped the man next to him on the shoulder. He was dressed in blue, too, another cop. The man turned around, but he wasn't a cop like I thought. He was a mailman. "Frank, got another gloom letter for old Zozobra here. You're making one last run to the park before he goes up in flames, right?"

The cop wasn't part of the Ring. He just thought I was another patron on my way to watch the Zozobra burn and was trying to help! I stood there dumbfounded as the postman took my letter and said, "Sure am. Last delivery of the night."

Before I could stop him, the bank alarm finally went off down the street.

"Hey, somebody just robbed the bank!" the cop muttered to himself completely unaware that that someone was me. He yelled into his police radio and ran down the block towards the bank. I could see Sean was already riding towards me on his bike, so he was safe.

It all happened so fast that by the time I turned back around to grab the letter from the mailman, he was gone. He had hopped onto a motor scooter and was pulling out into the street, taking the only clue we had to go up in flames in old Zozobra. I was about to run after him, but Sean pulled up next to me.

"What happened? Did someone take it?" he said, reading the panicked look on my face.

"That man has it." I was too ashamed to admit that I had screwed up, so I lied and added, "Dirty Santa Fe Ring scum!"

"Well, come on, he's only on a scooter," Sean sneered, and off we went. The mail scooter turned a corner onto another street past a few cops. Sean and I casually rode down the same street about to pass the cops when they stopped us. Once again, I was filled with dread.

"Sir, hold on," he said, addressing Sean. "Can't you see we've got all the roads to Zozobra blocked off for the procession?"

He was right. The procession to Zozobra had begun. Santa Fe always shut down the roads bordering where the Zozobra burned.

"But that man, he got through," Sean said.

"Yeah, but he's an official mail carrier taking the last letters to Zozobra."

Sean turned to look at me. I shrugged. So my stupid mistake was out, but he didn't say anything in front of the cop. We just turned around and made our way back to where we came.

"Now what?" Sean asked, irritated.

"We park this and walk?" I smiled sheepishly.

***

It had taken considerable effort to fight our way into the procession, but finally ahead of us was a swelling crowd of people, thousands of them, all here to watch the giant puppet they called Zozobra burn. The Zozobra sat atop a hill in the park, silent and still, but soon it would be teeming with the illusion of life and moaning in pain. I had never seen it in person, but I did see it on the news once. It was quite a sight. Any other time it would've been fun to watch, but tonight, for me, Zozobra truly was a monster about to consume the one thing I needed most.

"How do we even get close to it?" I sighed, feeling hopeless.

"I know how to get close to it," Sean said confidently.

"How? You didn't even know what Zozobra was until today?"

"Just watch and learn, Mechito."

I didn't know what the heck Sean had planned, but I followed him anyway. He was heading for the security gate, which was a very stupid idea. Did he think he was just going to ask to get inside?

Sean tapped on the glass. A large woman with glasses on her nose peered out at him, none too happy looking.

"Excuse me," Sean said in the innocent sounding voice I noticed he used whenever he wanted something, "I am so sorry we are late. I cannot tell you how sorry we are."

The woman gave him a blank stare as if she were waiting for something. "And you are..." she motioned with a hand.

"Ramirez. You should have a name tag back there for... Garcia and I."

Now I knew what he was up to! He was pretending to be part of the backstage crew.

The clerk's skeptical gaze was unphased. "And you all are here to..."

"We're here to help prep the Zozo- you know before we light it up," Sean said like an idiot.

Before he could say something even stupider, I interrupted. "We're part of the ceremonial dance team."

That changed everything. The woman's expression lightened. "Oh, so you're here for your robes?"

"Yes, yes, robes. That what I meant." Sean smiled nervously then turned to hiss at me under his breath, "Why didn't you tell me there were robes?"

The clerk began rifling around for some robes. "I'm glad to see they're finally getting some more male dancers for a change. But you're still awfully late. Let me check the list. Ramirez... Ramirez. Ramon Ramirez?"

"Yes, that's me," Sean said, a little too happy.

She shook her head. "I could've sworn I already gave you your robe." Then she looked to me, "And you are?"

I tried to remember the name Sean gave me. "Garcia."

Her eyes were glued to her clipboard. "Several Garcias here. Can I get a first name?"

I said the first thing which came to mind, which was Bob for some reason. "Uh...Bob. Bob Garcia."

Sean turned to look at me as though I'd just issued a death sentence upon us both. Under his breath, he said, "Bob? What kind of a Mexican name is that?"

"Shut up," I whispered back as the clerk looked over her list.

The clerk looked up. "Robert?"

"Yes, I also go by Robert," I answered.

"And Roberto," Sean interjected nervously. I shot him a look.

"Okay, well, here you go," the woman said, handing us two white robes through the glass. "Take the long way around the back," she added.

We took our robes and headed around the perimeter of the crowd. Sean smiled at me and said, "See, and we even got costumes."

"You're just lucky is what you are," I said snidely, but even then I couldn't help but grin. Whatever Sean set out to accomplish, he always did, even if it wasn't smoothly.

We picked up our pace a little and jogged towards the little dirt hill where the massive Zozobra puppet was strung up. Old Man Gloom, as they also called him, was shaped like a man, but with his white face, green hair, big ears, and giant stature, he looked like a cross between King Kong and the Joker from Batman. In minutes the ceremonial performers would begin dancing at the feet of the giant puppet right at the same time that someone else would set off some fireworks if I remembered right. And eventually the big man would catch on fire, burning everything within him, including the letter.

Two security guards stood near the main stage area to ensure only performers and crewmen got past. With our robes on they weren't suspicious of us but looked a bit perturbed just the same. One of them pointed behind him and said, "You guys are awfully late, but the dancers are all assembling back there behind the puppet."

Calling Zozobra a puppet at 50 feet high might seem kinda weird, but that's really what he was, a giant puppet that would soon begin moving thanks to a cable above his head with wires attached to the arms.

"Thank you, officer," Sean said, and we made our way towards the back of the puppet and towards the other dancers. They looked at us a little suspiciously.

"How's it going?" one of the guys asked.

"Good, good. A little nervous. This is my first ceremonial dance," I lied, or sort of. It would be my first ceremonial dance, technically.

"So what formation are you guys in?" he asked.

"Uh…Soprano," Sean answered, and the guy looked at him like we were nuts. Before he could ask any questions, the program officially started.

A man in a red robe with white trim that looked oddly like Santa Clause ascended the steps towards the giant Zozobra. In one hand he carried a golden scepter, probably plastic, and in the other an old black leather-bound book. He wasn't old, but he did have a long white wig on to make him look that way. If I had to guess, I'd say he was the mayor.

"Citizens of Santa Fe, it is now time to consider the fate of Old Man Gloom!" he shouted and turned to the giant effigy as though it were real and called out, "Zozobra! Because you are a hideous boogeyman that frightens our children with your miserable wailing that makes our dogs howl at the moon… because you upset our peaceful way of life, I ask the citizens of Santa Fe, should we now send the Zozobra to a fiery death? Should we burn him?" The crowd erupted in cheers and shouts. I could hear some people screaming, "Burn him!" The wind began to pick up at that point, tussling the mayor's robe as though supernatural forces were at work.

The mayor continued, "The people have spoken. I now declare on this night that Zozobra, also known as Old Man Gloom, be dispatched by fire. With the execution of Zozobra, we shall release all the anxiety, heartache, and gloom of our fair city, and all who bear witness shall be liberated from heartache and fear. I now ask the citizens of Santa Fe to proceed with the fiery execution of Zozobra! Chase all our gloom away! Bring on the fire dancers, burn this monster! Burn him!"

Drums began to pound and fireworks filled the air. The ceremony was now in full swing. I got nervous, thinking it was time for the dancers to go out, but first only a lone woman in white went and danced in front of the monster, making me think of King Kong again.

A woman, probably the head of the troop, said, "Okay, we're going on in twenty seconds. Does everyone know where you're supposed to be?"

Sean and I gave each other a blank stare while everyone else shouted that they did. Soon everyone was waving their arms in the air, so Sean and I just started doing the same thing, but I still felt like an idiot. We followed everyone else around the monster still waiving our arms. As we circled in front of the huge puppet, I had to admit it was a little scary up close, even though I knew the monstrous groans and screams were just coming from a speaker somewhere. Sean and I both looked at each other and nodded. Since there were at least 40 or 50 of us out on stage, we could slowly sneak our way behind the Zozobra, and no one would notice.

I lifted the white sheet of Zozobra's robe. "Ready to peak under Old Man Gloom's skirt?"

"Let's just hope we don't catch our asses on fire, Mechito."

We both crawled inside. Hundreds of white papers were scattered across the ground. Legal documents, parking tickets, breakup letters, and in some cases sheets of paper with a single word written upon them. "Oy yoy yoy," Sean sighed.

"Okay, no need to panic. Our letter's old and yellow. Just look for old yellow paper."

I got down on my hands and knees and shuffled through every paper I could find, ignoring the ones with only one word written on them. This would take forever. The music was driving me nuts, too, since they were playing this mariachi song devoted to the Zozobra outside that cut into my concentration.

I heard Sean laughing. "Did you find it?" I asked excitedly.

"No," he said, still laughing. "These breakup letters are hilarious, Mechito. If you were older, I might read you this one."

I snatched it from his hands and grabbed him by the collar. "Look out there," I said and pointed outside. Through the thin veil of the skirt we could just barely make out a procession of more dancers carrying torches. "When they get to the base of the Zozobra is when they set off the fireworks that sets this sonbitch on fire!"

"Okay, I start looking harder," Sean said and got on the floor.

I did the same, trying not to tread over the same ground again and waste my time because, if anything, time was of the essence. I felt Sean nudge me. "What," I said, not wanting to be bothered with another Dear John letter he'd found.

"Uh, Pancho, we have trouble." I looked up, and standing in front of us were two tall men in ceremonial robes. They took off their hoods, revealing themselves to be the two men from the bank.

"Great," I sighed, and Sean nudged me to stand.

The two had their arms crossed, and the taller one said, "You know, this would be a lot easier if you just quit running from us."

I didn't know what to do. On the one hand, they didn't have a gun aimed at us, but I could still see a gun holstered underneath the big one's robe. And there was no way I was big enough to fight either of them.

"You ever hear the old expression don't bring a knife to a gun fight?" Sean began, and they both looked at each other puzzled. "Well, in my case, you shouldn't bring a gun to a knife fight either." As he said it, Sean threw a small knife from under his sleeve, which swiftly embedded itself above the big one's knee. As he fell, Sean punched him in the face while the shorter one grabbed Sean from behind, getting him into a headlock.

"You had better find the letter, Mechito, hurry!"

The younger man stopped and said, "You mean the letter is in here!"

Zozobra let out a particularly brutal scream and we all looked above us. I heard the screech of an especially potent firework and the top half of the marionette burst into flames. Now all four of us poured over the ground looking for the letter as Zozobra continued to scream and wail as though he were a real being. Embers of fire began raining down upon us and before I knew it, my eyes were stinging and I was coughing from the smoke. Just when all hope seemed lost, the younger looking guy piped up excitedly and said, "Here! I think I found it."

He looked up at us and smiled, caught up in the moment. "Thank you," Sean said sincerely and then punched him in the face, knocking him over. "Okay, run, *hermano*, run!" Sean shouted, grabbing me by the hood, and we darted out from under Old Man Gloom's skirt.

The two men were too dazed to catch us, and when I looked behind me, I could see them come limping out of the giant flaming monster.

I looked up at Zozobra, who was now shooting fireworks from his mouth and fingertips as he continued to scream in agony. He didn't look like King Kong anymore. Now he looked like Ghost Rider with his flaming skull.

Sean and I didn't stick around to watch the show, and we hightailed it to his bike. After that, we rode out of town to somewhere safe, where we could finally examine the letter.

IX.
COMPANEROS

uddled together in the darkness, me and Sean looked over the letter with the help of a lighter. I hadn't noticed 'till then, but the edges and the whole bottom part of the paper had gotten singed in the heat earlier, but otherwise, I could read it okay. I decided to read it aloud since I wasn't sure how good Sean could read English. (Speaking a language okay and reading it okay were two different things sometimes.)

"Dear Pancho," it started. "If you're reading this, I reckon that means I'm dead, and for that, I'm sorry. I would have liked to have gotten to spend more time with you and to see your brother one more time. But, life rarely works out the way we planned for."

I had to stop for a second. I thought Tumbleweed Williams only knew Uncle Pancho, but from the letter, it seemed like he met my dad, too. Baca never said anything about that. I just shrugged and went on to the next paragraph. "I never did get to tell you all that there was to tell about the Ojo del Oro within the tombstone. When used at exactly the right place at the right time, the Eye will show the way to Adams' grave, who the priest and I buried in a special spot. Old Man Adams' grave contains not only some gold from the lost canyon but also a map to said canyon.

However, the Eye only reveals the spot where Adams is buried, a special key is needed to open the tomb. Once you have it in your own hands, I think you'll figure out how it works just fine. I have hidden the key away somewhere I think no one would dare ever go. I hid it as far up the middle of nowhere that I could, that being in the desert between Cloudcroft and Alamogordo. I stashed it away in a dead-end arroyo that terminates in a cave. You'll find the arroyo dead south from Maruche Canyon and due north of Bridal Veil Falls. Look at a map of the area, and the arroyo is just about smack dab in between those two points. You'll find the key in an old Wells Fargo chest. And one more thing, when entering the arroyo don't—"

"Don't what?" Sean asked.

"Damn," I said. "The heat from Old Man Gloom's skirt earlier singed the end of the letter right off."

"Well, at least we know where to find it," Sean said. "Now, let's go find a map."

We managed to buy one cheap and easy in a convenience store. It took a while, but we eventually were able to figure out the spot he was talking about in the letter. "Well, that looks like that's it. Let's get going," Sean said and began to fold up the map.

"There's just one problem," I said, looking at his bike. "We can't go on that."

Sean looked intrigued. "Are you saying we're going to need horses?"

"Yeah, and I know just who can get us some. Only I don't think you two will get along..."

***

SUNDAY MORNING, OCTOBER 31, 1976

Cade had no more than stepped out of his truck than Sean's face turned more sneery than usual.

"Morning, sunshine," Cade said, slamming the door and I could tell by the way he was all hopped up that he'd just drank a ton of caffeine. I couldn't blame him. I had called him from a payphone last night to fill him in on everything that had happened from meeting with Old Man Baca to Dorado getting hauled off to Perdition—wherever it was. But I didn't call just to keep him informed. Cade had horses, and just as important, a horse trailer to haul them in. I had asked him if he could meet us on the outskirts of Alamogordo at dawn. He was early, and the sun had yet to rise, so it was hard for me to see past his headlights, but it looked like someone else was still in the truck cab. Before I could ask who it was, he started blabbering away.

He slapped me on the back. "Miss me?" I was surprised to find that after he said it, I actually did. He already had a can of beer in his hand.

"You're drinking right now?" I asked.

"Like they say, it's five o'clock somewhere."

"Yeah, they mean five p.m., not a.m., Cade."

"Well, all that damn coffee I drank got me too fired up so this should cancel me out perfect. Hey, and I found a book that mentioned that Perdition place. Turns out it's a ghost town."

"A ghost town?" I mused. "Are you positive?"

"Yep, that's what it said. Contrary to what you may think, I'm not a complete idiot." Only he pronounced idiot as idjiot.

Sean watched him with bizarre fascination, like a cat intently observing some strange animal it'd never seen before. "You mean to say we are related to him?" he asked where only I could hear it.

Cade took note of Sean finally and nodded at him after taking a sip of beer. "Well, I'll be darned. Guess Hondo and Uncle Pancho both liked them senoritas," he said, referring to Sean's dark skin.

Before Sean could reply, I asked Cade, "Hey, did you bring someone along with you?" I had just heard one of the truck doors shut and could see two people getting out and one was Dingus.

"Yeah, Dingus and Becky."

"Becky!" I practically choked. "You brought Becky?"

"Well, yeah. She kept coming by the house to ask if you'd called. What was I supposed to do?"

I was so mad I couldn't even respond and just began walking towards the truck.

"You're welcome!" Cade called out.

Dingus's eyes lit up when he saw me. "Whoa, Pancho, how'd you get that black eye?" I couldn't help but ignore him and kept on marching towards Becky. I hadn't even had time to really think about Becky yet over the past day in between meeting Sean and getting the letter. Maybe she had meant well, but she still told her dad about us when I asked her not to and it had caused us a lot of trouble.

She was leading one of the horses out of the trailer. She saw me and smiled. "Pancho—"

"What the hell are you doing here?"

She looked shocked. "I came here to help. What does it look like?"

"To help? Like you were helping when you told your dad I went to Mescalero?"

She looked defensive and before she could answer I kept going. "Does he know you're here now? Should we be expecting him?"

"I didn't tell him about Mescalero, Pancho. I haven't even seen him in two days."

"Drop the act, Becky. He told me that you told him about us."

"Pancho, I didn't, I swear. And I'm sure there has to be an explanation for what he's doing. He probably just said those things to scare you."

"Aha, so you have talked to him."

"No, Cade told me what happened after you called him. I went over to his house last night to see if you'd called. I had to because you sure never called me." She looked at me with hurt eyes.

I stopped to think about that. She could be telling the truth. I wanted her to be telling the truth.

"Look, I promised you I wouldn't say anything to my dad, and I didn't. If I did, do you really think I'd be here right now? Wouldn't I have just snitched on you again?"

She had a point. But before I could say anything, I heard Cade scream.

I turned around and could see that Sean had Cade in a headlock while Dingus danced around them excitedly, egging them on. I looked back to Becky and started to open my mouth. "Just go," she said, frustrated.

I ran over to Sean and Cade, who were now both rolling in the dirt, Cade still in a headlock. When Sean saw me, he rasped, "There is no way I can work with these…how do you say…Saltines?"

"We prefer the term cracker, you wet-back idiot!" Cade managed to shout.

"Would you two get off each other! We should have been on horseback already." I pushed them apart and Sean let go of his neck. We all sat around panting in the dirt until Cade finally got up, dusting off his pants and shouting, "Dad gone it! I coulda had a flashback to 'nam and killed you. You and that little mustache of yours reminds me of Charlie as it is!"

Sean's eyes turned angry again.

"Hey!" I shouted. "Dorado is out there somewhere in case you haven't forgotten. Your cousin," I looked at Cade and then to Sean, "and your brother, who you haven't even met yet. And here you are fighting wasting our time."

Cade and Sean looked at each other semi remorsefully, but before they could say anything, Dingus exclaimed, "Whoa, dynamite!"

I realized he must've been snooping around Sean's satchel on his bike. Cade and Sean both ran over to Dingus, who now held a stick in his hand.

"Can I have some?" Dingus asked as though there wasn't anything inappropriate about that at all.

"Absolutamente… not!" Sean said, correctly assuming he was nuts and snatching it from his hands.

"But there's all kinds of things I could do with that. Go fishing with it. Settle that score with Mrs. Johnson's cat. The possibilities are endless." Then something else caught his eye.

"What about this knife?" Dingus said, snatching one from the satchel. It was the one with the glass handle filled with nitroglycerin. "Can I have it?"

Sean's eyes got as wide as saucers as he plucked it from his grasp. "Pancho, can you please," he said, looking at me and making a shooing motion at Dingus.

Before I could do anything, I suddenly heard the galloping of a horse. Becky had gotten herself saddled and came riding up on a big grey mare.

"Where are you going?" I asked.

"West. Towards the arroyo," she said as though it was a stupid question.

"No, you're not," I said and turned to Cade. "Cade, take her home." I turned back to Becky. "Look, you don't need to do this. This isn't your fight."

"Yes, I do, Pancho. In case you've forgotten, this is my family history too, and it goes back a lot farther than yours does!" She looked down at Cade and Sean's dusty clothes. "And besides, somebody has to take charge of this mess." She threw her head back and took off at a gallop.

Sean slapped me on the back. "You have one hell of a woman there, Mechito, and trust me, they only get worse as they get older."

"You just had to bring her," I snapped at Cade while we started saddling our horses.

"Hey, little filly blackmailed me. Said if I didn't take her, she'd tell the whole town about my secret bunker. I can't have that, Pancho! I can't have that!"

I droned out Cade's rant and mounted my horse. I took off and tried to catch up with Becky before she made too many tracks and I lost sight of her. But I didn't want to talk to her just yet. I was embarrassed and still didn't know what to say. We'd never had a fight before. Not a real one like this. Actually, I didn't know if it was a fight or a misunderstanding.

Instead, I just rode along behind her a few paces. After a while I found the sound of the hoof beats on the ground below to be pretty soothing. There was something really adventurous about going out into the wild on a horse. Adventurous in a good way, not like taking a truck bed toboggan ride down a mountain or getting shot at.

I love horses, too. I wish I had one of my own, but Aunty Patty and Rod couldn't afford to buy me one. Plus, we didn't really have a place to put a horse, either. So I had to be content with the ones at Cade's ranch. The one I was riding now was Samson, a quarter horse I'd ridden quite a few times before. Me and him always got along pretty good, I felt like. But like I said, he wasn't my horse, and one day when I got older and had money of my own, I planned on buying one for sure.

It wasn't just being out on horseback that had me feeling good. It's where I was, too, because I love the desert. To me, it's beautiful. I know some people might think that sounds strange considering there isn't much to the desert, but maybe that's why I liked it. It was broad and open. It didn't hide anything, unlike people.

Just when I was really starting to get lost in my thoughts, Dingus caught up with me and had to ask all kinds of questions.

"Pancho, how'd you get that black eye?"

"A dirty old bum punched me in the face two nights ago in a bar fight."

"What? A dirty old bum punched you in the face in a bar fight? Dang it, Pancho, I would love it if something like that had happened to me. You're gonna have all kinds of stories to tell when we get home. We may as well have never even rescued that goat. This'll make that old news."

He was so excited and flustered I wouldn't have been surprised to see Dingus fly right out of the saddle. Dingus loved to tell stories to everybody at school. Probably only half of those were true stories, but with Dingus you could never tell. It was killing him that all this had happened to me and not him.

"Well, I just hope something interesting happens on this trip," he said.

I hoped not. Besides, we were on the trail of a secret artifact to who knows what hidden nearly a hundred years ago by Billy the Kid. You'd think that was interesting enough.

Ahead of us, an old stone wall, probably used as a crude shelter back in the old days, jutted out of the ground like the ruin of some ancient civilization. I guess in some ways it was. The Old West had died out about eighty years ago, historically speaking, which most historians blamed on the arrival of the railroad.

I looked up at the sky. It was clear except for one large bird circling above. I figured it was a vulture or a buzzard just hoping one of us would eventually die. Then I had another thought and remembered McCaw's hawk, Itza-chu. I shivered but figured that probably wasn't the same bird. But then I remembered what Baca had said, that McCaw was a brujo.

I tried to put McCaw out of my mind and decided now was a good a time as any to face Becky. I trotted my horse up next to hers. She didn't say anything to me and kept her head held high.

"Look, about earlier, I'm sorry. It's just been a pretty bad past couple of days."

"Ya think? I just found out that my dad might be part of some strange sort of mob and he arrested Dorado. Have you even thought of how I feel in all of this?"

I had to admit, I hadn't.

"I had to do something to help," she said.

Poor Becky. I could see now she really was just as mixed up in this as I was.

"I'm sorry, I didn't think about what you were going through, too. I was an idiot, okay?"

"I haven't seen my dad since before we went to the cemetery the other night, and I'm not even sure what I'd say to him if I did."

We rode in silence for a bit, then I said, "You know, it's not lost on me that Dorado kind of brought this on himself. What am I saying? He did bring this on himself. If he hadn't of screwed up, neither one of us would be here."

"Don't do that. He's your brother."

"He's almost like my dad in some ways. But don't ever tell him I said that." She smiled at me, and I continued. "With my parents gone, he's the closest blood kin I have, ya know?"

All of a sudden, I remembered Sean and looked back at him. He was twiddling a piece of long grass in his mouth and looking up at the sky as he rode. "Or he was. I'm still getting used to that." I turned back to Becky, and she smiled again. I knew we were made up now, and it felt like a weight had been lifted from my shoulders.

"He looks like you." When she said it, it surprised me that I actually felt kind of glad about it even though I guess Sean wasn't what you'd consider classically good looking.

"Yeah, he does," I said proudly.

Cade came trotting up between us. "So this alleged treasure the map leads to… what is it exactly?"

"I don't know, some sort of gold mine, I guess," I said. Truthfully I didn't care what it was. All I knew was that it would get the drug cartel and the Ring off our backs.

"Not a gold mine, a whole canyon of gold." Sean, followed by Dingus, trotted up to join us. "I assume you have all heard the legend of the Lost Adams Diggings?"

"Yeah, it was like a whole canyon of gold guarded by the Indians and stuff," Dingus said.

"And you know why it was called the Adams Diggings, right?" Sean asked.

"Yeah, because some guy named Adams was the one who found it," I answered.

"No, Adams was just the only one who survived," Sean said cocking an eyebrow. "The story goes like this. Back in the year 1864, there was a man named Adams, no one knows his first name, working as a prospector in Arizona and New Mexico. He had just lost all he had in an Indian raid. With hardly any provisions left and down on his luck, he was elated to eventually fall in with a group of white prospectors he met on the trail. The prospectors' camp was in a state of excitement. Adams soon found that they were on their way to a huge placer vein of gold somewhere on the Arizona—New Mexico border. Earlier, the prospectors had made the acquaintance of a young Mexican man who had been raised by the Apache Indians. He had a misshapen ear and was therefore called Gotch Ear. In return for several horses, Gotch Ear had agreed to lead the men to a well-hidden canyon, full of gold, that he had seen as a boy when he was with the Apache. Adams was allowed to join this expedition. It would change his life forever, but not for the better.

"True to his word, Gotch Ear led them to the lost canyon, which had huge streaks of pure gold running through it. Even the bottom of the stream running through the canyon was paved with gold. The canyon erupted into pure ecstasy, as is often the case with greedy white people. They gave Gotch Ear his horses as he was promised, and then he left."

"Wait," Cade interrupted, "so you're saying this guy took two horses instead of staying there and helping prospect the gold? That's a dumb Mexican for you."

Sean cleared his throat. "Well, being a Mexican rather than a greedy white man, Gotch Ear knew it was best to leave the canyon. And he was right. Soon after, the Apache show up. They were none too happy to have the white men in their canyon."

"They didn't want them to get their gold," Dingus interrupted.

"Not necessarily, you see, the Indians do not care for gold, never have. To them, it is sacred, the color of the sun. They do not touch it. Generously, the Apache Chief Nana agreed to let the men stay and mine the gold. There was only one condition. They were not to venture behind the sacred waterfall. Well, being white men, they could not stand being told what to do by Indians, and first time the Indians split, they wander behind the waterfall. What they saw inside, nobody knows. But Indians being Indians found out all about it and returned to the canyon, brutally massacring everyone there. Adams just happened to be lucky enough to have left camp to get supplies. When he returned, he witnessed the attack, but the Indians did not kill him. Instead, they captured him and said to tell everyone what he had seen in the canyon, so that no one would return or ever try to find it again. They took a hot poker and burnt out Adams' eyes so that he himself could never return, or so they thought anyway, then dumped his half-dead body outside of a small town where he told his story."

"Okay," I said, "but where did Billy the Kid come in?"

"Okay, so we flash forward nearly twenty years to 1881. New Mexico is a slightly different place. Now all of the Apache have been rounded up and put onto reservations. The railroad is beginning to spread. The West is changing. The land was also getting much less tolerant towards outlaws like Billy the Kid, who was fresh from his escape from the Lincoln County Courthouse. To celebrate, Billy wasn't exactly keeping a low profile. He went straight to his favorite saloon and bawdy house in White Oaks. While there, he met a blind old man named Adams. Adams explained how he had snuck away from his keeper, a priest, to get a few drinks. Well, Billy being such a nice guy buys him some more drinks, and before you know it, Adams has told Billy his tale, including exact directions to the canyon. You see, even though the Apache burn out his eyes, they could not burn out Adams' memory. Adams had made a deal with the priest that he would take him to the gold, and the riches could belong to the church. You see, with the Apache all imprisoned in the reservations, he felt he had no one to fear.

"Well, he wasn't entirely correct. A new threat had emerged in New Mexico, a group of corrupt white men—"

"Would you stop with all the white men talk?" Cade interjected.

Sean continued as though he had a point. "Well, okay, there might have been one bad Mexican in there, but only one. Anyway, this evil Santa Fe Ring, they somehow find out about Adams and his gold. Billy, having fought against them in the Lincoln County War, knows right away Adams is in trouble when he sees them come into the bar. When the Ring tries to take the priest and the old man, Billy saves them.

"Together, the three rode to the lost canyon, but unfortunately, the evil Ring managed to follow them there and surrounded them. With no more use for Billy, Adams, and the priest, they lined them up to be executed. One of the men, probably the only Mexican, could not bring himself to shoot a blind man and a priest. He said they would be punished by God for such an act. One of the other members said, 'I'll show you how it's done,' and shoots Adams. But, as if on cue, the canyon begins to tremble and shake. It is an earthquake, an Act of God to punish the wicked men and keep them from possessing the canyon's secrets. In the chaos, only Billy and the priest get out alive with the dead Adams and some of the gold. The canyon, though, is sealed shut, buried in the chaos. Billy and the priest vow that so long as the Santa Fe Ring is in power, they will not give the gold over to the territory, but will bury it with Adams. And the Ojo del Oro shows the way to Adams' grave, which is also said to contain a proper map to the lost canyon."

Sean stopped his horse to finish the story. "And now we know the Kid, with the help of Garrett, hid the Ojo del Oro in his tombstone. And the key to Adams' tomb is up ahead." Sean pointed forwards. "I am guessing that must be the arroyo?"

"Has to be," Cade remarked.

I had gotten so engrossed in Sean's story I hadn't even realized we'd made it to the arroyo. As if standing guard at the entrance was a huge ponderosa, probably more than 100 feet high. The roots were as tall as I was. We rode in wordlessly, none of us saying anything as we looked up at the huge granite walls and the tree that dwarfed us.

It was an eerie feeling. There wasn't a touch of the 20th Century in the whole place. No telephone poles off in the distance. No food wrappers contaminating the landscape. No plastic bags snagged in the trees. Nothing. There was only one thing that looked out of place.

"What's that?" Dingus pointed up at a brown lump wedged into a crevice that almost looked like…

"Dynamite," Sean answered solemnly.

"Why would someone put dynamite at the opening of an arroyo?" Becky asked.

"It's a booby trap. Just like in 'nam," Cade said.

"That must have been what Tumbleweed Williams was talking about in the letter in the part that got burnt off," I said to Sean.

"It's too old to still be dangerous. Come on," Sean said and rode ahead of us.

"If it did go off, we'd be trapped in here forever." I looked up at the tall steep walls of the arroyo as I said it and heard a slight echo of the word 'forever' that gave me chills.

Cautiously we followed Sean. After about five minutes of riding, we finally came to the end of the small, dead-end canyon and could see a cave that looked like a huge maw ready to swallow us up.

"No wonder he chose this spot," Sean said, referring to how creepy it looked. He crossed himself and muttered something I assume was religious in Spanish.

"Let's just get this over with," I said and dismounted my horse.

As everyone got off their horses, Sean began looking around the ground for something.

"What are you looking for?" I asked.

"We're going to need a torch," he said, picking up a brittle old piece of a broken tree branch. He walked over to a prickly pear cactus that had a spider web in it and wove and twisted the branch through it, covering it in webbing, then took out his lighter and set it afire.

I had to give old Billy the Kid props for choosing this as a hiding place, though. It was a good one because nobody in their right mind would ever want to wander into that cave. The torch cut a path of light through the darkness as we all followed Sean single file into the mouth of the cavern.

"I wonder how deep it goes," I said.

"About twenty more feet," Sean said. "Look up ahead."

I could vaguely make out an ending to the cave and it got clearer as we got closer. And there, sitting on a rock as if it was the Holy Grail itself, was an old chest just like the letter said. The box was green with gold trim. Some gold lettering said WELLS FARGO & CO. across the lid.

Even Cade knew what that meant. There could be money inside. He slapped his hands together. "Alright boys, let's see what we got."

All of us rushed towards the chest, but Dingus ran in front of us and grabbed the lid quick as lightning, ready to open it.

"Wait!" I yelled.

"What?" Dingus said impatiently.

Everybody looked at me like I was an idiot, so I said, "What if it's booby-trapped or something? You really think the Kid just left it lying there?"

"This is not movie and it's not booby-trap. Just open it!" Sean hissed kinda exasperated like. I noticed his English got worse whenever he was irritated.

Dingus opened the chest. Nothing happened.

"See, it's fine," Dingus said proudly.

Becky and I looked at each other, relieved.

"What's inside?" Cade asked, and we all crammed in front of the chest. As the light from Sean's torch revealed the contents, the first thing we saw was a revolver. I'm no expert on guns, but I could tell it was old. Sean picked it up, and Cade grabbed it from him almost immediately. But Sean didn't care. He just wanted to see if the key was there.

"Man, this is an old pearl-handled Colt .45!" Cade shouted. He was turning it over and looking at it. I heard him counting. "Whoa, this really must be the Kid's gun. There's 21 notches on it and everything. I wonder how much I could get for this thing at the pawnshop?"

All of a sudden, Becky looked sad. "What?" I asked her.

"I was just thinking how much my dad would like to have that…and then I remembered."

I knew what she meant and just touched my head to hers. She was thinking back to the way her life used to be, before it got complicated with all this mess.

Sean began removing several other trinkets from the chest. One of them looked like an old book. I picked it up, and best I could tell it must've been the Kid's diary. I peeked back into the chest. Sean had finally gotten to the bottom of it. There was something wrapped up in an old weathered cloth. The key to Adams' Tomb. It had to be.

Sean carefully dug his hands into the chest and scooped it out. Delicately, he began to unfold the cloth. It wasn't your typical key, though. It was bigger, and had four sides to it, like an 'x'.

"What kind of key is that?" I asked Sean. Since he had a skeleton key and knew how to pick locks, I figured he'd know better than anybody.

"It's called a cruciform key. You know, because it kind of look like a crucifix."

I took it from him and inspected it. "Leave it to a priest to make a key that looks like a cross," I said.

"Couldn't we have just busted open the tombstone and called a locksmith, though?" Cade asked.

Sean shrugged and took the key back from me. "We'll find out soon enough."

"Hey, there's something else," Dingus said and withdrew the lining from the box. "Look."

We had all just thought it was a piece of cowhide used to line the box, but now that Dingus was unfolding it, we could see it had writing on it. It was just a few sentences. It looked like a poem.

"Careful," Sean said and snatched it up before he could unfold it all the way.

Cade saw it too. "Just great, first some weird cross-key and now a poem. I've just about lost any respect I ever had for Billy the Kid."

"Quiet," Sean hushed him.

Becky peaked up to look. "It's in Spanish."

Sean grinned. "Now it is my turn to do the reading, eh?"

"What does it say?" I asked.

Sean read the poem for us in English:

> *Only by the dawn's early light,*
> *With the staff of San Esteban and the Ojo del Oro in sight,*
> *In the holy place atop the city in the sky,*
> *Will Adams' treasure be revealed to thine's eye.*

We all just stood there in silence. Baca had said the instructions for the Eye were here, but I had to admit those weren't the clear-cut directions we were hoping for.

"What in tarnation does that mean?" Cade said, breaking the silence.

"City in the Sky," Becky muttered. "I've heard that before. And San Esteban, too."

"I know. They mean Sky City. It's that pueblo on the mesa outside of Albuquerque," Dingus said. We all looked at him, shocked. "What? I read in A.R.… sometimes."

All of a sudden, I knew what Dingus meant. I'd seen pictures of it. It was literally a whole pueblo village that had been built on the top of a big mesa. Billy the Kid had never been there that I knew of, but then again, I was finding there was a lot about Billy the Kid that I didn't know.

"What's a pueblo on top of a mesa got to do with Billy the Kid?" Becky wondered aloud.

"I guess we won't know until we get there," Sean said. "But for now, let's get out of here."

Sean placed the key back within the old Wells Fargo chest. "You see that wasn't so bad. What is it you always say, Pancho? It's never easy." With a cocky smile, Sean began to lift the chest from off the rock ledge, only it seemed like it was stuck. It was tied to something. There was a weird little spark when Sean yanked it loose followed by a strange hissing noise like the lighting of a match. Or the burning of a wick. It suddenly hit me—the warning at the end of the letter that got burnt off.

Now I think I knew what it meant: Don't yank the chest loose because it's booby trapped! What looked like the end of a 4th of July sparkler quickly snaked from where the chest had set, down the floor of the cave, and into a crevice. We all stood there frozen in shock as Sean's expression changed from embarrassment to hysteria. "Everyone to the horses! Quick!"

We all ran as fast as we could and jumped onto our horses. Sean was already galloping away. "Hurry Companeros! Do you want to get your asses blowed off?"

"Come on," I yelled and prodded my horse into a run behind Becky and Sean. I looked up at the spark traveling along the fuse. It was literally a race for our lives, and if we were very lucky we could catch it and outrun it.

"What was that you said about the dynamite being too old to be dangerous?" I shouted to Sean, who was clearly quite worried about said dynamite at the moment.

"Hopefully it is! But I'm still not taking any chances!" he yelled back.

We were all terrified as we raced for the exit of the canyon except for Dingus, who was thrilled about the tale he now had to tell—if he lived to tell it. Dingus looked up to the traveling spark quickly making its way across the fuse, now visible again at the top of the arroyo. "Cool," he muttered entranced, while his brother yelled out, "We're all gonna die!"

"Nobody is going to die!" Sean shouted. "Watch this!" Sean whipped out the pistol he had stolen earlier in Santa Fe and began shooting at the fuse. I was sure he'd hit it. He fired. And he fired again. And again.

The gun clicked. It was out of ammo. "This is harder than it looks!" he yelled, exasperated, then threw the gun at the fuse. That missed too.

We were coming to the end of the canyon. We had only seconds left. I looked at Sean. He looked at me. We both screamed as the lit fuse met dynamite, and we all rode underneath it.

X.
DUCK, YOU SUCKER!

"Knockin' on Heaven's Door" by Bob Dylan drummed peacefully through the speakers. We weren't dead or even in the hospital. We were both still covered in dirt from the explosion, though. Me and Sean were taking a load off in a bar in a passenger train car just out of Cloudcroft. It was about noon, and my hearing was finally returning to normal, almost to where I could hear the clickety-clack of the railroad tracks.

Cade had taken Becky and Dingus and the horses back to Fort Sumner, but Sean and I decided to stop in Cloudcroft and take the train north. Both of us had hardly slept in the past day, so when Sean said he was too tired to ride his bike any further, I didn't blame him. So we bought train tickets and paid extra to have the bike stored in the back freight car. Once we were far north enough, we'd get off and head back to Sumner, and right after that we'd head off for Perdition to rescue Dorado… wherever it was. We still weren't sure, but Dingus and Becky told me they'd look over some maps and figure it out on the way home.

Anyways, the train wasn't real crowded, and me and Sean were just about the only ones inside. Like I said, we were in the car with the bar in it, and I think most people were in the dining car eating lunch. I watched through the window as a sea of trees passed by outside. We were in the forested region of the state again, going through the mountains, but before long we'd be back in the desert. I turned around and walked over to Sean at the bar, who was staring lovingly at his empty shot glass.

"Well, we did it," I said and slumped down on the barstool next to him. Even though I felt relieved for finding the key, tomorrow morning we were supposed to hand it and the tombstone off to the cartel. My mind was racing with everything we still needed to do. "Now we just have to figure out a way to rescue Dorado from Xander. Then, after that, somehow we've got to figure out how to deal with that drug cartel. Or maybe we could just turn the cartel loose on Xander—"

I guess I was starting to ramble and Sean cut me off. "Pancho, we've been all the way up to Santa Fe and almost got roasted alive inside of a giant puppet only to then go all the way back down south where we almost got our asses blowed off in that arroyo."

As he spoke, he reached behind the bar and took out another shot glass and started to pour some of his tequila in it. "We've earned a little rest, and tired minds come up with bad ideas." He pushed the glass to me and I couldn't help but remember back to a few days ago when Dorado had tried to get me to drink. It was sort of like history repeating itself in a funny little way, only now I was with my other brother. This time I didn't argue and picked it up. I figured I'd earned it. "Yeah, you're right."

"*Salud,*" he said and clinked his glass to mine.

I had never had tequila before, and for some reason, I thought maybe it was going to taste like pickle juice. It didn't. I coughed and wretched as I set the shot glass down. My throat got warm and my mouth felt like it'd been turned inside out.

"Good, eh?" Sean said.

"No," I shook my head profusely. I glanced out the window at the passing scenery and it looked a little different from before.

"So, do you really think a train is the best way to travel?" I asked him just to be saying something while the tequila took effect. I can't say I minded traveling by train, though. It was pretty cool. The Cloudcroft line started out as a logging railroad to transport lumber from the mountains. Now it was basically a tourist attraction and a neat way to travel around certain parts of the state.

"Trust me. Nobody would be looking for us on the train. Out on the open roads, though, near Fort Sumner, we'd get caught for sure. This is the last place they would look. You see, down in Mexico, let's just say I occasionally got in a little *pequeño* trouble."

"Just a little?" Somehow I now had a hard time imagining it was only a little trouble knowing Sean.

"Well, maybe more than just *pequeño*. But, what I'm trying to say is…" I could tell he was struggling to find the words. "This is not how your friend Cade would say…my first horse ride?"

I had to laugh. "Not my first rodeo. That's the expression you're looking for. But, I guess what you're trying to say is you've had to run from the cops before?"

He sighed and poured himself another drink. "Let's just say that growing up without a father in Mexico…it wasn't easy. Truthfully, I didn't just come up here because of the tombstone story in the news. One way or the other, I had to leave Mexico."

"Is that how you ended up with all that dynamite?"

A smile crossed his face for a second. "It belonged to a friend of mine, yes." He let out a long sigh, I thought he was going to say something thoughtful, but instead, he belched. He stood up and stretched his arms. "I am tired, Mechito. I believe I go lay down for a while. Wake me when we arrive, okay?"

I watched him walk away. I wondered if I'd look like that when I got older. I mean, obviously I would in a superficial sense. But Sean had a world-weary look in his eyes that I didn't that made him look tough. And even though I considered Dorado to be pretty tough, he didn't have that look either. I realized then that was probably the main thing that set their faces apart even more than the hair color. Some people say that the eyes are the window to the soul, and the way Sean's eyes looked, I had to wonder what happened to him to make him the way he was. When he woke up later, I decided I would ask him.

For some reason, I felt a little wired. More than anything, I wanted to practice throwing the knife Sean gave me again, but there wasn't anywhere to do that on the train, so I just started wandering around. I'd never really been on a train before anyway, so I figured it'd be neat to walk around the different cars. There's these little outdoor connection bridges between the cars you walk across to get to the other, so I left the bar area to walk through one of the passenger cars where the individual rooms were.

I was in a pretty good mood, because I finally felt like maybe there was a light at the end of the tunnel. I was also feeling pretty good because of something that had happened when I said goodbye to Becky at the train station. I had decided I finally wanted to say it. Even if we were young, and even if it had been an emotional roller coaster of a week between us—no, because it had been such a roller coaster—I said it. I kissed her on the forehead and said, "I love you."

"I love you, too," she said back. By the way that she smiled and the look on her face, I knew that she meant it, too. And she didn't hesitate either. She looked a little surprised but in a happy way.

Even though I had gone for a walk to look around, instead, I just kept replaying that scene in my mind over and over again. All of a sudden, as I walked past one of the cabin doors, I felt a strong hand grip my arm and before I knew it, it had pulled me inside. I was thrown to the floor and hit my head on one of the seats against the wall. I shook my head, trying to clear my vision up. "What the hell…"

Eventually I could see the form of a man before me holding a gun. He was tall with long hair that he had tucked under a black hat. It looked like McCaw. I stood up. "You."

"You sound disappointed," he said, still holding the gun on me. I stared at him in disbelief. It was him alright, but he had both his eyes and even his hand. One of the eyes looked different from the other, though, and I realized it was a glass eye. I looked at his left hand. I thought he was wearing a black glove at first, but now I realized it was a fake, too.

"Nice hand you got there. Is it for special dress occasions?"

"Well, I didn't want to frighten the other passengers. Have a seat," he motioned to the booth against the window. Since he was standing in front of the only way out with a gun, I didn't have much choice, so I did.

"How the hell did you find us?" I asked him as he sat down across from me.

He looked at me as though it was a stupid thing to ask. "Find you? I never lost you, boy. Didn't you hear me say that I'd keep my eye on you?" He pointed to his glass eye and smiled. I thought of the bird I saw flying above us when we were approaching the canyon. No, he was just trying to scare me, I decided, but before I could say anything, he started in on me again.

"You've been a busy boy. Been to Mescalero, Santa Fe…the desert outside of Alamogordo."

Another thought occurred to me. "And don't forget the bar in Tularosa." He cocked an eyebrow, and I continued. "Those were your men following us, weren't they? That's how you tracked me."

"Men? Do you see any men here with me now? Other than Itza-chu, I work alone. Didn't Old Man Baca tell you about me…that I'm the bogeyman?"

"He said you were a brujo, a witch."

"Maybe I am. But I still see doubt in your eyes. If it helps you to believe, perhaps I just use a radio tracker to follow Itza-chu. Does that sound less frightening to you? You can believe that if it makes you feel better."

"I don't get you, McCaw. Most people say the Apache don't care for gold. Why are you different?"

"Oh, I'm not after the gold. The gold is just a piece in a much bigger puzzle. A puzzle that all started to come together the minute an old man came forward claiming to be Billy the Kid." He smiled as though he were speaking of the proudest moment of his life. "As far as everyone believes, Pat Garrett killed Billy the Kid in 1881. But the truth is, I killed him in 1950 in a little town in Texas."

"You killed Williams! They said he died of a heart attack?"

"He was ninety years old. Put an old man under too much stress and, well…" He looked at me to let it all sink in. He had begun to relax and had sat the gun down and was starting to unscrew his fake hand. I thought about bolting once he had set the gun down only I saw something that made me reconsider. There was Sean, hanging upside down outside the window with his long hair blowing in the wind. Since it was his left eye that he was missing, McCaw couldn't see him.

Sean smiled and waved at me. I caught my eyes getting big and worried McCaw would notice. Instead, he thought I was reacting to his story.

"Does this frighten you?"

"No," I said and realized this was the perfect chance to stall him and pump him for information at the same time. "Did you…did you learn anything from him?"

As McCaw spoke, Sean was pasting something that looked like toothpaste on the window. I realized what it was—plastic explosives of some sort.

"I knew when Tumbleweed Williams met with the current governor what he was doing. He was coming clean about the canyon before he died. I wanted to know what he told the governor. He was a tough old bastard, though, wouldn't tell me a word. But as it turned out, the one man who he did talk to was your uncle Pancho, which is why he stole the tombstone."

"Is he still alive?"

He had by then taken off his hand and reached into his coat pocket to bring out his familiar hook, which he now was reattaching. "You mean is that the man in the photo, or is it dear old dad? Well, I'm not going to tell you that. As you know, that information and his current whereabouts are for myself to know, that is until you hand over the tombstone. Which brings me to something I don't know. Why were you out in the middle of nowhere?" He stood up and leveled the gun at my forehead. "What did you find?"

"I thought you were a brujo. Shouldn't you know?"

"Tell me!" He swiped at my face with his hook, and I fell out of the booth onto the floor. McCaw leered over me, pointing the gun back in my face. "Why all this jumping around? What did you find?"

I looked at Sean. He was planting a fuse in the plastic. He needed more time.

"Fine! I'll tell you! But first, you tell me why you waited until now on the train to corner us. If you knew where we were the whole time, why not kill us in the desert?"

He looked at me as though he knew I was stalling. "Because a small, enclosed space like this is the best place to kill a rat. Speaking of which—

He spun around swiftly and pointed his revolver squarely at Sean. His eyes widened and he lifted himself back up just as McCaw fired. The glass exploded into a million pieces and a gust of air filled the room. Seeing that he had missed Sean, McCaw leaned out the window, hoping to take another shot. I didn't need to think twice about what I was going to do next. I ran up and jumped, grabbing the ledge above the window and kicked McCaw outside. As he tumbled through the broken window, he twisted around and managed to jam his hook into the side of the window ledge and hung on for dear life.

Sean called to me from atop the train and extended his hand. "Mechito, come on!"

I reached out, clasping his arm as I scrambled out the window. As Sean hoisted me up, I felt something slice through the leg of my jeans. I looked down and could see that McCaw now had his good hand clinging to the window and was trying to cut my leg with the hook!

Sean pulled me up onto the train top as the hook ripped through my pant leg. I looked over the side of the train car, my hair whipping wildly in my face, and could see the sea of trees racing by underneath. Right now, we were on some sort of bridge. Actually, it was the most famous spot of the railroad called the Mexican Canyon Trestle, if I remembered right.

The second I stood up, it was like I had entered a violent new dimension. The force of the wind caused me to stagger backward right away and I almost lost my balance. No sooner than I had regained my footing, Sean was shouting something at me, but it was hard to hear. He looked angry that I couldn't figure out what it was. I shrugged back and yelled, "What?"

Sean's face took on a horrified expression and he tackled me. As I fell flat on my back, everything suddenly went black and became very noisy. I realized what had happened. We were in a tunnel! My insides did a loop realizing I had almost died.

He put his mouth next to my ear and yelled, "Take this!"

I felt something cool in my hand and I realized it was the key. I grasped it firmly.

"Why?"

"Because I have a brujo to kill."

No sooner than he had said it, we emerged from the tunnel and back into the blinding light of the sun. Sean's face took on a surprised expression, and he jumped to his feet. I flipped over onto my stomach and was shocked to see McCaw standing in front of us. "What the hell?" I blurted even though nobody could hear me. He must have crawled back inside the train and then climbed back out on the opposite side while we were going under the tunnel. He looked like a wraith with his long duster coat and hair whipping in the wind. Itza-chu, his hawk, was circling above him, keeping pace with the train.

Sean stood in front of me defensively. McCaw noticed the key in my hands.

"Whatever it is that you found, give it to me, or I shoot!"

He drew another revolver from inside his duster and aimed it squarely at Sean's chest.

Sean very calmly opened up his coat. At first, I wasn't sure what the heck he was doing until I realized he was showing off some of the explosives he carried around with him.

"You shoot me, and they'll have to build a new railroad."

McCaw looked disgusted for a moment and then said, "Fine. I'll aim for your head."

As soon as he said it, Sean threw a knife at McCaw. The old brujo was still too fast, though, and blocked it with his hook.

"Run, Mechito, Run!" Sean yelled and ran to tackle McCaw. As they both tumbled over, McCaw shouted, "Itza-chu!"

Oh crap. He was going to use the hawk to chase me down. On command, the hawk did what he said and divebombed me.

I turned and ran, but not quick enough because I felt the hawk's claws dig themselves into the back of my jacket. I fell over and the key went sliding from my hands across the top of the train car. I was scared to death it was going to slide right off the side, but the bird swooped in and grabbed it before it did.

I scurried to my feet, trying to find anything I could to throw at that dang bird. I dug my hands into my pants pockets. The only thing I could find was the keys to my house. A lot of good those would do. I remembered the knife Sean had given me, but I wasn't confident I could hit a moving target like this. The key was at least weighing Itza-chu down a little bit, so she wasn't too high off the top of the cars. She was only about one ahead of me. I ran as fast as I could and jumped from one train car to another. Running with the wind helped me clear it a lot easier than I would have if I was running against it.

I kept running and jumping from one car to another and was catching up to her slowly but surely—the only problem was I was about to run out of train cars. I dug deep and increased my speed until I had finally caught up with her. I jumped when she was finally within arm's reach and grabbed the key. That wasn't the best idea, since when I landed, I went skidding across the train car and slid right off the side. Itza-chu was still hanging on as I did. At the last second, I grabbed some railing running along the top of the car with one hand while I gripped the key in the other. Damn railing was rusty, though, and came loose a little bit from the car. As I clung to it for dear life, I swung around, and my face slammed against a window. A woman inside the dining car screamed. I guess I had disturbed her dinner.

She started pointing at me when I felt Itza-chu tugging at the key and trying to take off with it. Holding onto the key, I beat Itza-chu against the window several times, prompting more screaming from the diners until someone finally came to check on them. On the third hit, the stubborn bird finally let go and flew off, leaving me with the key. A panicked attendant in the dining car shouted at me through the window. "What are you doing out there!?"

I just smiled and shouted back, "Sorry, almost lost my keys!"

I stuffed the key back safe in my jacket pocket and hoisted myself up. I scanned ahead for Sean and McCaw. They were still fighting, and McCaw had him pinned under him and was trying to cut Sean with his hook. I started to run towards him with every intent of tackling McCaw off my brother.

Then I heard something strange. Even over the roar of the locomotive, I could tell what it was due to its powerful rhythm: helicopter blades. I looked overhead, and sure enough, that's what it was. At first, I thought it was the one from the cemetery coming to get McCaw, but it looked different, smaller and less militaristic.

The chopper hovered over the train, three cars behind me keeping pace with the locomotive. Three men jumped onto the car below. I needed to get to my brother, and quick.

I turned around and started off towards McCaw and Sean. In an instant, when McCaw looked up at the helicopter, Sean managed to slip free of his grip and punch him in the face. McCaw tumbled off him and Sean righted himself. He didn't waste any time and immediately jumped onto McCaw. But then the old man did something I didn't expect and shoved Sean off of him so hard that he tumbled backwards, falling between the two cars.

"No!" I screamed and ran at McCaw. I could only hope that Sean had landed safely on the little connector bridge between the cars, but for all I knew, McCaw could have killed him. Right then I was so mad I felt like I could fly. McCaw turned to me, aiming his gun, and shouted, "This is the end of the line, son. Now hand it over!"

I didn't stop running. I know it was stupid, but I was so mad I had every intention of tackling him off the train even if I went down with him. I jolted when I heard a gunshot and skidded to a halt. Only I didn't feel anything. I patted my chest and stomach frantically, looking down at my shirt. There was no blood. I looked back up at McCaw.

Where his only good eye had been was now a dark, bloody smear. Before I could even react, he fell from the train into the canopy of the tall forest below. Itza-chu dive-bombed into the trees, following her dead master.

"Well, bye, bye birdie," I heard a familiar voice coo behind me. It was Xander. I turned to face him. It was him and his men on the helicopter that I saw.

He smiled and blew the smoke from his revolver. "Bet you never thought you'd be happy to see me?" he shouted over the roar of the train, two men on either side of him as he approached me.

I shook my head and muttered, "How did you…"

I let my words trail off as it hit me. Me kissing Becky on the forehead at the train station only an hour ago. Me and Becky on the trail this morning and her telling me she hadn't told her dad a thing about where I was going. It hit me like a sledgehammer this time. It was too much of a coincidence that he would track us down twice. Becky had been playing me. My heart sunk.

"I love you, too," she had said back at the train station, but now I knew it was a lie. I didn't even have it in me to run. It was like the life was just plain sucked out of me and I just stood there staring at Xander in disbelief.

"Geez, kid, you alright? You're looking a little pale," he said.

A white-hot rage coursed through me. I drew back my arm to punch him, but his men stopped me before I could, grabbing both my arms and pinning them behind my back.

Xander shook his head. "Kid here's getting cranky. I think he needs a nap, gentlemen." He smiled at me. "Nighty, night, Pancho," were the last words I heard before one of his men knocked me across the back of the head and everything went black.

XI.
A TOWN
CALLED HELL

You know how when you're sick you can have the same dream over and over again? Well, that's what was happening to me, and every time the dream ended, it would start over. Sean and I were always on top of the train with the wind making me feel dizzy. Sean was always about to fall off the train, and I would run to catch his hand, only I missed every time. Finally, I reached out to him, only this time he disappeared, and I began to fall. "Sean!" I yelled out, and my eyes jolted open. I was finally awake. I felt nauseous for a moment, like I'd been going really fast and then finally stopped. A voice was calling to me from a long ways away, but I wasn't sure who it was.

All I could see at first were these black vertical lines against bright white light. I blinked hard, trying to figure out what the lines were and finally realized they were the bars of a cell. Was I in jail? It smelt musty and dank, so maybe I was. Something still didn't seem right, then I heard the voice calling me again. "Pancho! Hey, man, are you okay?"

I finally realized who the voice belonged to. "Dorado!" I shook my head and looked to my right and there he was. "It's really you!" I was so happy that I wasn't dreaming. I could tell it was real from the way I hurt and ached.

He was sitting in a chair next to me with his hands behind his back. When I went to grab him and couldn't move, I realized I was cuffed to the chair.

Right away he started asking a million questions. "Boy, are you a sight for sore eyes! Are you okay? Where have you been? Did you get the key thingy?"

"Yeah, I got it, man. I got it…" My words trailed off. I was thinking of Sean. Was he alive? I didn't actually see where he landed, but I think he just fell onto the little bridge that connected the train cars. Maybe he had woken up and gotten away before Xander got him? Or maybe he was being held in another room?

Dorado looked at me, confused, and said, "Hey, man, are you okay? You seem kind of out of it, and while you were passed out, you kept calling for someone named Sean."

"Yeah, man. He must've gotten away since he's not locked up in here with us."

"Who is he?"

I was so out of it I had forgotten Dorado hadn't even met Sean. Oh boy, would he be shocked when I told him. Actually, I wasn't sure just what to tell him. "Um…well, he's kind of our half-brother."

Dorado just gave me a slack-jawed stare. "You must've gotten hit on the head pretty hard, Pancho."

"No, he was fighting McCaw when he fell off the train. That was the last time I saw him."

"Whoa, you ran into McCaw again? You need to back this story way, way up, Pancho, starting with who this Sean person is, because we sure don't have another brother."

"I know. I wouldn't believe it myself but wait 'til you see him, man. He looks just like us, and not just a little bit. He saved me outside of Bent right after I lost you and he's been helping me ever since. We even went to Santa Fe and got Tumbleweed Williams' letter, then the key, everything."

"That's great, but I'm still missing the part about where he's been all these years."

"Look, I don't know a lot—

"How can you not know a lot if you just spent two whole days with this person?"

"We've kind of had a busy past couple of days, man. Trust me. What I know is he's not from the States. He's from Mexico. I guess our dad had a secret family down there or something."

"How the hell does that work? Is he like way older than us?"

"No, he's twenty one, same as you. He says our dad was down in Mexico one night and…" I wasn't sure how to say it, "You know…with some woman and then he came back to the States and forgot about her."

"No, Dad would not have cheated on our mom. Trust me."

That ticked me off for some reason. Dorado was always defending our old man and kept him on a pedestal when really he was the reason we were in this mess.

"Why do you treat him like he's such a saint? You were six when he left, Dorado. You barely knew him."

Dorado looked at me like I was from outer space. I realized it was because I'd never torn into him like that before. "What the hell's wrong, Pancho?"

"You, man! If you hadn't had to go digging around for our old man, we wouldn't be here."

"Uh, have you forgotten our conversation back at the house? I told you that you'd be better off not knowing what I was doing here, but you just couldn't let it go, and you kept pestering me, so I told you. You should have listened. You're fourteen years old for—"

"Fifteen! I'll be fifteen tomorrow!"

I felt my face get hot. I couldn't hit Dorado all tied up. I knew it was stupid, but I felt like I was so mad I'd explode if I didn't do something. I rocked myself into Dorado's chair and knocked him over and I went down with him.

"What the hell, Pancho?" he asked, lying on the floor.

"It's Becky, man," I managed to rasp out, still catching my breath. "I'm such an idiot for thinking she'd choose me over her own father."

He sighed thoughtfully. "I'm sorry, man."

"I told her I loved her. And then, an hour later, here comes her old man to come get me on the train."

Lying on the floor, a thought suddenly occurred to me. "Wait, why are we in a jail cell *and* chained to a chair?"

"Eh, let's just say I haven't been a model prisoner these past few days."

Suddenly I heard footsteps, and Xander walked in. I strained my neck to look up at him. "Glad to see you're coming around, kid. I was a little worried that last blow to the skull might have killed you," he said as he unlocked the door to our cell and swung it open.

"Well, there's always next time," I said and did my best to flash a sarcastic smile.

He laughed and then cocked his head sideways to our level since we were on the floor. "Now, what happened here? Having a little brotherly quarrel? And here I thought you'd be happy to see each other again." To two goons that had followed him in, he said, "Turn 'em back up."

"My other brother isn't locked up in another cell, is he?" I asked, referring to Sean as they flipped me back up.

Xander gave me an irritated look. "He got away."

He was about to say something else when a voice cut him off. "Xander, what are they still doing here? I thought we agreed to kill them some time ago?" The voice sounded familiar and belonged to a man in a tan suit who had just walked in with a briefcase. Before I could see his face, he turned around to set his briefcase on an old rolltop desk that sat outside our cell.

"Nice to see you, too, Professor," Dorado said.

I could tell they had apparently gotten to know one another over the past few days. And they definitely didn't like each other.

"Who's this, our attorney?" I said to Dorado loud enough that everyone else could hear it. When the man spun around, I just about jumped out of my skin. It was Professor Mendez.

"Professor?" I looked back and forth between him and Dorado.

"Yeah, sorry for not warning you," Dorado said.

Mendez looked pleased that I was so shocked and raised an eyebrow. "Well, you did ask me if I was part of the Ring, didn't you?"

Come to think of it, that day in class he didn't say no. "But what about all that talk about Tumbleweed Williams being a fairy tale? And, how you can't believe crazy stories like—"

He cut me off. "Merely a simple charade. In fact, truth is always stranger than fiction. Oh, by the way, did you finish your report?" He flashed a wicked smirk my way.

"Heh, I've been living your damn report. Do I at least get extra credit for getting the key?"

For once he stifled a laugh. "I must admit I am impressed. But, no."

"Can it at least get me out of...what should I call this...detention?"

"Detention?" he said in mock amusement. He looked at Dorado. "Dorado, didn't you tell your brother about the wonderful time you've been having here?" Mendez crossed his arms and looked at my brother in an antagonizing manner.

Dorado looked at me. "Welcome to Gilligan's Ghost Town. Population me, Gilligan," he nodded to Mendez, "….the professor…" and then at Xander, "…that crazed bastard we call the Skipper. Mr. and Mrs. Howell are out on the veranda somewhere and…" he looked around the room until he settled on the two armed men guarding the door, "Ginger and Mary Anne. And just for the record," he added in a whisper, "I don't know which one is prettier anymore."

They both grimaced, but Xander held up his hand. Xander walked over calmly and then belted Dorado across the back of the head, hard.

"I forgot! I forgot! You like to be Mary Anne. I'm sorry," Dorado rasped through the pain, his eyes shut tight.

Xander gave a stifled laugh. "Heh, you know, Dumez, I might just miss this one of these days. Hitting you that is, not your jokes."

Mendez sighed in disgust and turned his attention to me. "You really must pay better attention in class, Pancho. If you did, you might already know where you were. You are currently in a ghost town between Santa Rosa and Fort Sumner, Perdition." I must have gotten hit in the head pretty hard because up until that moment, I had forgotten all about Perdition! My spirits picked up for a second. Cade would know we were here. Maybe he and Dingus would come to our rescue. But then I remembered they'd had Becky with them, so who knows if that would happen or not. Maybe she'd already warned her dad to be expecting them. Or, if not Cade and Dingus, maybe Sean would come. If he could find Perdition, that is.

All I knew is that since Mendez mentioned killing us earlier that I needed to keep stalling him into talking. Actually, we all did that to Mendez anyway at school right before he was about to give us a test: get him to talking about something that interested him. By the time he stopped, it would always be too late for him to even administer the test.

"So, what's so special about Perdition?" I asked.

Mendez answered, "It used to be a gambler's haven. It started its decline like so many towns when it was bypassed by the railroad. In the 1920s a few citizens still clung to life here, but during the Great Depression they too left. The Ring bought up the land in the 1940s, and today we keep it as a sort of reminder of the Old West."

"A reminder to back when you guys actually ruled New Mexico, you mean?" Dorado said, finally getting serious.

"Oh, we still have more influence than you think. All we lack now is the proper funding, and hopefully once we discover the location of the Lost Adams, well…" he let his words trail off as he smiled.

"You do realize that even after you find the canyon, it's buried under tons of solid rock don't you?" I asked.

"It will take time to excavate it, make no mistake. Years most likely. But our organization has the resources to do so," Mendez answered.

"Which brings me around to the reason I've neglected to kill you just yet. Seeing as how I used to be your pop's deputy before he left us, how would you two boys like to join the Ring?" Xander asked.

Dorado spat out a laugh while I said, "If you guys expect us to grab some shovels and help you dig the damn thing out, then forget about it."

"You're wasting your time, Xander," Mendez said and picked up the key from the table, studying it intently.

"You've got the key, and you've got the Eye in the tombstone. Seems to me like you've got everything you need." I was going to suggest they let us go when something else that had been bugging me crossed my mind. "I have to admit, I do have one question though, why did you ever go public with the return of the tombstone if you wanted to keep it to yourselves?"

Xander answered. "I suppose that's a fair question. Unfortunately for us, the mayor found out about the discovery before I could cover it up. He's not a Ring member, as you can imagine."

"Yeah, what a pity," I said.

"Funny thing, though. It was his idea to make the whole thing into a big publicity stunt with this Tombstone Race later today. When he had duplicates made for the race, it gave us the idea to install a fake at the gravesite. In fact, I have to go help MC the whole damn race this afternoon."

"If that's so, how do you plan to steal it?" Dorado asked.

"Simple. One of our benefactors in legislature requested the tombstone, due to its historical value, be put on display in a museum in Santa Fe. I have a feeling it may get lost during transport, though." Xander smiled.

"After which we will finally break it open, the Ojo del Oro will find Adams' tomb, and this will unlock it," Mendez said as he secured the key in a metal cylinder to protect it. He handed it to one of the men. "Don't take your eyes off of this." Then to us, he said, "Which brings us back around to the point at hand. As much as I disdain the two of you, I suppose you were useful in acquiring the key for us. Do you accept Xander's generous offer or not?"

"That depends. What's your dental plan like?" Dorado asked.

"I've got some plyers handy if you'd like to find out," Xander answered.

"That's okay. The Professor's classes were always torture enough," Dorado rebutted. "After sitting through those, I can handle anything."

Xander was getting angry, and I knew I better do something to defuse the situation fast. All of a sudden an idea hit me. They didn't know where to open it. As Xander started to walk towards my brother, I blurted out, "How about a counteroffer? You let us go and I tell you where to use the Ojo del Oro. You can't use it just anywhere."

"You can't?" Xander said, real sarcastic-like. He touched his finger to his lip and looked up at the ceiling. "According to the note from the late Mr. Bonney, or was it Tumbleweed Williams—I can never decide—it says we're supposed to crack open the tombstone at Sky City at dawn."

I really must have taken a hard hit to the head. I had forgotten Becky would have told him about the note. Xander noticed my helpless expression and laughed. "Poor kid, you keep forgetting I have a source on the inside, don't you?"

I didn't say anything. What could I say at this point? All I knew was that I felt hopeless and dumb.

"Well, Xander, it seems we have our answer," Mendez said. He looked at me and Dorado. "But don't look so dull. Many men have died in search of the Lost Adams, my friends. You two aren't the first and you likely won't be the last," he said snidely. "At least take a little pride in the fact that you played a part in its history, no matter how insignificant it may have been."

"What are you going to do with us?" Dorado asked cautiously.

Xander looked at Mendez for a second, then directed his beady eyes back at us. "Metaphorically speaking, you boys have already been digging your own graves. I say now it's time to do it literally."

***

One hour and two holes later out in the desert, I found myself standing on my brother's shoulders under the dead tree with a noose around my neck. Both of us had our hands cuffed behind our backs, and the idea was that when Dorado finally couldn't stand any longer and lost his balance the rope would tighten, and well, I'm sure you can guess what happens to me.

"I know I'm a little slow, but doesn't this only kill one of us?" I asked. I wasn't going to give them the satisfaction of thinking I was afraid—even though I was.

"Look beneath your feet, boys," Xander said.

I looked down best I could, even though it's hard to do with a rope around your neck. Dorado was standing on top of an ant den. This kept getting better and better.

"Part of the fun of this is all in the waiting. Especially for you, big brother. You might can stand there for an hour or two, but it's gonna be a lot harder to keep still when you got ants in your pants. But don't worry. After you lose your balance and little brother gets that rope for a bowtie, you'll have plenty of time to think about it while the ants pick you clean," Xander said, still giddy as ever.

I thought about asking Xander, "Couldn't you just shoot us?" but decided against it because he just might. Instead, I decided to keep up my bravado and said, "Oh, and here I was thinking you'd do something creative."

Dorado was strangely serious. "You really are a heartless son of a bitch, Xander."

"That's not true. In fact…" He started patting around the pockets of his duster like he was looking for something. When he found what he was looking for, he pulled out a rolled-up joint of marijuana. "Here, have an anesthetic. One of the boys pulled it off of a hippie earlier today," he said as he lit it. He stuck it in Dorado's mouth, and when he acted like he was going to spit it out, Xander reeled back his fist like he was going to hit him.

Dorado kept the joint in his mouth and Xander let his arm down. "Don't say I never gave you anything." He patted him on the face.

The words went off like a lightbulb in my head. That's what Sean had said to me when he gave me his handcuff key that night at Bonito Lake after the bar fight. I still had it in my back pocket, so we might get out of this mess yet.

"As much as I'd like to stick around and see how long you can fair against the ants, I've got to keep up appearances and officiate the Tombstone Race today. Then, after that, it's off to Sky City. Toodaloo." Xander tipped his hat to us walked away with his men. "Come on, boys."

Once he walked away, I started digging for Sean's handcuff key as quick as I could. It was all a matter of keeping my balance while I tried to dig it out of my back pocket.

Dorado spat out the joint with disgust. "Don't worry, Panch.' I can keep my balance and if you can keep yours, we'll be fine. And before you know it, Cade will be here, and somehow, we'll get out of this."

"Yeah, if Becky didn't rat on him to her dad like she did everything else, which is a big if."

I twisted my wrist around to try and sink my hand deeper into my back pocket. After a minute, the muscles in my arm seized up. I cussed and flung my fingers back out of my pocket, letting my arm straighten up.

"Look, man, even if Becky was feeding her dad information, I still have a hard time thinking she'd leave us both for dead."

"Well, don't count on it."

"I know Xander, Pancho, and if he had arrested Cade, he'd be gloating about it to make us miserable."

"Yeah, well, we'll find out, won't we?"

"Man, want to know something funny?"

I didn't really; I was more focused on trying to get that dang key out of my back pocket. "What?"

"That's the first time I ever puffed a joint. I think... I think it's starting to affect me since I never had one before. Virgin system and all that." I could believe that. Even if he drank occasionally, Dorado had no interest in drugs.

Finally he noticed my twitching around. "Pancho, what the hell are you doing up there? Aw hell, it might be your last few minutes alive. I suppose you can do what you want. Since this is the last time we may ever talk, there's some things I want to get off my chest. That time Aunt Patty and Rod found the missing beer, and you blamed it on me and I tried to deny it… well, it was me."

Hmm, he actually did think he drank it. Then I realized that wasn't what I needed to be focusing on right now. I had to get that key. But he was saying some pretty interesting things.

"…And that time at the family reunion when you were ten, and Aunt Patty grounded you for six weeks because she thought you were the one who strung cousin May's tampons up in a tree to embarrass her…that was me too."

Finally! I clasped the key in between my middle and index finger and dragged it out of my pocket. I bent my wrist around and tried to work it into the cuff on my other hand. It's not easy to do when you can't see it.

"Okay, I guess that was everything. Don't you have anything you want to say to me?" Dorado sounded irked that I hadn't said a word to him.

"No, because I'm not going to die," I said. "I have a handcuff key, and I'm almost free."

"You never thought to tell me that! Ouch!" he yelped and his body jerked. The ants must have finally started crawling out of their den and up his legs.

I steadied myself atop his shoulders trying to keep my balance.

"Is it the ants?" I shifted my eyes downwards, but I couldn't see the ground very good. "Are you sure you're not just hallucinating them because of that joint?"

"One, you're thinking of LSD, and two, no!" he shouted.

I craned my neck down best I could without losing my balance. Now I could see a steady stream of ants crawling around Dorado's feet, and from the sound of things, making their way up his pants.

"Oh, boy," I said.

"Oh boy is right." Dorado started to wobble. "Work faster…faster!"

"Keep it together, man. I'm almost done." My wrist was cramping, but it was life or death. I had to get the key into the hole.

"Hurry, man! They're getting into the nether regions!"

Click! Finally, the key slipped in place. With a twist of my wrist the cuff came undone, and my hands were free.

"I'm good!" I yelled and grabbed the branch above me with my now free hands. Dorado collapsed onto the desert floor below, making noises that sounded either like torture or extreme tickling. I hung by the tree branch with one arm and used the other to lift the noose from my neck and to my utter surprise, the branch snapped loose! I landed next to Dorado.

"You see that?" I said in amazement as I began to work on his handcuffs.

"Pants off first! Pants off first!" he shouted. I hadn't thought of that. He looked up at me with pleading eyes. "Don't make it weird."

"Oh, alright!" I hissed and helped him get them off after which he proceeded to run around the desert in his boxers, jumping up and down and shaking his legs.

After a minute he seemed to calm down. "Okay, that's better," he said and turned around so I could work the cuffs off him.

After I got them off, and since my nerves were pretty shot, I picked up the joint Dorado spit out and took a puff. We went and sat on the big pile of dirt we'd created digging the graves earlier and just sat there for a few minutes as we passed it back and forth a few times, just trying to calm down a little. "What's next?" I asked him.

"You seem to be the man with the plan today." He took a drag. "You tell me."

What was next? I took in a deep breath then let out a long sigh, thinking. "We could walk away right now. Go to the authorities. Tell them everything, count on them to help us."

Dorado looked at me for a second before he busted out laughing. So did I after a second. I was so damn worn out I'm not sure if I meant that as a joke or not when I said it.

"You're right. The Santa Fe Ring is the authority all the way up to the top for all we know. We're probably screwed no matter what we do at this point," he said in between snorts.

"Ah, this really sucks," I said as I calmed down. I felt on the verge of tears yet I wasn't sad. I felt strangely detached. Was I having a mental break down?

There me and my brother were slightly stoned, sitting in silence in the desert next to the graves we dug earlier, him in his underwear still picking ants off himself, and me picking the lock on the cuff still on my right hand. Man, I was thirsty. And really hungry. So was Dorado.

"You know what I need? Water. A whopper. An Alsup's burrito with extra gristle," he said, staring blankly up at the sky. I finally realized the word for what we were: high. It was the first time I had ever gotten high.

"An enchurito," I muttered dreamily.

He looked at me. "What?"

"An enchurito. It's like a burrito and an enchilada combined." I threw my cuffs into the sand, then continued. "We get out of here, we're going to Taco Bell and getting an enchurito. A fluffin' enchurito, 'rado!" I hit him on the shoulder. "Dorado?"

His eyes stared glassily up at the sky. He wasn't listening to me anymore and was cooking something up in his own tired, deranged mind. Finally, he spoke.

"Seems to me we could go back to Perdition right now, get the key back, cause a little chaos," Dorado started counting his fingers. This was going to be a long one. "Go to Fort Sumner, steal ourselves a tombstone," he paused for a second as though he didn't remember what was next, then continued, "give that crazy Mexican drug cartel what I owe them by the Day of the Dead; then hope they don't kill us and that they tell us what happened to our dad… and hope like hell that I don't go to prison when the smoke clears."

I gave him a blank stare.

"After I get my pants back on," he added as though that made a difference.

"Just like that?"

"Just like that. Unless you have an idea you'd like to share." He slipped his pants back on.

I shrugged my shoulders. What the hell else could we do? "Well, over the past 24 hours I've fallen off a mountain," I started counting my fingers now. "Gone on a really wild toboggan ride, got shot at—a lot, robbed a bank, got in a bar fight, almost got burnt up inside the Zozobra, almost got exploded, fell off a train, and just escaped my own hanging. Why stop now? I don't suppose you have a specific plan for all of this?"

"Not really. I've always been a make-it-up-as-I-go sorta guy."

"You're out of your damn mind, you know that?"

"So are you." He smiled, got up, dusted himself off and offered me his hand.

"Yeah, I guess I am." It had been a long day, and it wasn't even over yet. We both stared off into the distance at Perdition.

XII.
GHOST TOWN DEMOLITION DERBY

It took us about ten minutes of walking through the sand and sage to get back to Perdition. We surveyed the scene, and for the first time I could see the entire town. Perdition was easily one of the best preserved ghost towns in all of New Mexico, and it was easy to see why. To some degree the Ring had been keeping the old structures in good shape. The only evidence of modern times was the two trucks parked outside one of the buildings.

The town was built along the edge of a low sloping hill that we had to climb back up to get to. The main street was still intact with about a dozen or so old wooden buildings like saloons, barbershops, casinos, and a post office lining both sides. We could see the building we had been in earlier was the two-story jail, though I guess that shoulda been obvious due to the cell they had us in. There was also an old, mission-style church with a big rock fence around it that stood out from all the other buildings. Right in the middle of town were several corrals that looked like they'd been built in recent times. All of them had livestock like cows and bulls in separate pens, and one even had horses.

"I guess if nobody comes along to rescue us, we can ride those out of here," I said, referring to the horses.

"Sounds like a plan. But first, the key," Dorado said, looking towards the jail. The easiest way to get in without surprising the guards inside would be to take the stairs along the back side and crawl through a window.

There were a few guards at various spots around the town, but none of them seemed to really be doing anything. As far as they were concerned, me and Dorado were probably dead, so there was no one to look out for. We crept slowly to the back of the jail and used the outside stairs to get to the second floor. Once we were safely back in our old room upstairs, we decided to see what the guards downstairs were doing.

We opened the creaky door slowly and tried to tiptoe onto the staircase leading downstairs. Only you can't tiptoe across a close-to-100-year-old wooden floor. Every plank creaked, so we stopped walking after a while and did sign language. Not real sign language—I don't know how to do that, and neither does Dorado—but our improvised version. Dorado pointed to an old plank of wood leaning up against the wall. Then he pointed to me and made a walking motion with his fingers down some imaginary stairs. Then he made a crazy face that I didn't understand. He got irritated with me and silently mouthed that he meant the two guards downstairs.

I nodded my head that I got it. Then he made a motion of them chasing me up the stairs, then he picked up the wooden plank and made it clear what was going to happen. Did I mention Dorado used to be a really good baseball player in high school?

As I crept around the corner, I could hear the men downstairs. I peered over the stairwell and could see them pretty good. There were only two—the ones Dorado had called Ginger and Mary Anne—and they were playing poker. The container with the key sat in the middle of the table where they could keep an eye on it. I pretended to creep down the stairs even though that wasn't the intention. I made sure they creaked extra loud when I was about halfway down. Their eyes sprang up from their cards to meet me.

"Hey!" one of them shouted. "How did you get in here?"

I gave them a deer in the headlights look and cussed for good measure before I bolted back up. Hopefully Dorado wouldn't get ahead of himself and smack me in the face. He didn't and I leaned against the corner wall next to him. I could hear the stairs creaking as the men ran up them, and at just the right moment Dorado swung the wooden plank around the corner. The board hit the first guy square in the forehead, knocking him out and into the second guy behind him. Dorado hopped over the first guard as the second one fell backward down the stairs. He landed on him with his fist in his face. Now they were both out.

Dorado fished through the second guard's pockets. I didn't know what for. "Pancho, look for a set of keys in his pocket," Dorado said, referring to the first guard.

"Keys to what?"

"You'll see."

I did like he said, and sure enough in his pocket were a set of small keys. I put them in my pocket and walked over to the poker table. The metal cylinder with the key was still sitting in the middle of the table. I grabbed it and stuck it in my pants pocket best that I could. It was about the size of a stick of dynamite in that container, so it was a little uncomfortable, but it stayed good and tight in there at least.

Dorado motioned for me to hurry up and follow him outside. Then I saw something even more important than the key: sitting on the porch in its orange and white majestic beauty was an ice chest. I opened it up.

"Son of a bitch," I muttered. It was all beer.

"I never thought I'd be so disappointed to see a free cooler of beer in my life," Dorado said from over my shoulder.

"No, no freaking way. There's got to be something in here other than beer." I thrust my hands through the cold icy slush until finally at the bottom I felt something plastic. It was a red solo cup which I filled with the melted ice water and began chugging, letting the rest dribble down my neck. Water had never tasted this good before in my life, and I doubted it ever would again. I heard something strange and turned to look at Dorado. He had picked up the whole ice chest and was drinking the slushy ice water from it, drenching himself in the process as beer bottles tumbled out onto the porch. After a second, he noticed me glaring at him and put it down.

"What?" he asked defensively as he wiped his mouth.

"You could've let me get some more before you spilled it all over the floor."

"I'm bigger than you. I need more water. I'm like twice your size."

"You are not twice my size. Now let's get out of here already."

As we crept out onto the front porch, I saw why he wanted the guard's keys. Parked in front of the saloon where the horses would've been tethered in the old days were two dirt bikes. The guards probably used them to patrol the perimeter.

"You remember how to ride one?" he asked.

"You have no idea," I answered, remembering the other night with Sean.

We scanned the area again. The guards were still in the same spots as last time. Two played sentry at the entrance. If we were gonna take the bikes out on that road, we'd have to get rid of them or start a diversion.

An idea hit me as I looked over at the livestock corrals.

Dorado was looking at them too. "Are you thinking what I'm thinking?"

"Stampede. I'm offended you even have to ask," I said. He smiled deviously like he was proud of me and nodded.

I squinted at the corrals and could see they had a standard gate latch. It was the same as the ones I'd seen on Cade's little ranch, just a simple metal rod you had to pull out and the gate would come open easy.

Dorado was studying them too. "Looks simple enough. Think you can handle that?"

"Yeah. I'll just yank 'em out as I ride past 'em," I said.

"Good. Plus the bike will stir up all the horses more and get 'em going crazy."

I nodded. "Okay, what are you gonna do?"

"I'm gonna do a little demolition work on that house over there." He motioned to where two guards sat atop the second-story porch on a balcony. They looked like they were taking a nap.

Me and Dorado snuck off the porch, careful not to make it creak too much, and jogged as quiet as we could across the dirt road to the saloon. We each hopped on a bike. "Ready?" Dorado asked.

I nodded.

The town was dead silent until we kick-started the bikes. The horses and guards alike about jumped out of their skins. Me and Dorado bumped fists, grinned, and tore out on our separate ways. He would keep the guards occupied while I freed the animals.

The guards at the entrance of town stayed where they were, guns raised, to make sure we didn't try to take that road out. The two guards on the balcony had jumped to attention and were aiming their guns at Dorado. He revved his throttle and shifted into the next gear heading towards them. Tiny explosions of dirt erupted on either side of his bike as they began shooting at him. At the last second, Dorado hopped off the bike. As he tumbled into the dirt, the motorcycle launched itself like a missile up onto the porch, striking the main support beam. The old rotten post splintered and snapped in two, bringing down the balcony and the men on it to the ground below.

Now it was my turn.

I rode by the first gate and reached out to slip the metal rod out of the latch. I did it without a hitch and was pretty pleased with myself as the gate swung open and a group of startled horses came busting out of it. Next up were the bulls, I used the same maneuver. Only this time the rod didn't pull out as easy. My arm jerked and the bike disappeared from underneath me. With a hard thud I was on my ass in the dirt. Damn rod was stuck in there sideways. I got up and started yanking on it.

I had another problem, too. Now that it was clear me and Dorado were off of the bikes, the guards at the entrance were running towards us. A sharp clang reminded me of what I really needed to be focused on. One of the bulls was angrily butting his head against the gate, trying to get out. I think my adrenaline must have finally kicked into overdrive because on my next pull, I managed to yank the rod out. I darted away in the nick of time as the gate came swinging open and a pack of angry bulls burst out of it.

It was just like the running of the bulls in Spain as I ran for my life. It was funny because the guards that had been running towards me had turned around and were running the other way. I looked for something I could climb up on to get out of the stampede. The rock wall attached to the courtyard of the old church was my best bet. I darted to it as fast as I could and clambered onto it. I cussed myself again for losing the bike as I crept along the wall and all the bulls rushed by beneath me.

I didn't know how the heck I was going to get out of there, but just then I saw a nice brown mustang coming my way in the stampede. I guess I was right about taking the horses out of here after all. I ran along the top of the stone wall, trying to time it just right, and jumped just as the horse ran by.

I landed bareback with a hard thud and racked myself so hard my ancestors probably could've felt it. I held on tight to the horse's neck and tried to get my bearings. Right as I did, I could see the horse was about to go running right underneath an old Spanish archway leading into the church courtyard. I ducked my head just as we passed underneath, avoiding decapitation.

In the courtyard, me and the horse were greeted by three more of the guards. "Whoa!" I yelled. It was a command for the horse, not my reaction. The horse reared up in the air while I clung to its neck for dear life. I clicked my foot into its left side to get it to turn around.

Thank God it had been trained and wasn't a wild horse, because it did as it was told and got me out of there. "Thanks, man!" I hollered to the horse as we ran out of the courtyard and back onto the main street. "You got any interest in coming back to Fort Sumner with me?"

I heard more gunshots. The guards had followed us out of the courtyard and were gunning for me. I needed to get off of the horse for his sake and mine both before one of us got shot.

"Well, forget what I said for now, boy," I said to the horse.

Up ahead of me was a signpost hanging off of one of the old saloons. It was thin enough that I could grab it—all I had to do was reach high enough. I had seen Clint Eastwood do it in one of his Spaghetti Westerns to get off of his horse in a hurry, so hopefully it would work. "If you ever pass through Fort Sumner, look me up!" I said to the horse as I threw my hands up and grabbed the signpost. As the horse disappeared from between my legs, the momentum swung me upwards like I had hoped. When I had spun 180 degrees I let go of the signpost, shooting into the air. I landed on the saloon's roof. The old wood splintered and broke on impact and I crashed right through the roof. In the sea of dust and haze from the collapsed wood I could barely see a thing. Coughing and waving my hands in front of my face, I jumped when I felt someone's hand on my shoulder.

"Fancy meeting you here, little brother." It was Dorado.

Before I could say anything, he threw himself and me onto the floor. A cascade of bullets traced the wall behind us.

"Time to go!" he said, and I knew what he meant. We both army-crawled as fast as we could to the back of the saloon to the door. He laid down on his back and kicked it open, and we both crawled out and rolled down the slope behind the building.

Dorado and I ran out into the dry open desert. We didn't know where we were heading except for that it was away from Perdition. We could hear the guards shouting at us, but at least they weren't shooting anymore. I could also hear the familiar sound of a really noisy engine. It was dead center in the middle of a huge dirt cloud heading our way. I prayed it was what I thought it was, and right then Dorado's Camaro came swerving to a stop right in front of us from out of the dust.

"Get in the car, losers! We're gonna go steal a tombstone," Cade hurrahed from the passenger seat as he slipped off his sunglasses. But if Cade was in the passenger seat, who was driving?

Me and Dorado both looked past him at the driver in shock. Rosalita looked Dorado square in the eye, revved the engine, and said, "And you always said I couldn't drive your car. Well, look at me now, baboso!"

"You found us!" Dorado yelled.

"I found Perdition on a map. I'm not a total re-tard, Dorado!" Cade shouted.

I didn't waste any time crawling through the passenger side window into the backseat, where I found Dingus along for the ride, too.

Dorado was slipping inside past Cade. "And baby, I never said that you couldn't drive my car, I said—" The sound of gunshots ceased whatever argument they were about to get into and Rosalita peeled out while Dorado's legs were still sticking out the window. I looked behind us. The guards burst through the cloud of dust we kicked up, and I could see the main one ordering his men to go back and get their trucks.

Dorado crawled his way inside across Cade, sitting awkwardly on the center console in between Cade and Rosalita. He looked at Cade, "How did she—"

"Hey, she tracked me down, man. Insisted on coming along. You know how them Mexican women are! And speaking of which, where's the other one?" Cade looked at me and I knew he meant Sean.

"We got separated," I answered.

"What happened?" Dingus asked.

"Xander tracked us down to the train and we got split up. Becky ratted us out again, man. I'm surprised you even made it over here."

"You can't never trust women!" Then Cade sniffed the air and said to Dorado, "What the heck? Y'all hippies been smoking weed? I thought you were about to die and here you are just tokin' it up at some damn hippie commune!"

All of a sudden the back windshield shattered in an explosion of glass. A bullet whizzed past our heads. Rosalita screamed, and even though she had been driving pretty good, she decided now was a good time to slam on the brakes.

"Don't slow down!" Dorado yelled and then pounded his foot onto the accelerator. "Let me drive," he said as he and Rosalita switched seats, and Cade slithered into the back with us.

Cautiously we peered over the backseat and could see two of the trucks from Perdition following us. One of the guards had a long-range rifle he was using to shoot at us. The shots wouldn't come as frequently, but they would be more accurate.

"Oh man, I can feel a 'nam flashback coming. Brace yourselves!" Cade yelled.

Dingus slapped him across the face. "Calm down, Nancy!" he said determinedly, eyes narrowing as Cade recoiled in shock. "Dingus always gots a plan!" He lifted his pant leg, revealing a stick of dynamite taped to his shin.

Cade shook his head in disbelief. "Dang it, Dingus! You mean you been packin' that thing this whole time?"

"Well, Sean had a whole bunch of it just lying around. I couldn't help myself."

"Man, I can't believe we survived this long, you psychotic little kleptomaniac!" Cade yelled.

"Just give me a lighter, funny man," Dingus said.

"Oh, I'll be the one to throw that, you little shit!" Cade retorted.

Those idiots couldn't quit squabbling for nothing, so I grabbed it. "No, I'll throw it." I took out my knife and shortened the wick so it would explode quicker. I took the lighter from Cade's hands, lit the fuse, and then threw the stick. It detonated in the dirt before they even knew what hit them, and they drove right into the hole created by the explosion. That truck was out of commission. The other one swerved around it and cautiously kept following us, but kept their distance.

"You got any more of that?" Cade asked.

"Does the Pope go to Fish Fridays at the Vatican branch of Long John Silvers?" Dingus lifted up his other pant leg, which had another stick taped to his leg. This time he took the lighter from me and lit it as Cade shouted, "Dang it, it was my turn, Dingus!"

Dingus stuck his torso out the window and waited until just the right moment and threw the hissing stick straight at them, but these guys were a little wiser and swerved out of the way. The stick detonated before it ever hit the ground. The explosion blew out their passenger side window, but it didn't stop them. It had still done some good because they seemed wary of getting too close to us. That didn't stop them from shooting, though.

We kept our heads down, never knowing when the occasional bullet was going to whiz past. A pang of dirt shot up into the air. They were aiming low now, probably trying to shoot out our tires. I poked my head up above the seat. Eventually they would hit us. I was sure of it. They were starting to get closer now, probably because they had figured we didn't have any more dynamite. The man leaning out the side window with his rifle was taking aim.

"Okay, this time is definitely my turn!" Cade shouted and grabbed what he thought was another stick of dynamite. It was the cylinder holding the key.

He was dumb enough to try and light it while I kept trying to tell him it wasn't what he thought it was.

"Well, hell," he said, stuck his torso out the window and threw it as hard as he possibly could at the driver. I couldn't believe it, but it sailed through the truck's front windshield and hit the driver square in the head! As the driver went unconscious, the front wheel swerved into a pothole. The truck bounced from the impact, throwing them off course big time. The guy hanging out the window dropped his rifle and they crashed into the side of the road.

"Hah! It was a dud, and I still got 'em!" Cade yelled jubilantly.

"It wasn't a dud, you idiot, that was the key!" I yelled back.

"It didn't look like the key!"

"They put it in a special container to keep it safe!"

Hearing this, Dorado slammed his foot onto the brake. My head, along with Cade and Dingus's, immediately hit the seats in front of us as we skidded to a stop. "Somebody go out and get it back," Dorado ordered.

The guy who had been using the gun was passed out cold, hanging outside the window. The driver stumbled out his door and collapsed into the dirt. We wouldn't have to worry about them.

Dingus hopped out the door, ran over to the truck and scavenged around until he found the key. As he started running back to our car, almost as an afterthought, he turned around, ran back, and kicked the driver in the groin. He doubled up and wailed in pain as Dingus ran back to the Camaro.

As soon as Dingus was safe inside, Dorado revved the engine and peeled out, leaving a dust storm in our wake. "Alright, let's get down to business and head for Sumner!" he yelled.

Soon our tires met the highway and we were off of the back roads where we could really burn rubber. After a few minutes and several miles, I heard police sirens and I knew they were for us. The men in Perdition might've radioed Xander that we had gotten away. But then again, it could've just been because we were going 110mph. All I knew was that Dorado's skills as a race car driver were about to be put to good use.

XIII.
EAT MY DUST

We were about midway to Fort Sumner on the highway when we saw the first of the cop cars heading our way. About half of them were State Police and the other half looked like Sheriff's vehicles from Fort Sumner.

I had been with Dorado out on the highway plenty of times, and once even during a test run on the racetrack, but nothing compared to the drive we were having now, and it would only get better from here.

Once Dorado saw the police cars headed his way, he immediately cussed and swerved around changing direction. Me, Cade, and Dingus all slammed into each other.

"Are you kidding me? I was doing a better job than that!" Rosalita yelled.

The State Police were gaining on us as motorists pulled onto the side of the road to let them by.

I slammed into Cade again. Dorado was dodging in and out of traffic now to pass other cars.

"I think it's about time we get off the interstate, boys!" he yelled. It was his way of warning us to brace ourselves as he turned off U.S. Route 84 and onto an unpaved dirt road.

"What are you doing now?" Rosalita shouted.

"They can't catch us if they can't see us," Dorado said as we hit the dusty dirt road.

It was true. I could hear the sirens, but I couldn't see the cars. All I could see was the billowing trail of dirt we left behind us and the faint glimmer of their lights. They really were eating our dust. I just hoped we didn't hit any cactus. Dorado took us out due east, still blazing a trail of thick dirt in our wake. That was all the cops would be able to follow. I squinted. Through the dust, I could see their strobe lights getting closer. I turned back around to the front. Off of the road in the distance I could see an arroyo. "Hey, man, we're headed straight for an arroyo!"

"I know," Dorado replied calmly.

"Are you crazy?" Rosalita interjected.

"We're gonna get rid of some of our company."

"Look, man, I like Burt Reynolds movies as much as the next guy, but you can't jump that! That's movie magic!" Cade yelled in fear.

"Who said anything about jumping it?" Dorado swerved sharply at the last second, drifting sideways along the arroyo's edge. The police wouldn't be able to see the arroyo from their distance and through all of this dust. I saw one of the cars cut through the dirt cloud, just missing our bumper to go sailing into the arroyo. I couldn't see it, but I heard the crash, followed by a few more. It wasn't a deep arroyo. It wouldn't kill anybody, just wreck their cars.

We headed the opposite direction back to the road, and I could see the remaining patrol cars slamming on their breaks to avoid the arroyo. Some of them were trailing far enough behind that they saw us emerge from our cloud of dust and started following us back towards the road. The only problem was there wasn't as much flat land to traverse, and if there was, it was behind us where the other cops were.

There was a tiny passage to drive through in between two big dirt dunes, but in an instant, one of the State Police cars had swerved to a stop there, blocking our way.

Dorado dodged him and took the slope at full force. We flew up it and sailed through the air for about three seconds. I felt butterflies in my stomach and then we slammed down on the ground.

"Easy on the suspension, Dorado!" Cade yelled like he was more worried about the car than us getting away with our lives.

Dorado tore through the desert and headed back for the main road. When I looked behind us, I could see there were only four police cars in pursuit now. With a hard thud, we'd driven back onto U.S. Route 84. We were back on hard pavement—and back in traffic. Even through all the honking horns, sirens, and screams, I swore I could hear something else.

It sounded a lot like Nana squawking at us. "Hey!" the voice kept yelling. "Don't pretend like you can't hear me!"

"What the hell?" Dorado said, looking down at something I couldn't see. "Did you install a CB radio in this thing?"

"Why, yes, Dorado, you're welcome. It's only the newest thing in technology!" Cade retorted.

"Nana?" Dorado picked up the radio handle reluctantly.

"Who the hell else would it be?" she said. "Is Cade there with you?"

Cade took the handle. "Dammit, Nana, we're too busy to talk right now!"

"Cade, I still need you to fix that leak in my roof. I been on you about it for the last three weeks!"

"Well, it ain't gonna rain anytime soon, old woman!" he yelled into the CB.

"Well, you're going to hear about it every day until you fix it!" she yelled back.

"Go right ahead. You ain't gonna live forever, and soon I won't have to worry with you!"

"Would you two quit distracting Dorado. He's going 110 miles an hour!" Rosalita shouted.

"And after toking marijuana at that," Dingus added.

Just then I heard another voice over the CB and my blood went cold. It was Aunt Patty. "They're going 110 miles an hour on marijuana? Mother, give me that!" she shrieked.

Dorado and I both shot each other horrified looks. Cade yelled into the receiver, "Yes, woman, now let us alone!"

Dorado snatched it from his hands. "Hey, Aunt Patty, what you heard was we're 110 miles from Tia Juana. Geez, calm down." Dang, my brother was a fast thinker.

"What, you took Pancho to Mexico?! I thought you said you were going to Capitan?"

"Uh, change of plans. Look, Aunt Patty, I really need to go."

Because Dorado had slowed down being distracted by Aunt Patty, one of the police cars was right behind us and the officer began yelling at us over a bullhorn. "Pull over now!"

"And what is all that noise? Who's yelling at you?" she asked.

Dorado needed to concentrate on his driving, so I swiped the CB. "Hey, Aunt Patty, we're uh…at a bullfight in Mexico. It's super cool!"

"A bullfight?! I thought you were in the car driving. How are you at a bullfight and in the car?"

"Uh, it's like a drive-in colosseum. It's a new thing..." I looked at Cade for help in elaborating. He just shrugged.

Dorado turned around and shouted, "They call it driving with the bulls. Over and out, Aunt Patty!"

Soon we heard a semi's horn honking. Dorado turned back around and we all screamed as he swerved back into the right lane, narrowly avoiding colliding with it.

Even Cade looked a little scared that time. I think Dingus had gotten so excited that he'd momentarily passed out. "Alright, that's not going to happen again," Dorado said to himself. He gunned it harder, trying to put more and more distance between us and the State Police.

There was a problem, though. We were stuck behind two semis, and up ahead there was a new State Police car coming from the other direction. There was nowhere to go because there was no way to pass both semis in time. Dorado upped the throttle.

"No, you're not!" Rosalita said, sensing what he was thinking about doing. "No, you are not!"

"I'm not...I'm not," Dorado repeated and then pulled into the left lane to pass, romping on it. "Oh yes I am!" he yelled. We sped past the first semi and Dorado turned the wheel sharply, putting us in a sick drift right between the two giant trucks. One second we were alongside the truck, the next we were nose to nose with it moving sideways, and then it was beside us again, heading the other way as we spun into the dirt again. Dingus screamed the entire time, and I wasn't sure if it was from fright or excitement.

I looked behind us as Dorado got back onto the main road again in the opposite direction. The remaining police cars had all crashed into each other, trying to turn around and get their bearings on the busy highway!

"How's it looking, Pancho?" he asked from up front.

"Those first four won't be catching up to us anytime soon, but the new guy's making tracks!" I yelled back.

The cop that had been coming from the opposite direction when we drifted in between the two trucks had never had to turn around like the other ones. He was right behind us, and now we could hear his siren blazing.

Before I knew it, he was right beside us. He didn't motion for us to pull over though, he rammed into us. Me and Dingus both flew out of our seats and hit our heads on the roof. But something else was happening. We were spinning. His vehicle had become entangled with ours and we were twirling like a boomerang across the busy highway.

I looked out the window. It looked the same as if we were on a merry-go-round. It made me feel sick, that's for sure.

I heard another loud horn honk, and the cop was gone. His car had gotten hit by another semi and had been swept away into the traffic. We all just sat there in silence, trying to catch our breath as the Camaro came skidding to a halt. It was over. They were all gone. We had demolished eight police cars by my count.

The honking of further traffic caught our attention, and realizing that we were still in the middle of a busy road, we took off. Dorado was leaning his head out the window and looking at the damage done to the car.

Cade took off his hat and hit Dorado over the head with it. "After all the work I put into this thing, Dorado!"

***

We rode most of the rest of the way in silence, each of us collecting our nerves. And even though it had been a terrifying experience, there was one good thing about it. Pretty much all the cops from Sumner were now stranded out on the highway. Aside from Xander and a few others, we'd have the run of the whole town—at least I hoped. The trick now would just be getting the tombstone and avoiding Xander before they all managed to get back or call reinforcements.

When we rolled into Sumner, it looked like a whole 'nother town than it usually did. A banner hung from the middle of Sumner Avenue proclaiming "Billy the Kid Tombstone Race Today." As to be expected, it was buzzing with tourists, too. Some of the people were dressed up in costumes, and I suddenly remembered today was Halloween. I reckon that's why they picked Sunday instead of Saturday for the event, so they could say they had the Tombstone Race on Halloween.

There was hardly any place to park, either. Cars lined Sumner Avenue and the whole parking lot of Pat Garrett High was a sea of New Mexico and Texas license plates.

"What I want to know is, how do y'all idjiots plan to steal the tombstone in the middle of a dad-goned race built around exactly what you're trying to steal?" Cade said with his usual lack of cadence as we surveyed the scene before us.

"Well, they say the best place to hide is right out in plain sight," Dorado said.

"Besides, Cade, we made it this far. What else could go wrong?" Dingus mocked his older brother.

About then the Camaro sputtered, and smoke started coming from under the hood.

"Daaaaaad gone it, Dingus!" Cade yelled and whacked Dingus with his hat. "You just had to say it!"

Dorado sighed. "Okay, so now we walk."

And walk we did. Right after we pulled over, Rosalita dipped into a little store to buy us all whatever cheap Halloween masks she could to help us hide our faces. That was one good thing about today being Halloween, at least. She came out with what looked like a couple of cowboy hats, two masks that only covered your eyes, and a black cape for me and Dorado.

"And here I was thinking I wouldn't dress up this year," I muttered as she handed me the black hat, mask, and cape while Dorado got the white hat and mask.

Cade looked us both over as we put our masks on. "Great, Pancho's Zorro and Dorado's the Lone Ranger. Who am I supposed to be, Tonto?"

"Sorry baboso, they were all out of feathers," Rosalita said. "They did have these, though. Nobody wanted them." She held out two Jimmy Carter masks for him and Dingus.

"Aw hell, if I ain't voting for him, I sure ain't wearing his face," Cade said, disgusted.

Dorado grabbed the masks from Rosie. "It doesn't matter," he said, shoving them both into Cade's chest. "Besides, we have bigger problems to solve, starting with where is the tombstone?"

That was a good question. It reminded me of studying for a test at the last minute, only this time my life depended on me passing said test. I looked around the town, racking my brain for where it would be. All I knew was that everybody was heading for the football field behind Pat Garret High to watch the race. "Maybe it's over there? I mean, like maybe they've got it on display or something?"

"That's as good a guess as anything. Let's go find out," Dorado said and walked towards the parking lot, which looked like a huge college tailgate party. There were people with barbeques and grills set up, tent vendors selling crappy little Billy the Kid trinkets—just about everything you could imagine. Towards the entrance to the field was a big podium. The high school band was playing in front of it for a while until the mayor went up and started talking.

I didn't really listen to him and was straining to see what was out on the field itself. Through the chain-link fence that surrounded it, I could make out what looked like a little obstacle course set up. It had tires on the ground for those footwork drills that football players did, plus hurdles. Some were big and some were small. If I understood it right, you were supposed to throw your tombstone over the big hurdles, jump the hurdle, pick the tombstone up, run to the next one, and so on.

I looked around for the players. So far a bunch of guys were just stretching their legs and putting on their numbers for the race. There was no dress code or anything like that. Some guys were in their football leggings, a few just wore gym shorts without a shirt, and some were even dressed up for Halloween just to be funny. More than a few had come as Billy the Kid. I could see some of the duplicate tombstones lying around, too. They weren't as elaborate as the fake one Xander had placed at the grave. They were mostly in the shape of Billy's tombstone but without any of the engraving.

Suddenly I heard the mayor say the words "Sheriff Xander Garrett" and nearly jumped out of my skin. People started applauding as Xander approached the podium.

"Thank you, thank you," Xander shouted over the applause as he stepped on stage. Once they quieted down, he began again. "For nearly a hundred years, the Kid has been the source of much controversy and so has his gravesite. After being stolen 26 years ago, we were all tickled pink when the tombstone came back to us and we could put it back where it rightfully belongs." People clapped and cheered. "Only there's something that you don't know. I must now confess, we haven't been completely honest with you. The tombstone at Billy the Kid's grave is a duplicate." There was a hushed silence. "And the real one is right here!" Two men unveiled a tarp that had the real tombstone underneath it. "The mayor and I felt it best under the circumstances to put a fake there, and boy was it a good idea considering what happened last week." The crowd laughed. Xander walked over and patted his hand on it. "Figured I'd keep a close eye on it...all things considered." The crowd erupted in laughter and applause again.

"We should all be very honored that this historic tombstone is soon to see new life as an exhibit in the Museum of New Mexico History in Santa Fe where it can be safely preserved for many generations to come." The crowd booed.

"And that's why," he started to say, but the crowd still hadn't quieted down enough. "And that's why today we're giving it a grand send-off with the Tombstone Race. And if you want to see the real thing for yourself one more time, you can. At the end of the race tonight, we'll bid the tombstone farewell one more time in a special ceremony. But until then, we're going to keep it locked up safe and sound right across the street… in the jail."

While the crowd laughed at that last remark, my heart sank. I looked at Dorado. His face had turned white as a sheet.

Xander paused and then said, "All things considered, we figured if the Kid wasn't alive to be locked up here, we could at least lock up the tombstone. Just don't nobody try to steal it." He paused for the laughter this time while two men picked it up and carted it away.

"Alright, looks like we got ourselves a race to start," Xander said, and the crowd started applauding again. "First up, senior boys division. Ages—"

Dorado cussed and kicked the dirt.

"Well that's that, 'rado," Cade said, pulling his Jimmy Carter mask off. "Might as well kiss your other pinky finger goodbye and call it a day." He said it as though that were that, and it was time to go home.

Dorado snapped and slammed Cade up against the wall of a porta-potty. "They're not gonna cut another finger off. They're gonna kill me, you idiot. And after they're done with me, they might move on to the whole family. Is that what you want?"

"Stop making a scene!" Rosalita hissed.

Dorado eased off.

"It's still your fault," Cade pointed a finger in Dorado's face.

"We break the tombstone outta jail," I blurted out.

Everyone looked at me like I was nuts.

"Well, what else are we gonna do? And besides, I robbed a bank earlier this week."

"It's a police station, Pancho," Dorado said. He turned around and started walking back to the Camaro, which had finally quit smoking.

"I know," I said, following him, "but think about it. Xander is overseeing the race. A lot of the cops are probably still stranded out on the highway. There's probably hardly anybody in the station right now."

Dorado turned around and looked at me. He knew I was right. "Okay, assuming all that is true, we still don't have a getaway car or a gun. Both those things are very important when it comes to a jailbreak."

"We'll get some," I said.

"From who?" Rosalita asked.

"Can you call Missy?" I asked Cade.

"No, I done sent her away to her sister's till all this mess cools off."

"Why don't y'all just call Aunt Patricia?" Dingus asked.

"You really think Aunt Patty is gonna bring us guns and a getaway car to go rob a jail?" Dorado said. Then he looked at Rosie. "Do you think one of your brothers could—"

"My brothers hate you."

"This is true."

"Darn it. I know who we can call. But it's gonna cost me," Cade said as though he was resigning himself to some horrible fate.

"Who?" me and Dorado both asked.

He just gave us a funny look and it dawned on us who he meant.

"I can't believe I'm doing this," he muttered to himself as he leaned in through the Camaro window and grabbed the CB. "Nana, do you copy?"

XIV.
THE GREAT TOMBSTONE ROBBERY

"That's him. That's your uncle Pancho. Or maybe it's Hondo." Nana was looking at the photograph and shaking her head in disbelief. "Aw hell, even I couldn't tell 'em apart." She shook her head some more and leaned back on Cade's truck which she had driven over.

"I'm sorry, Nana. We weren't gonna tell you until we knew for sure. Ya know, so we didn't get your hopes up or anything," Dorado said.

With everything going on, we figured we finally had to tell Nana the truth. "Well, you boys tell me what needs to be done, and I'll do it," she said. "If there's a chance one of my boys is still alive, I'd do anything."

"You've done it, Nana. You brought us a getaway car and a shotgun—even if it is only loaded with birdshot," Dorado said.

Nana got a funny look on her face. "Y'all aren't getting rid of me that easy." She picked up the shotgun, cocked it, and flashed a funny kind of grin. "And besides, who'd shoot a helpless, pitiful old woman?"

***

"Everybody on the floor now! Or my nana'll shoot your ass!" Cade yelled while Nana aimed her birdshot-filled shotgun at what looked to be the only real cop in the station. The only other person there was a grey-haired lady who answered the phone.

"Cade, I can't see shit in this thing," Nana mumbled from behind Dingus's Jimmy Carter mask that he'd given her to hide her face.

"Don't use my name! Don't use my monkey-fluffing name, woman!" he yelled back from under his own mask.

While me, Cade, and Nana got the keys to the jail cell, Dorado would be waiting out back with Dingus and Rosie to drive us out of there. I walked over to the guard lying on his stomach on the floor.

"That's right, stay real still," Cade said as Nana kept the shotgun on him. "Nana just got outta the slammer, and she ain't goin' back!"

"What the hell is this?" the poor man muttered as he eyed Cade and my grandma.

"The keys to the cell—the one with the tombstone. Hand 'em over," I said.

"I'm just a temp service aid. I'm not even a real cop yet. Please don't hurt me," he said as he handed them over. They jingled in his trembling hands as I took them. "I don't even like guns. I don't know why I took this job!"

"Harold, you're embarrassing us!" the older woman hissed at him. "Man up for once in your life!"

Harold burst into tears. "I'm sorry, mother!" Something told me he wasn't a part of the Santa Fe Ring.

"Keep your eye on them for a minute, I'll holler when we can split," I yelled as I ran to the back. Funny thing was, I knew where I was going. Since my real dad was sheriff a long time ago, Xander had given me and Dorado a tour when we were kids. Funny how life turns out. Even though he'd always made me uneasy, I never imagined that Xander would be my mortal enemy one day.

I got to the cells in back in no time. There was nobody in them, but just like Xander said, the tombstone was propped up on a bench inside one of the cells.

My hands were shaking as I unlocked the door. As I walked inside the cell, I studied the tombstone, worried what if it turned out to be another replica. It looked just like the one I saw in the cemetery that night. It had the same triangle-shaped top and inscription, only older. I ran my hands across the weathered granite. It was the real deal this time, I knew it. I picked it up. It was too light to be solid granite, so there was definitely a hidden chamber inside. Just as a sense of relief started to wash over me, I heard a voice call my name that cut like a knife. It was Becky.

I turned around. She was standing outside the cell, and for a split second I worried maybe she'd slam the door and lock me in. "Pancho, thank God you're okay. My dad's had me locked up in his office ever since I got back, and then I heard yelling so I came back here to hide—"

"You can cut the act, Becky," I said, shaking my head.

A confused look etched itself across her face. "I don't understand."

"Fool me once, shame on you. Fool me twice, you know the rest." I walked outside the cell.

"Not that again, Pancho—"

I cut her off. "First Mescalero, then the train. I was an idiot to ever think you'd choose me over your dad. But then again, I don't have a real dad, so what do I know?"

I was about to say something else when someone started pounding on the back door.

"Pancho, open up!" It was Rosalita. Then I heard Dorado yell, "We've got trouble!"

I dashed over to the door, sat the tombstone down, and opened it up. They both tumbled inside out of breath, and Dorado said, "I just saw Xander coming and—"

He stopped when he saw Becky.

"And I think you know why," I said and gave her a dirty look.

"Pancho, I swear..." she looked like she was going to cry, and for a second I felt like I was, too.

The sound of a gunshot snapped me back to my senses, and Cade came running around the corner with Nana slung over his shoulder.

"That little fella in the office knows how to use a gun after all!" Cade yelled and then ran right past us and for the door to get in the truck.

"There's our cue to leave!" Dorado dashed to pick up the tombstone while I looked back at Becky again, not sure what to do.

"Dorado, Pancho, hurry!" Rosalita cried from the doorway.

"Come on, let's go!" Dorado shouted with the tombstone in his arms. He was standing by the door waiting for me and here I was frozen in front of Becky. Neither one of us knew what to say. Suddenly I heard Xander shouting at somebody to stop.

"Oh shit!" Dorado cussed. I could hear Cade's truck peeling out.

"They left without us! That baboso!" Rosalita cried.

It seemed like everything was happening in slow motion. Xander was about to come in through the back, and now the guy who said he was only a service aid was running our way with a gun pointed at us from the front.

I don't know why she did it. Maybe she felt guilty. Maybe she had a change of heart. But at the last second, Becky tripped him, and the man flopped onto the floor belly first.

"Come on!" Dorado yelled as he hopped over him with the tombstone, followed by Rosalita.

I couldn't hesitate any longer. I ran and jumped over the guy while he was still struggling to get up. I turned to look back at Becky one more time. I should have thanked her, but instead I said, "This doesn't change anything." I felt a pang of guilt and then I bolted, following Dorado and Rosie out the front and into the bright sunlight.

"Where are we going?" I shouted to my brother as he ran out into the street.

"Where does it look like?" he yelled back as a car honked at him. He was running towards the football field where the race was going on.

"Are you crazy?" Rosie yelled as we followed him.

"Do you have a better idea?" he asked. We had made it to the parking lot outside the field now, where all the tailgaters were. "Besides, we'll blend right in."

As we stopped to catch our breath, I looked behind us and could see Xander and a couple other guys burst out of the police station. But from the way they were looking to the left and the right, I could tell that they hadn't seen us yet.

Dorado noticed too. "See, we're safe," he panted, out of breath.

"What now?" I asked. "We can't just stay here."

"I'll walk around the parking lot and see if I can spot Cade's truck anywhere. With any luck, that stupid baboso will circle back for us," Rosalita said and darted off into the crowd.

Just when I was starting to calm down, I heard a female voice ask, "Is that the real tombstone?" I turned to see a middle-aged woman in glasses approaching us, gazing at the tombstone in awe.

"Uh, no. It's a duplicate," I lied real quick, shaking my head.

"It doesn't look like the duplicates they made for the race," she said, running her fingers over it.

Before I could say anything, the lady's husband walked up and said, "Wow, that's the real tombstone! Where'd you get it?"

I looked around nervously. People were starting to notice. I shot Dorado a worried look.

"Nope, just a duplicate," Dorado practically shouted as he tried to back away from the couple. People were still staring at us, so he added, "We're actually selling these at a tent on the other side of the parking lot. Come see us later, we're called… Tony's Tombstones."

"No, they're not!" a familiar voice boomed over the rest of the crowd. Dread seeped into my every pore as I turned around to confirm my fear. There was Coach McPherson dressed as a Viking and gnawing on the biggest turkey leg I had ever seen. My eyes met his, and even with my mask on, I could tell he recognized me. I could also tell he was still sore about the other day. He pointed to us with the turkey leg and shouted, "It's the Dumez brothers and they're at it again! And this time they're stealing the real tombstone!"

"Run," Dorado said simply, and we did. We bolted towards the entrance of the field with Coach and his band of merry followers in hot pursuit.

"Get back here!" McPherson yelled, while others in the angry mob shouted, "Those kids, they've got the real tombstone!"

I looked behind us as we ran onto the field just in time to see Coach McPherson launch the massive turkey leg right at the back of my brother's head.

"Dorado!" I cried as the huge, dismembered piece of meat flew through the air. I was trying to warn him, but I just made things worse, because the second I yelled his name, he instinctively turned to look behind him. Instead of hitting him across the back of the head, the flying mass of meat socked him right across the jaw and he tumbled to the ground. The tombstone sailed from his grasp and skidded through the grass. It landed right at the feet of a hyped-up-looking high school athlete.

"It's okay, bro, I got you!" He gave us a thumbs-up, snatched up the tombstone, and took off into the obstacle course. I looked around the field and suddenly realized this wasn't an individual competition at the moment, but a team relay.

"He thinks we're part of the relay race!" I turned and shouted to Dorado, who was still on the ground.

"Pancho, you're faster than me, go!" Dorado shouted and pointed towards the field. He didn't have to tell me twice, though. I darted onto the field after the guy right away. The first obstacle was the tire course, which I breezed through pretty quick. Once my feet cleared the last of the tires, I looked ahead and could see the next challenge was one of the big hurdles. The athlete who had taken off with the tombstone had already cleared his. I ran at the hurdle as quick as I could. I didn't know whether to feel really cool or really stupid as I sailed over it with my cape billowing in the wind.

Once I landed, I ran as hard as I could at the guy. I gained on him pretty quick, which wasn't hard to do since the tombstone was slowing him down a little. I couldn't just ask him to hand it over, I'd have to tackle him. Now, I hadn't played football for school ever, but I had been in plenty of pickup games in the park with Missile and Dingus, so I knew what to do. I stiffened my shoulder and kept my head down as I rammed into him. It took him completely off guard and he crashed into the grass, the tombstone tearing up little pieces of the turf as it skidded into the earth.

"What the hell?" he muttered as I plucked up the tombstone.

"Sorry," I mumbled and took off.

Some guys on the sidelines, who I guess were his teammates, noticed. "Hey, get him!" they shouted.

The announcer noticed too. "Wow, it looks like a member from a rival team is trying to steal the tombstone!" he said over the P.A. system.

Before I knew it, several guys from Pat Garrett High's football team were chasing me down again and I was hit with a bizarre sense of déjà vu. The last time this happened, I was running across the field in my underwear holding a goat named Billy the Kid, and now I was holding the tombstone of the real deal while dressed as Zorro. Mendez was right. History really did repeat itself.

Just as the gigantic football players were closing in on me, I heard my brother cry out my name. Dorado had caught up to me and was running alongside me just a few feet away, clapping his hands together the same way he would signal me to throw him a football. I pushed the tombstone with all my might, launching it at him. He caught it and continued his drive up the field. It worked, and the guys that had been chasing me shifted their attention to him. Another high school football player ran at Dorado from the opposite direction to tackle him, but Dorado put his head down and plowed right through him with the tombstone. The crowd went wild.

"Looks like the relay just became a game of tombstone football! Whataya think, Ken, should that be an official event at next year's race?" the announcer asked his co-host, clearly amused.

Pretty soon, an even bigger guy was gaining on Dorado, one that would knock him over for sure this time. Now it was my turn to catch the tombstone. Dorado locked eyes with me. There were two problems, though—big problems. The guy was about to pounce on Dorado just as he threw it, and I was about to run smack dab into another one of those hurdles. There was no way to go around it, either. Just as the guy slammed into my brother, Dorado hurled the tombstone into the air, the impact giving it extra momentum. Instead of coming at me, it was about to go sailing right over me and the hurdle both. There was nothing I could do but jump sideways over the hurdle. As I flew through the air, I wrapped my arms around the stone block tight, clutching it to my chest. A second later, I hit the ground and rolled through the grass best that I could to lessen the impact but it still hurt like hell.

As I rolled over onto my side struggling to breathe, I could see Coach McPherson and the football players coming at me. But, to my utter shock, Coach threw back his massive arms at the last second, bringing him and his players to a stop right in front of me. Then, in the nicest voice I'd ever heard him use in front of me, Coach said, "Dumez, will you come play football for me next year?"

I was too dumbfounded to respond. Dorado skidded up next to me. He scooped up the tombstone in one arm and lifted me up with the other. "He sure will, Coach. On one condition."

"Name your terms."

"Help us get away from him." Dorado pointed behind McPherson and the football players and I could see Xander stepping onto the field.

McPherson looked behind him and paused for a moment. Then, finally, he said, "Boys, let's go thank the sheriff for putting this here race together. Come on now!"

As his players ran towards Xander, McPherson turned to me one more time. "And you, I expect to see you first thing this summer for two-a-days."

"I did not expect that to happen," I muttered to Dorado as he dragged me through back gate and out of the field.

"Well, miracles do happen," he said, then added, "Speaking of which."

I heard a funny-sounding honk, and when I looked in the noise's direction, Rosalita rolled up on a motorcycle. At least that's what I thought it was until I realized it was a moped.

"I never found your bastard cousin, but I did manage to get this," she said as she came to a stop.

"A moped?" Dorado said with sheer horror as he handed me the tombstone.

"Hey, I had to show a twelve-year-old my chi-chis to get this thing!" she hissed as she hopped off. "Anyways, you idiots better get out of here."

Rosalita pecked Dorado on the cheek as he got on the bike. I hopped on behind him, locking the tombstone firmly between his back and my stomach. "Thanks," I said to Rosie.

"You take care of him, Pancho Dumez!" she said and I realized she really did care about my brother, even if she got pretty extreme about it.

"I will," I said.

"Hi Ho Silver, you babosos!" she shouted, making fun of the fact that Dorado was still dressed as the Lone Ranger and riding a moped. She was still laughing as Dorado and I peeled out—or peeled out the best one could on a moped.

He grinned at her and yelled, "Hey, we'll do something special later, I swear this time!"

"Where have I heard that before?" she shouted back as we sped away.

The damn thing was so slow I shouted, "Geez, man, we would've been better off walking!"

We pulled onto Sumner Avenue, and I managed to spot Cade's truck circling the block. "Cade! Three o'clock!" I shouted and Dorado looked to his right. He gunned it a little harder to try and catch up with him.

"Thanks for leaving us earlier, you bastard!" Dorado yelled as we pulled up alongside him.

"I thought Nana here got shot. I was trying to save her life!" he yelled back.

"The hell you did, you ninny-picker!" I heard Nana yell back and knew she was fine.

"What the hell are you doing on that?" Dingus yelled from the pickup bed.

"We had to improvise! Pancho, hand Dingus the tombstone!" Dorado yelled.

I handed the tombstone off to Dingus in the back of the truck bed and did my best not to fall off the bike as I did.

"Now hurry up and get in!" Cade yelled.

"It's better if we split up. They haven't spotted you yet," Dorado said.

"Yeah, but you can't outrun them on that!" Cade shouted back.

"No, but me and Pancho can lose them in some tight spots on this thing! Head for that old gas station north of Lake Sumner, and we'll meet you!"

"Okay!" he shouted back, and Dorado immediately veered off to the left, taking us off Sumner Avenue. It wasn't long before I could hear a police siren again. When I looked behind us, I could see a motorcycle cop way off in the distance, but it wouldn't take long for him to catch up. I tapped Dorado on the shoulder. "Guess the reinforcements made it back to Sumner," I said.

"Time to take a detour! Hold on!" he shouted and banked hard to the right, taking us towards a little outside park. "Feel like going to a party?"

"What?" I yelled as we sped off the pavement and onto the grassy field of the park. We were headed in the direction of a big tree and a small pond where some people were having a little kid's Halloween party from what I could tell. A little boy dressed as the devil was whacking away at a skeleton piñata under the tree. All I could hear was the whine of the engine, mariachi music, and screaming children as we raced through the park. I looked behind us and saw the motorcycle cop.

"He's still following us!" I shouted.

Dorado drove us right under the tree close to the piñata as several of the adults screamed. We just barely missed getting hit by the little devil boy's baseball bat, oblivious to our presence thanks to his blindfold. As the cop came in close behind us, the boy's mother screamed and grabbed him just as he swung. The baseball bat went flying from his hands and sailed right into the cop's spokes. The stuck wheel threw him violently from the bike and into the pond!

Me and Dorado both laughed all the way back onto the main road. Only it didn't last long. I could hear another car racing up the road behind us. It wasn't a squad car, but I could tell it was after us. I had a strange feeling of finality in that moment. The sun was setting off in the distance, blazing orange and red, and the car would be on us any second. It was over, plain and simple.

And then I heard it: the sound of a train whistle on the tracks ahead. I didn't know whether it was the sound of our salvation or our impending doom, but I knew what Dorado would be thinking. The scream of the poor moped engine confirmed it. He was gonna try and beat the oncoming train, creating a barrier between us and the car—a barrier that could very likely kill us.

I looked ahead at the long train that was swiftly approaching. All we could do was scream as Dorado gunned the engine over the train tracks to get across just seconds before the train did. The rush of the train's momentum knocked us both off the bike and it slid into the gravel.

We both just lay there, catching our breath as the huge train raced by. But there was no time to rest. Xander and his people would be on the other side of the train once it finished passing. "Come on," Dorado said as he got up.

He hopped back on the moped and tried to get it restarted, but it wasn't having it. It gave us all it had to get us across the tracks in time, and it was finished. "What now?" I asked.

He let the bike fall over and grabbed me. "We run! Let's follow the train for as long as we can. Use it for cover!"

It was going too fast to jump onto, so we ran alongside it for cover like he said. I realized it was a bad idea by the time it had outpaced us along the overpass that goes over U.S. 84.

Immediately once the train had crossed the bridge, a black bronco pulled up onto the tracks blocking our exit from the pass. We turned to run the other way, but behind us two more cars parked in a V blocking our way off the overpass. We were trapped.

"Hands up!" we heard several of the men shouting as they got out of their cars, guns pointed at us yet again. I was getting way too used to this. But there was nowhere to run, so we put up our hands. Mendez and several other men had stepped out of the Bronco. Mendez looked at us disdainfully, "I'm getting pretty tired of you two meddling in my affairs."

"Careful, professor, you're starting to sound a lot like a Scooby-Doo villain," Dorado said.

"Aw, don't be so hard on 'em," I heard Xander say from behind us. We turned around to face him. "These boys did us a favor by stealing the tombstone. Now we know who we can blame for it. Granted, it'll be a little embarrassing that a 14-year-old kid dressed as Zorro managed to escape Fort Sumner's finest, but I'll probably be able to retire soon anyhow." Xander sauntered over closer and seemed rather pleased with himself. "And take off those masks for crying out loud. You look like a couple of morons."

We lowered our hands and started to take off our masks when we heard Mendez say, "They don't have the tombstone on them, you idiot."

"What!" Xander said and looked like he would kill us then and there. "Where is it?"

Me and Dorado looked at each other. Xander held up a finger. "Hold that thought. Let me give you something to consider before you answer." He turned towards one of the cars and shouted, "Bring 'im out!"

My jaw dropped as one of the men dragged Sean from the car, his hands cuffed behind his back, and kicked him to the ground.

"Sean!" I shouted, glad he was still alive! Dorado looked at him in amazement. It was the first time he had ever seen him, and now he was as dumbstruck as I had been by the resemblance.

"Give me that tombstone, or he gets a bullet." The man put a gun to Sean's head.

"Don't give these pigs a thing, Pancho," Sean said.

"Pancho, there's no time," Dorado whispered, and I knew he was right.

"Well?" Xander hissed.

And then I thought of something crazy. I looked down beneath the railroad bridge and saw a big semi about to pass underneath it. In a split second it'd be right below us. I looked up and locked eyes with Dorado. We both knew what the other was thinking. My heart was beating so hard I felt like I could fly. He nodded at me and we both bolted.

"We'll call you!" I yelled as we jumped off the side of the bridge.

XV.
SHOWDOWN
AT SKY CITY

I had read somewhere that the brain seems to perceive time more slowly in times of extreme duress. Now I know that's true because it seems like I floated in the air for an eternity before I smacked into the truck's box trailer with a thud. Before I could even think of the pain from my hard landing, I grabbed onto the trailer and held on tight so that I didn't fall off. I looked up to see if Dorado had made it.

I saw the tips of his fingers clinging to the side of the box trailer. I clambered over to him with the wind whipping through my hair. I grabbed his right arm with mine and gave him some support as he righted himself with his left. He really did look scared as he pulled himself up and then lay down on top of the bed, panting. "Thanks," he muttered.

If I wasn't on top of a box truck traveling 60 miles an hour down the highway I probably would've tried to take a nap. Stress can make you exhausted, and I was tired anyway. It was dark now, too, but this day wasn't over yet.

Me and Dorado finally managed to crawl off of the truck when it pulled over into a rest stop not too far from the old gas station near Lake Sumner. After that we had gotten off and had to walk to the gas station where we'd wait for Cade to come get us. (And yes, I had finally ditched that stupid cape by now.)

Dorado was leaning against the wall near one of the outside restrooms. He looked tired and stressed, too. I leaned back with him and looked at the sky. It looked like a cold front was moving in. I could tell because there was a pink aura to the whole western horizon. I don't know how it is everywhere else, but in New Mexico that means there's moisture in the air.

"So that's our brother, huh? Sorry, I didn't believe you earlier," Dorado said suddenly. This was the first quiet moment we'd had to talk.

All of a sudden I felt the past few days catching up with me. We had finally accomplished what we needed to. We had the tombstone and the key, and now Dorado could give them to the cartel and pay off his debt. Only what about Sean? I could probably trade the tombstone for his life and make a deal with Xander, only then our lives would still be in jeopardy with the cartel. Whatever we did, we lost.

"We shouldn't be here," I blurted out.

"What do you mean? I'm sure they won't find us."

"I don't mean *here*. I mean this situation. These people, Xander, the Santa Fe Ring, Villegas and his cartel..."

I looked towards the northwestern horizon again. The sky had developed into an even more pinkish-purple haze. "It's gonna storm tonight," I said absentmindedly, saying anything to take my mind off of the problem at hand. Dorado glanced up in that direction and then looked back at me. He could tell I was feeling hopeless.

"Listen, man, after I call Villegas to give him what he wants, we'll find someone who can help us take care of Xander. Surely not the whole state can be corrupt."

"Don't you get it?" I said and started to feel tears sting my eyes. "Even if you give Villegas what he wants, he'll probably kill us anyway, and Xander will damn sure kill Sean."

"Pancho," Dorado began reluctantly, "there's something fishy about that guy. I don't know what exactly, but—"

"What are you trying to say? That he's an impostor? I mean, you've seen him now. Is there really any doubt in your mind we're not brothers?"

"No, I can believe we're brothers. It's just that... something doesn't feel right."

I realized then why Dorado didn't seem to like Sean. Without our real parents, and as much as I loved our aunt and uncle, in a way, it had always just been me and him. Now we had another brother. A brother he didn't know, but that I did. I guess if the situation was reversed I would've been a little weirded out, too, instead of excited about it.

I shook my head. "Sean was the only person in all of this who never lied to me." Dorado looked away. "We have to help him, Dorado. It's what dad would have wanted."

"You're right," he said, sounding a little ashamed of himself. All of a sudden, his eyes lit up, and he hit me on the shoulder. "Hey, do you remember what they did at the end of *King Kong vs. Godzilla*?"

Dorado must've gone out of his mind. He kept talking. "You know, when the Japanese government realizes they can't beat either one of them so they come up with the plan to…"

I finished his sentence with him. "…bring 'em together!"

He grinned at me. I got exactly what he was saying. "You mean like I call Xander and tell him we'll trade Sean for the tombstone and the key. While you call Villegas and tell him to meet us at Sky City tomorrow morning at dawn."

"Exactly. With both of them at the same place at the same time—

"They'll shoot it out and kill each other. Problem solved."

We both slapped hands and laughed, but then Dorado's face got serious. "Wait, how do you know Xander won't kill us as soon as he gets what he wants?"

"After all the double-crosses we've pulled on Xander, he wouldn't dare kill us until he actually cracks open that tombstone. Plus, right now, he'll only get the tombstone. He won't get the key until tomorrow morning when you bring it to him at Sky City."

"What? No, I'm not leaving you again."

I could hear Cade's truck and see his headlights as he pulled up. I pointed at the truck. "Do you want to trust that idiot with something this important? That key has to get up there or then I will be dead." I looked at him while it sunk in and then added, "You know I'm right."

Cade came walking up with the tombstone, Dingus at his side. "What the hell took you so long?" Dorado asked. "Me and Pancho didn't even have a car and we made it here before you."

"Well, I'm sorry Do-ra-do," Cade said, dragging out the syllables in his name like he always did when he was mad at my brother. "You only stirred up all the cops in this section of the state, so I had to take the back roads to be extra careful. Now, are y'all ready to shake and bake or what?"

Dorado sighed. "There's been another change of plans."

"And you're not gonna like it," I added.

Cade shrugged his shoulders. "I'm flexible. I'm down for anything."

"We're giving the tombstone back to Xander."

"What?" Cade exploded and nearly dropped the tombstone. Dorado steadied it from him. "After we just got it back?"

"He's got Sean," I explained. "And like it or not, he's family. Same as us."

"Pancho's going to trade the tombstone for Sean at Sky City with Xander, while we haul ass up there with the key as insurance."

"What about those drug dealers that were after you?" Dingus asked.

Dorado grinned. "Oh, don't worry. They're invited to the party, too. Which reminds me, I need to make a phone call."

***

After Dorado got done calling the number on the card Villegas had given him, he stepped out of the phone booth outside of the gas station and gave me some quarters. "It's all set. Now it's your turn."

"Here goes nothing." I looked up the police station's number in the phonebook and then dialed it. An operator answered. "You've reached the De Baca County Sheriff's Department, how may I direct your call?"

"Just tell Sheriff Garrett that the Dumez brothers are turning themselves in at the old gas station north of town, and to come alone," I said and hung up the phone.

"There, it's done."

"You ready for this?" Dorado asked, putting his hands on my shoulders.

"Yeah, I'll be fine," I said, even though I wasn't sure how it would all play out.

In the background I could hear Cade getting into his truck while Dingus asked him, "Can I drive this time?"

"Hell no, you look like you still oughta be strapped to a car seat to begin with!" Nana answered. Suddenly it struck me that this could be the last time I ever heard them argue, and I felt sad. Maybe I was just getting tired. It's easier to get sad when you're tired for some reason.

Dorado stood there and thought for a minute, then he did something that surprised me. He hugged me. We don't usually hug each other. "Be careful," he said before he let me go and started walking towards Cade's truck.

He suddenly turned around. "I almost forgot." He tossed something at me and I caught it out of reflex. It was our dad's old pocket watch—the one with the picture of him and uncle Pancho inside. Only when I opened it, Dorado had taken it out and replaced it with a cut-out from an old polaroid of me and him when we were kids.

"Happy birthday, little brother."

I grinned. I had forgotten it even was my birthday tomorrow. "You love this thing. Are you sure?"

"Yeah. I figure it's time to start looking to the future rather than the past," he said and trotted off to Cade's truck. I looked at the photo of me and him. I think it was his way of saying that what he'd lost was less important than what he still had.

"I'll see you in Sky City," I yelled as he shut the truck door.

The first fleck of moisture hit my cheek as I watched them drive off into the night. I went down the hill behind the gas station and waited for Xander. Waiting for something scary is hard to do. It's worse when you're cold and shivering.

I gave the tombstone another once over while I waited. I had always wondered how you'd hide something in solid rock, but now I could see that the tombstone came in two pieces. The triangular top wasn't a part of the stone block below it. It was a separate piece that looked to have been attached with concrete.

Absentmindedly I began to chip away at it while I sat there in the grass. It must've been a good twenty minutes or more before I finally heard it. I had expected Xander to send a car, but in the air above I heard the thwacking of helicopter blades again. My heart started to pound. Not necessarily just because Xander was coming, but because I had never flown in a helicopter before.

My hair whipped into my face in a frenzy again. Maybe when this was all over I'd get a haircut after all. The chopper was landing about thirty feet away from me. I picked up the tombstone and walked towards it as Xander got out. He was wearing a bulletproof vest and a short-sleeved shirt, but he still held his cowboy hat to his head as he walked towards me. I was so damn cold in the misty rain I was almost happy to see him.

He didn't say anything. He just held out his hands to take the tombstone. When I gave it to him, he looked down and seemed to weigh it in his hands, then looked back up at me. "Okay," he nodded. "Where's the key?"

"Where's Sean?"

"You'll see him in Sky City. Where's the key?"

"My brother has it. You'll get it when we get to Sky City and I see Sean. Call it insurance so you don't kill me here on the spot."

Xander raised an eyebrow and grinned. "You know me so well. Come on." He cocked his head towards the chopper and we both ran to it. It was the same chopper he'd used to get on the train outside Cloudcroft. As far as I could tell the only one with Xander was the pilot. Xander shut the door and sat in the seat across from me rather than up front with the pilot.

"You ever been in one of these before?" he asked like you would a little kid who was looking forward to his first ride.

"First time," I said, and my stomach lurched. We were taking off. "Never been to Sky City before either."

"You've had yourself one hell of a vacation, kid. Maybe when you go back to school, you can tell the class about it."

"You act like I might just live through this after all, Sheriff."

"Oh, come on, now. You're not still sore about almost getting hung out there in the desert? You really think I didn't notice that was a brittle branch we hung the rope on?" He cocked an eyebrow as though that made it okay.

"So that was all fun and games out there, huh? You're something else, Xander, you and your daughter both. After you get your gold, do you still plan on terrorizing Fort Sumner?"

"Nope, kid, the minute I get my gold, I'll be headed out of the territory for good."

"And Becky, too?"

He nodded his head. "And Becky, too."

"Good."

"You sound awfully bitter for a kid. You really should be more trusting." He leaned back and grinned.

"The only people I'll ever trust again are my family."

"Sometimes those are especially the ones you have to watch for." As he said it, he propped his arms behind his head. As his shirt sleeve raised up on his right arm I saw it: a small tattoo on the underside of his bicep. It was of a Zia symbol with an all-seeing eye in the middle. It was the same one that I saw on Sean. It was probably the same one that several other members of the Santa Fe Ring had.

I felt sick to my stomach. Even though I really didn't want to know the answer, I made myself ask, "What's that?"

"Oh, this old thing?" Xander said with an evil twinkle in his eye, knowing I'd just figured everything out. "It's an old Masonic symbol the Santa Fe Ring used to embrace back in its more whimsical days. I take it you've seen it before on someone else that you know?"

"Sean's one of you, isn't he?"

"Bingo."

"And all this time I thought it was Becky. So she's not—"

"Aware of my activities? She wasn't up until you drug her into this."

"Wait, then how did you track me to Mescalero? Sean didn't know I'd be there."

Xander smiled. "How dumb do you think I am, kid? The first place I checked after you three idiots broke into the grave was Cade's ranch. His wife didn't have any problem ratting out her husband, I can tell you that."

"Figures." I never did like Missy. Things still weren't making sense, though. "Then tell me this, if Sean was staying with Delbert Baca then why is he also working with you?"

He laughed. "Heh, that kid is one heck of a liar. Sean did meet Baca once, but the old coot didn't trust him and wouldn't tell him anything."

I didn't say anything. Man, was I an idiot.

"Yep, Sean's been working with me the whole time. Hell, it was him who found the tombstone in Granbury, right where your Uncle Pancho hid it years ago. Unlucky for Sean, but lucky for me, he got arrested. When the cops saw Billy's famous missing tombstone, they called yours truly. That's how I met ol' Seanny boy, and we've been working together ever since. Then, when you got away from me in Mescalero, I sent Sean in. Figured you'd trust him due to the resemblance, and I was right. Turns out when you found the key, you were working for the Ring the whole time and just didn't know it."

"No, how could he do that to his own brother?"

"Because you're not brothers. You're cousins. He's Pancho's son, not Hondo's." The words hit me like a sledgehammer, yet at the same time, they made sense. Maybe I knew it the whole time and just didn't want to believe it. Then I thought, no, maybe Xander was lying. But why?

"But what about his mother in Mexico and all that?"

"You mean the story that your old man had a one-night stand with a woman in Mexico and then left her? Do you really think your daddy would do that? It was your uncle, Pancho, who found a senorita he liked in Mexico. Only he married the girl. He, his wife, and little Sean were one big happy family until your dad and McCaw came for a visit. The three of them got into a fight trying to get your uncle to tell them where he hid the tombstone, and one of them failed to make it out of it alive."

I was going to ask another question, but he kept on talking.

"You don't know this, but your father and uncle were like two sides of a coin. Pancho wanted to unearth the hidden canyon, just like us. Your father, well, he sided with the Indians. He agreed with them, for whatever crazy reason, that the canyon should stay hidden. It's kind of funny when you think about it. One twin had the tombstone, and the other had the key to open it with." Xander patted the tombstone. "Your uncle did a good job of hiding it, too. He was bringing the tombstone to Williams in Granbury, only when he found out Williams was dead, he hid the tombstone and then hightailed it for Mexico. He never told anyone where it was. Or at least that's what I thought. Then, about two months ago, surprise, surprise, Sean shows up with it."

"But why did Sean pretend to be my brother? Why not just tell the truth that he's my cousin?"

He looked at me and squinted as though he wasn't sure what to say. "That's family business. I'll let him tell you when you see him. You've had a long day, kid. Why don't you get some rest?"

Xander got up and ruffled my hair. I shoved his hand out of the way and he just laughed, but he didn't belt me for it.

I leaned back against the seat and took in everything I'd been told. Just this morning I had been sitting with Sean on the train, thinking how cool it would be for him to be part of the family once all this was over. And now he was my enemy. A lot can happen in a day.

For the next hour or so I drifted in and out of a fitful sleep until a clap of thunder woke me up. I didn't exactly like the idea of being aboard a helicopter in a thunderstorm.

I rubbed my eyes and stepped up front where Xander and the pilot were so I could see out the front window. Even though it was the middle of the night, it was bright purple outside and the moon was full. It was extra bright because of the lightning. We were safe from the storm, though. It was way off in the distance, the occasional flash of lightning making the bright night even brighter.

Xander looked over at me. "You're just in time."

Up ahead of us was the pueblo on the mesa, illuminated dramatically against the hazy sky and the lightning. It was certainly a sight to behold, probably the most amazing thing I'd ever laid eyes on in my life, which was appropriate since there was a chance I wouldn't live through the coming day anyway.

"Acoma Sky Pueblo," Xander said with admiration. "The Spaniards said it was the greatest stronghold they had ever seen. Back in the days of the Conquistadors, the Acomans lured the Spaniards to the top of the mesa to trade only to massacre them. Men even threw themselves off the mesa to escape instead of being killed by the Indians. A few of them were lucky enough to land in the sand instead of the rocks when they jumped, but I wouldn't try it myself," he said, hinting to me not to try anything.

The helicopter started to descend upon the ancient village. Unlike the last time I had seen a helicopter land, this one didn't stir up a bunch of dirt. The ground was still too damp from the light rain.

Once we landed, I followed Xander out of the chopper and asked, "You're not going to cuff me?"

"Where would you run?" he said, outstretching his arms. "Besides, I imagine you're looking forward to your family reunion. Sean didn't have the luxury of traveling by chopper like us, though, so it'll be awhile."

I looked around in awe. I had been to pueblos before, and this one wasn't necessarily any different, it was just amazing that it existed on top of a mesa like this. We were 400 feet or more off of the ground, and if I remembered right, the only way up was a narrow road that came up the plateau. That was how the natives had built the village, by hauling everything up the trail stone by stone, plank by plank. Before us were rows and rows of houses, some were ancient-looking and made of rock, while others had smooth adobe exteriors. Most were only one story, but a few were two stories high and had little wooden ladders running up their sides. When I gawked at them for too long, the pilot carrying the tombstone nudged me forwards from behind.

"So, where are we headed?" I asked Xander.

He pointed southward. "See that church over there? It's the San Esteban del Rey."

The second he said the name, I remembered the old poem in the cave, how it said something about the staff of San Esteban. It was all starting to come together.

I looked ahead where he had pointed and could see an ancient looking, mission-style church. San Esteban del Rey was made of adobe and sat outside of a large, walled cemetery full of equally ancient looking crucifixes jutting out of the muddy earth. The church was tall, nearly forty feet, and had two bell towers on either side of the entrance. Attached to the church was what looked to be an adjoining convent on the north side.

Xander stopped me before we went inside. "And kid, your brother better get here by dawn, or I can't guarantee your survival."

"He'll be here," I said. And with that, we entered the ancient church, which was lit by candlelight. It was like entering another world or going back in time to the days of Colonial New Mexico. It wasn't filled with wooden pews like most churches and was wide open with a large altar at the front. There was only one other way out that I noticed, which was a doorway that led into the courtyard of the convent on the north side of the church.

I searched the room with my eyes, wondering why the tombstone had to be opened here of all places. The only place that looked significant was a big mural at the front of the church. It had six different compartments and I seemed to remember murals like that were called the Stations of the Cross. I recognized the Virgin Mother in the top middle box. All the other boxes had what I guessed were different saints in them, but the middle one at the bottom didn't have anybody in it, which was odd.

The noise of Xander plopping onto the floor of the church cut into my thoughts. "Might as well take a load off, kid," he said nonchalantly as he pulled his hat down over his eyes. "We both know you ain't goin' nowhere. And if you do, Jones there'll put a stop to it."

He was talking about the pilot, who lifted up his shirt, revealing a gun tucked into his belt. He didn't need to worry. Xander was right. I wasn't going anywhere so I laid down on the floor. I'd barely slept in days and it wasn't tough to drift off. Anymore sleep was about the only escape I got from this mess. I don't know how long I slept, but my stomach eventually woke me up. I was starving. I didn't get anything to eat last night.

Normally the morning after Halloween, I'd have a sugar hangover from all the candy and junk I ate. And usually Rod or Cade and Dorado would take me and Dingus out with them to use all the leftover pumpkins for target practice. Actually, Dingus only went along once, which is self-explanatory. I didn't know what sort of fate awaited us today, but something told me that we'd be the ones getting used for target practice, not the pumpkins.

The sound of cars pulling up outside broke into my thoughts. One of them wasn't a car, though. It was the sound of a motorcycle I'd gotten to know pretty well by now. My stomach tightened into a knot.

I sat up and saw several men walking in. I didn't see Sean yet, but I saw Becky looking cold and tired. She locked eyes with me.

"Becky!" I yelled and ran to her. "I'm sorry. I'm sorry," I must've said it a million times as I threw my arms around her, wanting more than anything in the world to make her feel warm and safe again. "Becky," I began as I finally pulled away, "I didn't know. I'm sorry."

"I know," she said and sniffled like she might've been crying. Oh, man, she smelled good. Having her in my arms seemed to unravel every tense nerve in my body. "I tried to tell you in the jail."

"I know. I should have listened. I'm sorry."

"Unfortunately, she's right." Sean had finally stepped through the doorway. I studied him closely as though he was a completely different person, and in some ways he was. At first, he was a stranger who saved my life. Then, he was my long lost brother. Yesterday he wasn't just a relative, he was my trusted *compañero*. And today, he was my enemy.

I looked at Becky. Four days ago she was my girlfriend, a day ago I told her I loved her, but only a few hours ago I was heartbroken because I thought she betrayed me. Now she was my girlfriend again. I knew what people meant when they said they'd gone through an emotional roller coaster.

"How's it going, amigo, or should I say enimigo?" I said to him.

"Oh, come now, Mechito, we're still amigos. You just know something about me that you didn't before."

"An amigo doesn't leave another amigo for dead with a noose around his neck."

"Well, Mechito, in my defense, I had just fallen off a train and was taking a little nap." He raised an eyebrow as though that made everything okay. "Besides, I knew you'd be fine. You learned from the best, no?" He pointed to himself as though I should be thanking him. He was trying to lighten things up, but I wasn't about to let him. "You know, you and your brother could always join us, Pancho."

"Thanks, but Xander already offered. And knowing what I know now, the answer is especially still no. But before I spit in your face, I have one question. Why lie? Why say you were my brother instead of my cousin?"

He looked at me like he was carefully calculating his response. "Because we didn't know if you knew or not."

"Knew what?"

"You'll learn eventually. For the record, I don't hold it against you. You're not your father any more than I am mine. And after all, we're still family."

"I'm only going to say this once, Sean. You're not my family. You're not my 'compañero' and you're sure as hell not my friend. Now, we're nothing but enemies." I didn't know for sure if I wanted to say the next part or not, but I said it anyway. "I hate your guts."

He looked disappointed for just a second and then hid it. His eyes turned steely and angry. "Alright, have it your way then." He shifted his gaze to Professor Mendez, who was walking towards the altar with another man carrying the tombstone. With a heavy thump, he put it on the altar.

"Careful, you idiot!" Mendez snapped and pushed him away with the back of his arm.

"Calm down. I'm sure it's been knocked around worse than that before," Xander said.

"I'm sure it has," Mendez said, looking at me with disdain, "but for all our sakes, we had better hope not. Now, when can we expect your brother with the key?"

I sighed. "Unfortunately, right about now." Dressed in robes and disguised as monks, Cade and Dorado had just walked through the door. They both threw their hoods back and Dorado cocked a revolver in Mendez's direction while Cade brandished a shotgun at Xander.

"Howdy, professor," Dorado said.

Cade cocked his shotgun and shouted, "Alright, give us the Mexican, and nobody gets hurt!"

With his other hand, Dorado held up the key. "That's right, my brother, my family and I are walking out of here together." Only when Dorado noticed me next to Becky, and Sean standing free by Mendez, it all dawned on him.

"Son of a bitch," Dorado muttered.

"Wait, did I miss something again?" Cade asked.

Sean walked over to Dorado and took the key. "Thank you for the gesture, but it wasn't necessary. I'm right where I need to be. Always have been."

Dorado didn't waste any time and slugged him one across the face knocking him backward. Xander's men drew their guns, and Sean said, "Stop! That's not necessary."

"Enough with this nonsense!" Mendez shouted. "We're burning daylight, literally. Gentlemen, you are lucky to be here to witness history in the making. I suggest you lower your guns."

Seeing they were hopelessly outnumbered, Cade put down his shotgun, and Dorado handed his revolver over to one of the men.

"Cuff 'em up for now," Xander said, then pointed at me. "And him too while you're at it."

As they cuffed me, Dorado, and Cade, Mendez looked over the key.

"Where's Dingus?" I whispered.

"We slipped him some sleeping pills and left him at the ranch," Dorado said. That was probably for the best, I figured, even though I sort of wished he were here.

"And Villegas?" I asked tepidly.

"I don't know, but when he gets here, we make a break for it."

I looked back over at Mendez, studying the tombstone on the altar in front of the mural.

"Now, how the hell does this thing work?" Xander asked as he walked up beside him.

Mendez began to explain to Xander what I had figured out earlier. "See this top triangular portion? That's a separate piece connected by concrete. I would guess the bottom portion has a hollowed-out compartment containing the Ojo del Oro."

"And if not?" Sean asked.

"Then Tumbleweed Williams was one hell of a practical joker," Xander answered.

"Get the chisel," Mendez said and snapped his fingers. One of the men brought over a chisel and mallet and held it over the tombstone.

"No, I'll do it," Mendez barked and tore the tools from his hand. His fingers traced the concrete seam that connected the triangular top to the main stone.

"The concrete they used to connect the top piece to the bottom shouldn't be difficult to break. It is nearly 100 years old now. I'm surprised it's even held together this long," Mendez said as he began to chisel away at the concrete seam. Just as he said, it cracked away easily. I was surprised it didn't break when we dropped it during the race.

"That sun'll be rising soon. We ain't got all morning," Xander said.

Mendez only held up a finger as if to say "wait" and kept his gaze fixated on the tombstone. He hesitated a moment, looking at the seam he'd been working on. Then, harshly, he slammed the hammer into the chisel. The triangular top popped right off.

Everyone let out a sigh. Mendez picked up the top, examined it briefly to make sure it didn't have anything inside, and then tossed it aside. I could see the hollowed-out compartment in the main body of the tombstone, right where the top had been. It looked like some rawhide was stuffed into it. Gently, Mendez pulled out the rawhide and began to unfold it, finally revealing the so-called Ojo del Oro.

I couldn't believe it. The Eye looked like a piece of stained glass, the type you would see in a church. It was a perfect round circle, like a bright yellow sun. "The Ojo del Oro indeed," Mendez muttered.

Now it was all coming together. Somewhere in the church had to be a stained-glass window… except there wasn't. Like I had said earlier, the front of the church had the Stations of the Cross mural, not stained glass. I looked behind me towards the front door of the church. A small balcony was stationed over the entryway with a window facing east, right where the sun would rise, but no stained glass. The only thing up there was a statue of a wooden saint holding a staff… a staff that terminated in a strange, upside-down arch that looked like it was made to hold something.

"Only by the dawn's early light, with the staff of San Esteban and the Ojo del Oro in sight," I muttered, remembering the poem.

"That's Saint Esteban then," Becky said.

Mendez had figured it out too. "There. See the top of the staff? That is where we place the Eye, gentlemen."

Sean rushed to the front of the church and swiftly climbed up the ladder to the balcony. One of the men ran after him with the Eye.

"Here, toss it quick," Sean said atop the balcony and clapped his hands together. Mendez winced as the man did as Sean asked, but he caught it easily. The sun was just beginning to brighten the church window as Sean placed the Eye upon St. Esteban's staff. At the instant Sean got it wedged into place, the early morning sun hit the Ojo del Oro and created a blinding beam of light. I looked away and turned to the front of the church to see where it pointed. It took my eyes a second to focus, but when they did, I could see right away where the beam was pointing.

The Ojo del Oro had been a prism all along, and now it was projecting a near perfect cross onto the mural at the front of the church. It landed right on the spot I noticed last night, the one panel in the Stations of the Cross not to have a religious figure in it. And right below it was a rectangular panel—a panel about exactly the width of a coffin.

"Here!" Mendez exclaimed excitedly.

"Well, that's a damned dramatic way for 'X' to mark the spot!" Xander said.

"The grave of Adams has to be here." Mendez was already pouring over the spot, holding the cruciform key. The panel even had a little cross-shaped indentation in it. You wouldn't have thought it was a lock of some kind, but that's what it was the whole time!

Mendez inserted the key and really had to struggle to get it to turn. It had been almost a hundred years since the body of Adams had been hidden there. Finally, Mendez managed to turn the key and the panel opened. He swung the hidden door open, and, sure enough, inside the compartment was a casket.

"Another coffin!" Cade whispered to Dorado. "Ain't that how this whole dang thang started?"

"You really think the gold's in there?" Becky asked me.

"We'll find out," I said.

Mendez looked at it with wild eyes while some of the Ring men approached the Stations of the Cross. With two men on each side, they began to pull the casket from the wall.

"How much gold does this thing have in it?" one of the men said with a grin as they hauled it out. With one last heave, the men tore the casket from the wall and it came to the floor with a hard thud. Whatever was in there had to be heavy; it sure wasn't just Old Man Adams. Mendez held out his hand and one of the men gave him a crowbar. It would be he who would open it.

Xander rubbed his hands together. "Moment of truth, boys."

Everyone was practically holding their breath as Mendez pried open the casket. Me and Becky had to stand on our toes to see what was inside as the lid swung open. The first thing I could make out was a heavily decomposed body, just a skeleton really. Inside with it were various nuggets of gold from the fabled canyon. "They buried Adams with his own gold. Ingenious," Mendez muttered.

"And just think, this gold is only a fraction of what's still in that canyon," Sean said, his eyes wide.

In the skeleton's crossed arms was what looked to be a traditional map. Gently, Mendez plucked it from the corpse's grasp and began to unfold it. "Now this, this is the map."

It looked just like an old, weathered map that you'd see in a Western on TV; dotted lines and all, I guess tracing the Kid's journey to the canyon with Adams. It looked to me like it was towards the northwestern part of the state.

"Where is it?" Xander asked while Sean looked on intently.

"Right on the New Mexico–Arizona border…just like Adams always said," Mendez answered.

Everyone was in awe, but a sound broke the silence. The front door of the church had just creaked open. I expected to see Villegas's men barging in, but it was a procession of parishioners shuffling in with a priest. Their faces were painted like skeletons for the Day of the Dead.

"What the hell?" Xander muttered.

"I thought you made sure the church was off-limits today?" Mendez hissed at him angrily.

"It is," he said to Mendez, then to the procession slowly entering the church, "Hey, church is closed today. Comprende?"

However, the men ignored him and continued to funnel inside.

"Sean, how do you say 'get the hell out' in Spanish?" Xander asked.

The priest finally looked up and spoke. "There's no need. We all speak English."

The voice gave me chills. It was one that I had come to know well over the last few days. The priest pulled back his hood revealing his eyeless face. It was Seven McCaw.

XVI.
DAY OF
THE DEAD

MONDAY MORNING, NOVEMBER 1, 1976

The shooting started instantly. Not from the Santa Fe Ring, they had all been taken completely off-guard. McCaw's men had begun firing the second after he spoke.

I saw the pilot named Jones clutch his chest and go down first. It seemed like it was happening in slow motion. The Stations of the Cross shattered and parts of the adobe walls exploded from the onslaught of bullets. The inside of the church had turned into a total massacre.

"Pancho, get down!" Dorado yelled and pushed himself over onto me so that we both toppled to the floor. My first thought was for Becky. I craned my neck to look across the ground and could see Xander had pinned her down like Dorado had me. We both locked eyes for an instant, but then some of the dust from the exploding adobe got into my eyes and I shut them tight, wishing it was all just a nightmare. It was all we could do to lay there and hope that McCaw and his men kept their end of the bargain and let me, Dorado, Cade, and Becky walk away.

Eventually, the gun fire stopped and all I could hear was the sound of mine and Dorado's breathing.

"It's okay. You can all stand up now," McCaw drawled calmly. "Just keep your hands where we can see them."

I looked in Becky's direction again as Dorado got off of me. She was fine, just shaken up like me. She and Xander were both beginning to stand with their hands up. I looked for Cade and Sean next, and they were doing the same. Dorado nudged me and I knew we should too, so I did.

In front of us stood Seven McCaw looking like a corpse. Though his men were all painted up for Day of the Dead, McCaw didn't need any makeup. He wasn't wearing his eyepatch anymore and instead had both vacant sockets exposed, looking like a skeleton come to life. He held out his arm, and seemingly from out of nowhere, that damn hawk flew into the church and perched itself on his shoulder.

"You… I killed you," Xander said in disbelief.

"Well, it is the Day of the Dead, after all," McCaw replied with a shrug.

Even though McCaw didn't have eyes, he was looking around the room like he could see everything. As I studied his face, I realized that Xander's bullet didn't totally pass through his eye socket into the brain, and must have just grazed him badly enough to take his remaining eye. But the real question wasn't how did he survive, it was how could he still see us? I looked at Itza-Chu perched upon his shoulder and realized he had been telling the truth all along. A shiver went up my spine. He really was a brujo.

McCaw raised up his good hand, counting as he looked at each and every one of us that was standing. "One, two, three, four, five, six," McCaw whispered, identifying me, Dorado, Cade, Becky, Xander, and Sean from what I could tell.

"Perfect. Just the ringleaders and the children," he said. I looked around the room. He was right. All of the Ring men were dead except for Sean and Xander. I looked at Mendez crumpled up on the floor of the church, his big, hawk-like eyes now totally vacant and lifeless. I shivered. Even though I didn't like him, even though he would've had me killed, it was still strange to see someone that you knew dead.

"Cuff them," McCaw said to his men, and within a few minutes, we were all on our knees with our hands behind our backs against the wall. It reminded me of being in trouble with the teachers at school, only way worse. I wanted to be next to Becky, but instead I was between Xander and Dorado, who was next to Sean. Cade and Becky were both on the ends. As they cuffed Xander, Becky, and Sean, McCaw walked over to Mendez and plucked the map from his cold, dead hands.

"What do you plan to do with us?" Dorado asked. "I did come through on my end of the bargain. You've got the map."

"That I do," McCaw said, looking down at it, examining it with that bizarre, eyeless face. "But, that's for the boss man to decide," he said, and I knew he was talking about Dr. Villegas.

I didn't know how long it would take Villegas to arrive, but I wasn't going to waste any time. As soon as the cartel men were satisfied that we weren't going anywhere and had backed off, I began to wiggle my hand into my back pocket. I still had the handcuff key I'd used to get out of the cuffs back in Perdition. And, since I had practice, hopefully it wouldn't be as hard this time.

I turned to Dorado. I subtly nodded my head and shifted my eyes downwards, getting him to look behind me. He saw what I was doing and nodded his head slightly to only where I could see it. As I began working the key into my left cuff, I heard a helicopter. "Here comes the boss," McCaw said. He handed the map to one of his skeleton men and told him, "Take this to the chopper."

I could hear the helicopter touch down outside somewhere just as the cuff unlocked. I passed my hand behind my back while everyone was distracted by the noise of the helicopter. I knocked my hand against Dorado's. He turned to me and whispered, "Xander first."

I shot him a look. Was he crazy?

"He still has a gun on him," he whispered, reading the confused look on my face.

I glanced at Xander next to me. Even though he was cuffed, they had forgotten to take one of his guns. Even if he had tried to kill us earlier, like they always said, the enemy of your enemy is your friend. I nudged my fist against Xander's, rapping the key against his knuckles. At first he looked a little confused, but once he grasped the little key in his knuckles, he gave me a sly look acknowledging that he understood. He took the key between his fingers.

Just then I heard Villegas's voice coming from outside. "Hello, hello," he shouted calmly as though he were waltzing into a neighbor's house to borrow a cup of sugar. A few seconds later he came swaggering in, or at least swaggering the best that a one-legged man with a cane can swagger. Villegas's eyes lit up in surprise when he saw Sean among us. "Well, well, well. Fancy seeing you again, Diego."

At first, the name took me by surprise until I remembered the night I first met Sean and how he had given me that long list of names. I guess to me he was Sean, but to Villegas, he was Diego.

"Hello, *Huracan*," Sean said, acknowledging him with his own strange nickname.

"Wait, you two know each other?" Dorado looked at Sean suspiciously.

"Let me guess. You used to work for him, too?" I asked Sean.

"I would never work for that pendejo!" Sean spat after he said it. "But yes, we know each other."

It was becoming very clear to me that there was a whole lot more to this story that I didn't know and that maybe I never would. Right now, it didn't exactly look like the odds were in our favor for survival.

"It's funny to finally see them both together, isn't it, Seven?" Villegas said, and I realized he was talking about Dorado and Sean.

"I'd seen you both apart, but together..." Villegas waved his finger back and forth between Dorado and Sean, who were right next to each other against the wall. "They look like they could be twins from a different mother, don't they?"

"Yes, we're all thrilled by the resemblance, Huracan," Sean said. "Kind of like how you resemble a one-legged Chihuahua I once knew in Juarez."

McCaw stepped forward as though he was going to hit Sean, but Villegas held up his hand. "There's no need, he'll be dead soon enough."

Villegas hobbled over to the coffin filled with the golden nuggets. "Dorado, while you did technically follow through and get me the map... again I see there are uninvited guests. Why?" He bent down to pick up one of the gold nuggets and rubbed it between his fingers.

Dorado shrugged. "They're just our groupies, what can I say?"

Xander shot him a dirty look, then turned to Villegas. "You know, it's gonna be awfully hard to dig that whole canyon out. Especially seeing as how you're located all the way down in Mexico and the canyon is up here in New Mexico. But, if you let us all go, I'm sure I could broker a deal with the Ring to let you in—

Villegas laughed and cut him off. "With all the bad blood between our two organizations, I don't see that happening." Villegas sat down on the steps leading up to the altar, then took out a cigarette and lit it. "Besides, my organization existed long before the Ring, and will continue after the Ring is finished, which looks to be soon."

"I thought you were just a drug cartel?" Dorado said, sounding shocked.

"Oh, that too. We all need money, and right now drug trafficking just happens to be one of the easiest ways to do it," Villegas explained and took a puff from his cigarette.

Something was starting to click. That weird serpent symbol in the shape of a 'Q' on his helicopter. The golden snake coiled around his fake leg. Were Villegas and his men part of a secret society from Mexico similar to the Ring?

"The drug trade is a relatively new development in the scheme of history," Villegas continued. "But, my organization goes all the way back to Emperor Moctezuma. As it is, my people knew about that canyon long before Old Man Adams, Billy the Kid, or even Seven's Apache ancestors."

"Wait a minute…" Something was dawning on Dorado. "You never needed me to repay a debt for losing a race. You just needed a fall guy to steal the tombstone so the Ring wouldn't know it was you."

Villegas's eyes lit up and he grinned. "You finally connected the dots, Dorado. Good for you! I almost manipulated Diego here into the same trap, only Diego managed to get away. It was Diego who found the tombstone hidden in Texas, did you know that? After Diego came to America and sided with the Ring, I knew they'd be expecting us. That's where I had the very good fortune to meet you, Dorado. The tombstone would go missing, and after having been seen around Fort Sumner recently, so would you. The Ring would think you took it, and my organization would continue to fly under the radar." Villegas put out his cigarette on the altar steps. He stood up and walked closer to us. "You see, Dumez, there was never actually any scenario where you were going to make it out of this alive. In fact, none of you are."

For a second, I worried this was it. But then, Dorado said, "Well, if you're going to kill us, will you at least hold up your end of the bargain and tell me if the man in the photo is my father? Or is it my uncle?"

Dorado was smart, he was stalling him just like I did Mendez back in Perdition earlier.

"I suppose there's no harm in that." He paused for a moment. "It's Hondo."

Dorado and I looked at each other in shock. Our father was alive.

Suddenly, a devious expression crossed Villegas's face and he turned to Sean. "Actually, why didn't you tell them, Diego? You could have answered that question a long time ago."

Sean shot Villegas a dirty look.

"You mean you knew this whole time?" I burst out.

"Look, it was for your own good!" Sean snapped.

"Why? Why didn't you tell Pancho when you had the chance?" Dorado asked.

"Can't you get it through your thick skull? I didn't tell him for his sake!" Sean shouted and cocked his head at me.

"No…no…" Dorado got a funny, sad look on his face and started shaking his head, but I couldn't figure out why.

I felt stupid. Obviously, they knew something I didn't. "What? Just tell me already!"

Sean sighed and finally said, "Your father… he killed mine."

I let the words sink in and it finally clicked why Sean pretended he was my brother instead of my cousin. It was in case I knew the truth about what happened. "Hondo came to Mexico to find Pancho wanting to find that tombstone. Only your father, he agreed with that damned Indian Baca that the canyon should not be found."

"But how do you know for sure which one died?" Dorado asked.

"Because if my father was alive, he would've come back for me!" Sean spat, angrily. "You're just lucky I never found Hondo Dumez myself."

Even in his cuffs, Dorado lost it and lunged at Sean. One of the guards stepped in and pulled him off while McCaw and Villegas just laughed.

"Seven, who do those two remind you of?" Villegas said.

"Oh, I don't know. A pair of twin brothers I once knew down Mexico way. It's funny how history repeats itself… in fact, I'd almost forgot. Diego, you know what today is, don't you?"

Sean didn't answer and just gave him a stare that seethed with anger.

"Surely you remember. Fifteen years ago, today. The Day of the Dead, 1961. I was there, too. The day Hondo killed Pancho," McCaw said.

A chill ran down my spine. The uncle I was named after died the day I was born and it was my own father who killed him. Suddenly I wondered if Sean had hated me this whole time and I just never picked up on it.

"No, my dad would not have killed his own brother," Dorado said, shaking his head. "And for what? What's so damn important about that canyon other than gold that's worth killing over?"

"Let's just say it's a burial ground," McCaw answered.

"Wait. All this for some sacred Injian burial ground for y'all's people or something?" Cade asked, disgusted.

"Oh, not for my people, and certainly not sacred," McCaw replied cryptically. "Anyhow, this little trip down memory lane has got me feeling nostalgic. Dr. Villegas, if it's alright with you, I have a little proposal I'd like to put forth."

Villegas waved his hand at McCaw. "Be my guest."

"I propose a new bargain for Dorado and his estranged cousin."

"Oh yeah, what's that?" Sean asked.

"A duel. A duel to the death just like your fathers."

My stomach lurched and I felt sick.

"And why the hell would we do that?" Dorado asked.

"Simple. If you win, I will tell you exactly where in Mexico your father is and let you and your brother go." He turned his eyeless face to Sean. "And if you win, I will also tell you where Hondo is so that you can avenge your father just like I know you want to." After a moment, he turned to me. "And you, just like little Diego did, can watch it all happen."

"And if we both refuse?" Sean said.

"Then we kill little Panchito here. How's that?" McCaw answered.

Immediately after he said it, one of the cartel men aimed a gun at me from across the room.

"Don't do it," I said, shaking as my eyes started to tear up. "Don't give them the satisfaction. They'll kill us all anyways."

"He's right," Becky said. "Don't do it."

"Becky," Xander cut in, wanting her to be quiet, but it was too late. McCaw turned his creepy gaze to her, as did Villegas.

"Xander, I never noticed how beautiful your daughter is," Villegas said. And then, as though this whole thing couldn't get any worse, he added. "In fact, after you're dead, don't worry, I'll let her live and see to it that she gets a good home… down in Mexico."

His men laughed and I felt Xander tense up, as though he was about to pounce, but then he stopped himself.

"Better come over here with me where it's safe, girl," Villegas said.

"Dad?" Becky turned to Xander, terrified.

I wondered if this would be the moment that he finally drew his gun, but instead, he just looked at her and said, "Do what he says. It'll be okay, I promise."

Becky seemed to understand something in his tone when he said "I promise" and nodded. Slowly she stood, and one of the cartel men came and took her by the arm. As he led her away, I could just barely see the handcuff key in between her fingers.

As she stood next to Villegas, Xander said to him, "You're lucky I'm chained up, Villegas, because if I wasn't—

"Yes, but you are," he cut him off snidely. "And speaking of that, let's get this party started as you Americans like to say." Villegas pointed to Sean and Dorado. "Undo their cuffs. If they make any sudden moves, put a bullet in his head," he said, meaning me. "Actually, you can undo his cuffs as well. I don't want him to feel left out."

I panicked. I couldn't let them see that I'd undone my cuffs. Swiftly I locked them back into place. If they saw that mine were undone, they might check Xander's. And right now, Xander was our last hope. I was still praying that any second he'd jump into action and start shooting. But if he didn't when Villegas threatened Becky, I didn't know when he would. I suddenly realized what he was waiting for: the duel. When one of them shot the other, he would use that as a distraction to start shooting himself.

Before I could think anymore about it, a guard came over and undid my cuffs, but I stayed on my knees since they hadn't told me what to do.

"Pancho, I want you to be a good boy and count it down for us. I'll even give you my watch," Villegas said, digging into his pocket and tossing me his watch.

I caught it, then immediately tossed it back to him. "Don't bother, I have my own," I said and pulled out the watch Dorado gave me from my jacket. "Family heirloom," I added.

"Suit yourself," Villegas said, putting his own watch back in his pocket. "Get them each a gun," he said to one of his men.

"I don't need a gun," Sean said, letting a hidden knife slip down from the inside of his jacket sleave and into his hand.

"Interesting," Villegas said with a grin.

"I never thought I'd actually meet someone dumb enough to bring a knife to a gunfight," Dorado said, rubbing his wrists, which were finally free of the cuffs.

"You don't know me very well, primo," Sean replied.

One of Villegas's men handed Dorado a gun and a leg holster. Before the man let go of the gun, he said, "There's only one bullet in the chamber, so don't get any ideas."

Villegas looked at his watch. "Let's make it 7:20 on the dot, exactly one minute from now."

One minute. In just one minute my life would change forever. I looked at Dorado, strapping the holster around his leg, and my stomach lurched. Even though I wanted Dorado to win more than anything, I didn't want Sean to die either, especially not like this. And as quick as Dorado was with a gun, I wasn't sure if he would be fast enough to beat Sean since I had watched him throw a knife with lightning-like speed several times now.

"Pancho," Villegas said, "aren't you forgetting your job?"

I looked down at the watch. "Thirty seconds," I croaked out. My voice was cracking like it did back when it first started to change a year ago.

"When it gets to ten, count down from there," Villegas said. "Are you boys ready?" he asked, looking at Sean and Dorado.

Sean slowly placed the knife upon his shoulder letting it balance there and raised his hand in front of him. Dorado let his hand hover over the gun as the two slowly began to circle each other in the wide open spaces of the church. I was starting to shake. The next few seconds were the most nerve-wracking of my life. Falling down the mountain, jumping off the bridge with a rush of adrenaline—those moments of certain death were almost fun compared to this. I looked down at the watch again. Seventeen seconds.

I turned to look at Xander pleadingly, my eyes tearing up. "Do something," I whispered.

He shook his head subtly. "Look at the knife," he mouthed.

I did. It wasn't just any knife. It was the knife with the nitro-filled handle. When he threw it, it would cause an explosion. Sean wasn't going to kill my brother, he was going to help get us out of here! The only problem was Dorado didn't know that.

"Start the countdown, Dumez," Villegas said to me, irritated.

"Ten," I began, my voice still shaking, now hoping that Dorado wouldn't be quicker than Sean on the draw instead of the other way around. "Nine." Dorado let his hand hover comfortably over his leg holster, while Sean's hand was still raised in the air, ready to snatch the knife off his shoulder and throw. "Eight." The hairs on the back of my neck began to stand. The room was growing tenser by the moment. "Seven… Six… Five."

"Dorado Dumez, I have one last thing to say before I kill you," Sean said.

"Oh yeah, what's that?" Dorado replied.

"Duck!" Sean shouted just as I counted down to one.

Dorado hit the floor as Sean threw the nitro-knife past him and into Adams' coffin. I ducked too as the coffin exploded into a shower of bones, wood, and gold. My ears were ringing from the explosion and I was disoriented. I shook my head and looked up from the ground to see Dorado spin around on his back and shoot one of the cartel men. Xander freed his hands and started shooting, too. Sean scrambled over to one of the dead Ring men that littered the floor and grabbed a gun to join in the shooting. The cartel was so taken off guard that they hadn't even begun to fire back yet. Some of the ones standing close to the coffin were killed by the explosion, while others rushed for the door leading into the courtyard. Through the smoky haze, I saw Villegas dragging Becky through the door with him.

"Becky!" I cried, and found it strange that I could hardly hear myself yell.

"Dad!" I barely heard her cry out as he pulled her through the door.

"Becky!" he yelled back, then crumpled to the floor as a bullet from one of the cartel men struck him in the leg.

I went to run after Becky, but Dorado grabbed me and pulled me in the other direction towards Sean and Xander. "Come on, Pancho!"

A few of the men were giving cover fire for McCaw as he fled through the north door and into the courtyard. Sean and Xander managed to shoot at least one before they had all gotten outside.

Me and Dorado dropped beside Xander as Sean began to ask him, "Are you—

Xander didn't wait for Sean to finish. "I'll live but my leg's shot for now. Which means," Xander grimaced through the pain and grabbed me by the collar, "Dumez, you and your brother better get my little girl back."

I nodded. Xander handed Dorado his gun and let me go.

"We will," Dorado said as we both bolted for the front door. As we ran outside, I heard Cade cry out, "Hey, what am I, chopped liver?" There was no time to help him though, we'd just have to come back for him later.

We bolted out the front door and into the sunlight. I spotted Villegas's helicopter not far away parked outside the courtyard. There were only two of the cartel men that I could see including the pilot and McCaw, who were already sitting down in the front while Villegas was dragging Becky inside the bay just as the blades began to turn.

We ran towards it as fast as we could, hoping against hope we'd get there before it took off. We rushed up to the open bay doors as Villegas was trying to force Becky into a seat. I could see she'd already freed her hands of the cuffs and was fighting him off best that she could.

"Hands off her!" Dorado said and pointed his gun at Villegas first, but then turned it on McCaw and the pilot up front when they noticed us.

"Becky, come on," I said, holding out my hand. She went to take it, but since Dorado didn't have the gun aimed at him anymore, Villegas suddenly whipped out his own pistol and pointed it at Becky's head.

"I don't think so," he said, gripping her arm firmly. "Besides, I'm still waiting on one of my men."

"Behind you!" Becky screamed. Two meaty, powerful hands grabbed me and Dorado from behind, throwing us to the ground several feet away. I looked up to see a gigantic, bald skeleton man standing over us. He didn't waste any time and kicked the gun from Dorado's hand with his right foot. Dorado didn't miss a beat either and countered by kicking the big guy's left knee.

Dorado righted himself as the big guy doubled over in pain and shouted to me, "Get Becky, I'll hold him off!" I jumped up and sprinted for the chopper, which was still on the ground preparing to lift off.

"Get us out of here!" Villegas yelled as I ran towards him. He took the gun off of Becky and aimed it at me. Becky didn't give him the chance to shoot and knocked the gun from his hands. He turned around and struck her so that she toppled back into the seat.

I knew exactly what I was going to do next—sweep the one-legged man's good leg just like Dorado had done to the other guy. Only problem was I couldn't remember which one was his good limb. I jumped into the bay just as the chopper lifted off, flipped onto my side, and then used my momentum to sweep his left leg. Pain shot through my ankle.

"Wrong one," Villegas sneered and lifted his pant leg revealing his golden limb.

"How about this one?" Becky said and slammed her foot down into Villegas's right knee, the real one. He toppled over into McCaw, who was coming to his aid, and McCaw fell back and hit the pilot, causing him to lose control of the chopper for a split second. I grabbed Becky by the hand and stepped towards the bay doors to jump out as quick as we could, only the helicopter spun around violently. Since we were only a few feet off the ground, I watched as the tail spun towards my brother and the big guy he was fighting. "Dorado!" I yelled and he ducked at the last second, missing the tail which slammed into the big cartel guy, knocking him out cold.

The pilot finally managed to stabilize the chopper and it began to ascend again. Dorado was standing below, yelling at us to jump before it was too late.

Becky looked down. "I hate heights!" she shrieked.

"Remember the other day when you pushed me out that window for my own good?" I shouted to her.

"Yeah?" she replied with dread.

"Your turn." I kissed her on the lips real quick and then shoved her out. She fell into Dorado's arms and he broke her fall before tumbling over himself.

"Get him!" I heard Villegas shout. I looked behind me and saw McCaw coming at me. There was no time to wait for Dorado to get back up and catch me. A few broken bones would be better than letting McCaw slash me to bits with his hook. I jumped from the bay, only when I did, it felt like my leg had caught something. My stomach did a loop as I fell through the air and smacked into Dorado, who stood up in the nick of time to break my fall. Only I was a little higher than Becky had been and knocked into him harder, disorientating us both as we tumbled to the ground. It seemed like I was on top of him for only a second before I felt myself being dragged away.

"Pancho!" he cried out as I was pulled through the mud. I turned from my brother, who was slowly disappearing in the distance to look at my leg. My foot had gotten tangled in a ladder inside the bay that had uncoiled with me when I jumped!

I panicked as I tried to free myself. As unpleasant as being dragged through the mud of the mesa was, within less than a minute the chopper would sail off the edge of Acoma, and instead of being drug across the earth I'd be dangling hundreds of feet in the air. I'd also be the cartel's prisoner—probably forever. I had to get my foot loose now or my life as I knew it would be over. Frantically, I quit trying to untangle my foot since that didn't work and searched inside my jacket for the knife Sean had given me. I drew it out and began to cut away at the rope.

"Looks like you're coming back to Mexico with us!" Villegas shouted from above with a laugh. Right after he said it, a bullet hit the fuselage. McCaw jerked his head up and pointed at something in the distance. I tipped my head backwards to see Sean on his bike, steering it with one hand best he could while also shooting at the chopper.

"Hang on, Mechito!" Sean yelled.

I looked back at the chopper. It was turning sideways so that the open bay doors would face Sean. McCaw was aiming his gun at him, Itza-chu on his shoulder so that he could see. I estimated I had less than ten seconds before two very bad things would happen. First,

McCaw would get Sean in his sights, and second, I would go flying off of the mesa and have no choice but to hang on for dear life. I knew what I had to do.

I quit cutting the rope and let myself slip back into the mud so that I had a good view of McCaw. I raised the knife so that my arm was in throwing position. I didn't have time to think about it. I acted on adrenaline-fueled instinct and threw the knife at my target—and it wasn't McCaw. Itza-chu squawked as the knife buried itself into her breast and McCaw dropped the gun, clutching his empty eye socket.

Sean roared up next to me in the nick of time and slashed through the rope with his own knife, freeing my foot. He caught me by the arm and brought his bike to a skidding halt right on the edge of the butte. We watched as the helicopter sailed off the mesa. So did Seven McCaw. In his shock, he had staggered backwards out the other bay door, his long duster coat flailing in the wind as he fell from the chopper to his death below the mesa.

In between breaths, I managed to say, "Thank God that's over."

"I'm not so sure it is." Sean drug me to my feet and righted the bike. "Get back on."

"What?"

He kick-started it. "Get back on!"

I looked behind us off the mesa. The helicopter had turned around and was coming back at us. The ground erupted into explosions of mud at our feet. The helicopter had a machine gun turret mounted on the front.

"Oh," was all I said as I hopped on, and he roared into a wheelie in the wet earth. We rode for cover in between several houses, and I hung on tight as bullets traced the adobe wall next to us.

I wasn't sure if Villegas' pilot was toying with us or if he was just a bad aim, but the bullets were hitting the tops of the houses causing us to drive through a sea of wet, shattered adobe. Sean was having trouble seeing and changed the bike's course. We zigzagged through several different rows of houses but the bullets always seemed to find us, exploding either in the mud or the adobe. Soon my own eyes were getting clouded with debris. I didn't know how Sean could stand it. We drove for cover in a narrow alleyway, but that was even worse as more and more adobe debris pelted us in an even smaller space.

About then the shots finally stopped. I looked to the helicopter which was level with us on the edge of the mesa. I could see something was wrong by the way the pilot was hitting and shaking something on his control bank, and Villegas was yelling at him. I put two and two together. "Their guns jammed."

"Great, but we're still in a Mexican standoff with a helicopter."

"You have one last stick of dynamite?"

Sean pulled one from his jacket. "Of course. But I don't know if it would be enough against that."

I took the dynamite. I wasn't thinking about throwing it, though. The chopper was still hovering right at the edge of the mesa, level with us on the ground. It made me think of that day at Pat Garrett High, when at the last second me and Dingus slid the bike right under the janitor's mop. If we rode fast enough and slid down at the last second, the bike with the dynamite would slide ride into it.

"What if we turned your bike into a bomb?" I asked.

Sean looked at the chopper. "Are you thinking what I think you're thinking?" he asked.

When he said that, I knew he got it. "Yes."

"Then we better move fast." He held up his lighter. "Compañeros?"

"Compañeros." I answered. Sean lit the fuse, then I wedged the dynamite into the handlebars in front of him.

"On the count of three we lean and let this sucker go!" he yelled.

This was going to happen fast. Sean spun the bike around to face the chopper and took off full bore for it. Villegas saw us coming. He barked an order at the pilot, and soon the chopper spun around so that the open bay was facing us.

"One!" Sean yelled as we picked up more speed, heading straight for that chopper, hoping it wouldn't move.

"Two!"

Suddenly I saw Villegas stagger into the bay with a rifle. It didn't take long for him to get us in his sights.

"Three!" Sean yelled.

In that moment, just as Sean and I shifted our weight to send the bike sliding towards the chopper through the mud, Villegas and I locked eyes. He knew death was coming for him, but he smiled and pulled the trigger anyway. The bullet hit me right below my shoulder with the force of a sledgehammer as Sean and I fell off the bike.

The bike skidded through the mud and hit the side of the chopper, exploding right where Villegas stood. I did my best to watch as I rolled across the butte, catching glimpses of the chopper smoking and spinning in circles before it finally crashed into the side of mesa and was no more.

When I finally finished rolling, I had a strange feeling of dizziness and loss of time. The air smelt funny now, too. I looked for the chopper. I couldn't see it, but I could see a lot of smoke and I could feel the heat, maybe that's what was making me feel sick.

I turned around to look for Sean. It hurt my arm as I twisted my neck. I clutched my shoulder, and my hand was soaking wet. It was the mud, I thought. My heart fluttered, and I realized it wasn't wet mud. It was blood. And it was all coming from me.

I could finally see Sean, though. He was on his back in the mud a few feet away. I stood up and stumbled the distance over to where Sean lay plopping down in the mud next to him.

"You crazy little son of a bitch," Sean said and then laughed. When he did, some blood came out of his mouth and flecked all over his shirt.

"You are a force to reckoned with, aren't you, Pancho Dumez?" He looked at me with respect when he said it.

"Yes, I am," I said proudly. "What happened to you?"

"That crazy bastard Villegas," Sean laughed and pointed to his chest, wet with blood. "He got the two birds with one stone," he said, then pointed at me.

What the hell did that mean? Boy, he was talking weird.

"But we got him too." Sean laughed and pointed to something weird sticking out of the ground. A fake golden leg with a snake curled around it. I had seen it somewhere before, but I couldn't remember where.

My eyes lazily looked down at the ground next to me. My blood and Sean's blood had collected into the same pool. I looked at his wound. It was near his heart. In the distance I could hear Becky and Dorado calling to me, but they seemed like they were miles away.

For a second, I felt like I had blacked out, then I heard Sean talking to me. "Before I go, I want you to have something."

"Going? Where are you going?" I asked.

"Oh, Mechito, you must've gotten hit in the head," he said. He was fiddling with something around his neck. It was that funny little conch shell necklace he always wore.

Why did he want me to have it? But then, for a split second, I remembered it was my birthday. Or maybe it had been yesterday? I wasn't sure.

"It was my father's. You are his namesake, you should have it now." I reached out and took the necklace from him. He grinned and nodded, then winced suddenly. Then I remembered something. He was dying.

I had grown both to love him and to hate him within the span of a single day. As he lay dying, I didn't know which of the two emotions I felt more. This would be the last time I ever talked to him. I could cuss him one more time. Show him how angry I was at him, but I didn't want to do that. I could tell him I forgive him, I didn't hate him, that he was my family, but I wasn't sure I wanted to do that either. He started talking again, cutting into my thoughts.

"Mechito, I want you to know… even though I hated your father, I hope you know, I never hated you," he said with a tear in his eye. I realized in his own way he was trying to tell me that he loved me.

While I was looking him in the eye, trying to decide what to say and instead saying nothing, Sean died. He nodded his head at me one more time with a weak smirk, then his eyes seemed to change, like a light went out in them and his head dropped to the ground.

After a second or so I started to cry. I didn't know why I was crying. I hated Sean. Sean was a traitor. Was it okay to still care about someone you hated? That was confusing. It made my shoulder hurt for some reason.

I laid over flat on my back and looked up at the sky. It was dizzying and huge. I wanted to throw up. All of a sudden Dorado and Becky were above me. Becky gasped and Dorado said, "Aw Dammit, Pancho," and looked away. His voice sounded hoarse, too.

"D'rado," I couldn't seem to say his name right. "Sean's dead."

"Yeah, I see that."

"You think I ought to keep talkin'…you know, so I stay around?" I meant to say stay conscious, but it's hard to get your words right when you're bleeding out.

"Yeah, you do that. You keep talking. Don't stop talking." He got up. "Becky, hold his hand, keep him talking."

She knelt beside me. Her cool hand felt good in mine.

"Hey baby," I said. I don't think I'd ever called her that before.

She was crying. "Hi, Pancho."

"I'm sorry I pushed you out the helicopter," I blurted out, and she laughed.

"I guess that was payback for the other day?" she said and then started crying again.

Why couldn't I get her to quit crying? I tried to think of something to say to make her feel better, but I was getting tired.

Someone shook me. "Pancho, honey, don't go to sleep. Stay awake. Please stay awake."

Suddenly she was gone, and Dorado was in my face again. I cried out as I felt something pushing on my chest. "Keep the pressure on it." It was Cade's voice. How did he get here? Damn, I just wanted to go to sleep, and everybody kept hassling me.

Everyone's voices kept getting further and further away. Maybe I was going to sleep. After that I could only pick up little bits and pieces of conversation, but I wasn't ever part of it. And people kept slapping my face a lot.

"Are you sure you can fly it?" somebody asked.

"Of course I can still fly a heli-chopper!" yelled someone that sounded like Cade.

"Pancho?" asked another. More shaking.

Someone else said, "Albuquerque is only 60 miles away. That's not long traveling by air."

Suddenly I felt myself being set down on the cool floor—I could tell it was a floor because it wasn't mud—and I realized I was in a helicopter. It seemed like I rode in the same helicopter with Xander earlier. Or maybe it was a hospital floor. I didn't know. My stomach lurched and I got dizzy like we were flying again. Then I finally went to sleep.

EPITAPH
BOOT HILL

The day had started off pretty strange in that my life was finally getting back to normal—because for the past week and a half, strange had been my new normal. They had released me from the hospital a few days ago, and this morning was the first time I'd woken up in my own bed and it actually felt normal again.

I didn't remember my first day in the hospital. I just remembered one night I woke up and I was in a hospital room. I knew why I was there, though. Getting shot may have made me loopy at first, but I was never going to forget that day. Ever.

Dorado was asleep in a chair next to the bed. I didn't know Aunt Patty and Rod were there, too, but when I started to stir around, they were up first thing. Aunt Patty couldn't restrain herself and threw her arms around me and accidentally knocked off the little gadget that monitors your pulse. For a minute, she thought I'd gone into cardiac arrest because of that noise the machine makes when your heart goes dead. She went into all-out hysterics until Rod picked up the loose monitor and explained it to her. By then a bunch of nurses had come in and, because of all the excitement, said maybe they should limit me to just one family member at a time.

The next day, when I had asked Dorado how we'd gotten there, he told me that Cade had managed to fly the Ring's helicopter to Albuquerque. He said if he hadn't, I'd have bled out and died. It made my stomach feel funny again when he told me that.

Things got better when I got moved out of the ICU and could get more visitors. It didn't take long for the nurses to limit that rule again, though. Missile came to visit, green with envy he didn't come along like Dingus had, and Dingus was himself torn up that he had missed the battle on the mesa. I don't think he'd ever forgive Cade for drugging him and leaving him at the ranch. Anyways, I think the final straw for the nurses was when Dingus kept blowing up and popping all those rubber gloves they have laying around in the room.

It seemed like the only person who didn't come to visit me was Becky. At first I thought she hadn't been to see me because I was in the ICU, but when she didn't come by when I got moved out of there, I got worried. I guess she had her own family issues to deal with. Even though Xander was alive when I last saw him, he didn't come back with us on the chopper. He just sort of disappeared, but he wasn't dead. If he was, his body would have been found on the mesa by now.

Even though I hadn't enjoyed being in the hospital, I was so doped-up on painkillers and had so many visitors all the time that my mind was always occupied. Now that I was back home, I didn't have time for anything but thinking and I was about to drive myself nuts. It was bad enough that I wished I could go back to school… almost. I sat around and thought about Sean and Becky mostly, even when I tried to take my mind off of everything watching TV. I wondered when I'd see Becky again, and with Sean I just wondered what the real truth was about him. I had so many questions I'd never get to ask him, like why Villegas called him Diego, what else did he know about our family. Lots of stuff I'd never know.

I caught myself fiddling with that necklace he gave me, just like he always did, and stopped. It wasn't something I would've picked out for myself, but it was the only thing of his that I had to remember him by. I didn't even have a picture of him I realized suddenly and felt sad.

I had spent so much time thinking he was my brother it still seemed like he was. I know a few days doesn't seem like a lot, but when you spend those days running for your life, it seems like a lot longer than it really was.

That afternoon I looked up "Mechito" in a Spanish dictionary and finally figured out that he had been calling me "Short Fuse" because of my temper. I laughed and then threw the dictionary across the room.

I wished Dorado was back already. He had been in Albuquerque testifying about Xander, the Santa Fe Ring, and everything that had happened to us, and was on his way back today. They had wanted me to go, too, but Aunt Patty convinced one of the judges that I had been through enough and shouldn't have to rehash everything, what with my injury and all.

I decided to take a walk outside to kill some time. It had snowed last night, and I felt bored enough that I almost wanted to build a snowman, but somehow that seemed stupid. After surviving a gunshot wound and blowing up a helicopter, somehow building a snowman seemed like something for a little kid.

All of a sudden, I heard footsteps crunching through the snow. Even though I hadn't turned around to look, somehow I knew it would be Becky.

"Hey, stranger," she said kinda awkward-like and I turned around. Even though we were only a few feet apart, it seemed like it was miles.

"Hey," I said. She was wearing a white beanie with black mittens. She had never looked so cute to me, but maybe it was because I knew she'd be leaving soon. We hadn't had a fight. We still loved each other like crazy. But somehow, upon seeing her for the first time since that day on the mesa, I knew deep down we were broken up. Too much had happened that day for our lives to ever go back to normal. She had almost died. She saw people get shot, including me and her dad.

"Where've you been keeping yourself?" I asked.

"With my mom mostly. You know, just around."

"But not at the hospital, huh? Or here. I've been home several days now."

She looked around uncomfortably and took a deep breath. "Yes, Pancho, I was there at the hospital. I was there when I thought you were going to die, and I felt so mixed up and crazy between you and my dad I didn't know what I felt, okay? And when you finally came to, I just..." her words trailed off. She looked down at the snow and smiled. "It's funny. This all started because your dad disappeared. And now, so has mine." She finally said the quiet part out loud. It was all my fault.

"Do you...do you hate me?"

She looked back up. "How could I hate you?"

"If Dorado and I hadn't stirred this up, you never would've learned the truth. You could still be happy."

"It'd still be the truth even if I didn't know it." She smiled and wiped away a tear. She was silent for a moment then said, "I'm going to Texas with my mom. Today."

She looked down at the snow-covered ground again. I knew that was probably coming, but it still hurt like an icicle had jammed itself into my heart. The cold air was nothing compared to the sting I was feeling there.

"Yeah, I figured you would," I said and hoped my voice wouldn't crack.

She walked towards me and put her hands in mine. "Pancho, I'll always love you, and you'll always be my first love. But right now, the truth is that I just want to forget all of this. Go somewhere new and start over."

I realized that meant forgetting me, too. Now in her mind I was inseparable from the horrible past few days. "I'm really sorry, Pancho," she said before wiping away a tear.

"I'm sorry, too," I said and did my best not to cry as she hugged me. We stood there holding each other for a minute until she let go and started to walk away. Suddenly she turned around. "I almost forgot. On the chopper... I took this." Her voice was still shaky. She pulled out an old, weathered piece of paper. It was the map. She handed it to me. "I thought about burning it, but I wasn't sure what to do with it. I thought you should have it."

I stared at it. I was probably the person who wanted the least to do with the damn thing, and yet here I was the one who ended up with it. "Well, anyways..." She shrugged nervously and turned around.

I dropped the map and grabbed her by the wrist, pulled her back to me, and kissed her. She didn't fight it and kissed back.

"What was that for?" she asked when I pulled back.

"I couldn't live with myself if I didn't kiss you one more time."

She hugged me tight. "I'm going to miss you."

"I know," I said, and we just stood there for a while holding each other. After a minute, she pulled away. "Goodbye, Pancho."

"Goodbye, Becky."

She began to walk away, but then she turned around and smiled through the tears. "Hey, don't go digging up any more graves."

I laughed and shook my head. "Never again."

She smiled and walked away. It shouldn't have made me feel better, but for some reason it did. I looked down at that damned map in the snow. I should burn it, I thought. I bent over to pick it up.

It was a strange thing to hold in your hands; something that most people would kill over and yet I didn't care about it myself. This was the best look I'd ever gotten at it. It had drawings of rock formations and different landmarks finally leading up to the canyon. For a minute I wondered why Billy the Kid didn't just write a note saying it was at this or that spot, but then I realized back in the 1800s maps were still the easiest way to find stuff since a lot of places had never actually been mapped out or named yet.

I folded the map up and stuffed it in my jacket, then went inside to have a drink. Aunty Patty and Rod were both back at work, and Nana was asleep on the couch, so nobody would notice if I swiped one of Rod's beers.

Just as I opened the fridge, I heard Dorado's car pull up outside. I took out the beer and leaned back against the counter and waited for him to come inside. Aunt Patty's messed-up washer was going at it again full speed. Dorado was right. It did sound like I was in the hull of an ocean freighter. Eventually, I heard the front door open and shut.

"Permission to come aboard?" Dorado asked, leaning in the doorway. He looked different and I realized it was because he had to dress up for court. He was wearing a long dressy coat and even had on a scarf.

"Permission granted," I said and took my first swig of beer.

"You hitting the sauce?" he asked with a look of concern.

Last time I was in the kitchen with Dorado he had been disappointed in me that I wasn't drinking, and now he looked like he was disappointed that I was.

"No, it's just root beer," I lied.

He walked over to me, looked at the bottle, and took it away. "That is not root beer."

"Hey, the other day you were disappointed that I wasn't drinking," I said.

"That was then, this is now," he said as he poured it down the sink. I think he still felt guilty about dragging me into all this mess and was trying to be less of a bad influence now. "Besides, you don't want to turn out like Nana, do you?" He motioned towards the living room, where Nana was passed out with another rolled-up nicotine patch in her mouth. About then, Billy, who I'm surprised Aunt Patty didn't get rid of and still let in the house, came up and started eating it.

"It's just been kind of a rough day, man," I said, frustrated.

"What happened?"

"Becky came by to say goodbye. She's moving with her mom to Texas."

"I figured she would."

"They say anything about him… Xander, at the hearings?"

Dorado shook his head. "Disappeared without a trace. And I don't blame him. Sounds like the governor's gonna open an investigation into the Ring and try to ferret out anyone that's a part of it."

"Heh, assuming the governor's not one of them."

Dorado smirked. "Well, if several years from now somebody digs up that canyon and strikes it rich, then I guess we'll have our answer."

The canyon was something else that had been bothering me. "Dorado, at first I thought this whole thing was about gold, but McCaw and Baca both act like the canyon is cursed or something."

Dorado shook his head. "Well, whatever it is, we don't have to worry about it anymore."

"Not necessarily." I drew the map out of my jacket where he could see it.

He snatched it from my hands. "Pancho, how…"

"Becky took it off the chopper from Villegas. What should we do, burn it?"

We both stared at it. In a way I hated that map. It represented all the tragedy and death that had occurred over the last few weeks. At the same time, it was also a part of our family history.

Dorado crinkled it in his fingers. "I guess it's sort of a family heirloom, huh?"

"We can't exactly keep it, though, either."

Dorado stared off into space, chewing on his lip like he always did when he was contemplating something. "Hey, I tell you what, let's take a drive."

"Where?"

"You'll see."

***

About ten minutes later, I was standing in front of a casket and an open burial plot in the Fort Sumner cemetery. Not the one Billy the Kid is buried in, which is now more of a historical marker, but the one where normal people got buried. The headstone read "HONDO DIEGO 'SEAN' DUMEZ."

Dorado had talked to the coroners about him, and they had managed to dig up his records. Turns out he was named after me and Dorado's dad just like I was named after his. Seeing as how he hated my dad, I figured he just changed his name to Sean. Why he picked that particular name, though, I guess I'd never learn.

They couldn't find his exact birthday, though, so the tombstone just said 1955-1976. Suddenly the irony struck me that it was all ending just as it had begun nearly 100 years ago around a 21-year-old outlaw's grave. Only Sean really had died, unlike Billy, who rode off into the sunset. I remembered what Professor Mendez had said about being doomed to repeat history. He was right, even about himself, since he was among the men who had died in search of the Lost Adams. Then I remembered what Old Man Baca had said in the church about coming face to face with a legend: afterwards you would either be dead or become a legend yourself. Now I knew what he meant, only Sean was the dead one, which I guess made me and Dorado the legends.

"I don't know. I hoped maybe this would help give you closure with the whole thing," Dorado blurted out after we'd been staring at it for a while. "They're supposed to come by and bury the casket pretty soon."

After he said that, we heard footsteps in the snow. I thought maybe that would be the gravediggers coming to bury Sean. But when we turned around to look, the gravediggers I saw before us weren't there for Sean. They were there for us. My blood ran cold. It was the two men who had followed me and Sean through Tularosa and Santa Fe. The only question now was, did they work for the Ring or the cartel? I suddenly remembered that my brother had never seen them and said, "Dorado, this isn't over yet." I grabbed his arm, getting ready to run.

"It's okay, Pancho," he said calmly and stayed where he was. "I called them."

Before I could ask him how or why, the two men stepped aside to reveal Delbert Baca standing behind them.

"You!?" I exclaimed in shock.

"Don't look so disappointed," Baca said.

"You mean they're…" my words trailed off as I pointed at the two men.

"Meet my two sons, Hondo and Hildalgo Baca," he said.

"If you had ever given us time enough to speak, we could have told you," the smaller one said.

"I thought you were there to kill us," I said, exasperated.

"An easy mistake," the big one said and shrugged.

"You didn't really think I'd send you off totally unsupervised, did you?" Baca said. After a second, he told his sons, "You two take a walk. You're making the kid nervous."

"I will admit, you could have told us about them at the church, though," Dorado said.

Baca shrugged as his sons wandered off to look around the cemetery. "I wanted to watch you for a while. See if you were both who I hoped you were. He came to me before you," Baca said, motioning to Sean's grave, "but his intentions were less pure than your own, so I never told him where to find what was needed to locate Adams' Tomb."

"He claimed that our father killed his. Do you know if that's true or not?" Dorado asked.

Baca looked uncertain. "As I said, I was not there when your father found his brother in Mexico. All I can say is that like me, Hondo knew that the canyon should stay hidden."

"And why is that?" I asked. "Seven McCaw acted like it was all because of some Indian hocus-pocus, mumbo jumbo."

"That canyon is the burial ground to a great evil that my people swore to never disturb. Let's put it like that. And besides, after tangling with McCaw, do you really think it's all just hocus pocus?" Baca said, giving me a look. "Anyhow, like I said, Hondo knew of this as I did. His brother, unfortunately, did not."

"About that," Dorado said. "You never did tell us the whole story about how our dad and his brother got mixed up in all this."

"You haven't figured it out yet?" Baca said, looking right at me instead of Dorado.

"Should we have?" I said, confused.

"I thought that it would be obvious in the Kid's letter to your uncle," Baca said. "Hondo and Pancho were his grandsons."

I suddenly remembered back to the odd line in the letter where Williams regretted not getting to spend more time with Uncle Pancho. It couldn't be…

"Wait, so that means…" Dorado blurted out.

Baca nodded. "You're the descendants of Billy the Kid, yes."

"But how does that even work?" Dorado asked.

Baca flashed an ornery grin. "I'll let you have fun solving that mystery on your own. Besides, this old man is getting cold and hungry." He turned away from us towards his sons and called out, "Boys, start the truck! I want to get one of those Enchurito thingies from Taco Bell on the way home."

"Wait. You can't just tell us we're related to Billy the Kid and leave us to go to Taco Bell!" Dorado yelled out.

Baca just laughed as he walked away. "Oh yes, I can."

It was just like that old codger to drop a bombshell like that on us and try to leave. I racked my brain trying to think of a way to keep him around. "Hey, one more thing. What about this?" I shouted and drew the map out of my jacket, holding it out towards him.

Baca turned around and shook his head when he saw it. "I don't want it."

"You don't want it?" I asked, confused. "I thought you were like the super-secret Indian guardian of the canyon or something?"

Baca laughed. "My part in that story is officially over. It's your problem now."

"So you're not worried that we're gonna run off together and go find the lost canyon?" Dorado asked.

"Not anymore. Like I said before, you're both exactly who I was hoping you were, even if Sean wasn't," he said and started to walk away again.

"What are we supposed to do with this, then?" I shouted, shaking the map at him.

"I'm sure you can think of an appropriate place to put it," he said without turning around as he trudged away into the snow with his two sons.

"What do you think he meant by…" Dorado's words trailed off. The same realization that was slowly sinking in with him hit me as our eyes drifted towards Sean's grave.

I looked back at Dorado. He cocked a brow and flashed an ornery smile. He was thinking the same thing that I was. History had a funny way of repeating itself.

9 781953 221421